DIONYSUS

First published in 2022 by PRESS DIONYSUS LTD in the UK, 167, Portland Road, N15 4SZ, London.

www.pressdionysus.com

Paperback

ISBN: 978-1-913961-40-4

MOTHERS DAUGHTERS & DRUGS

Gulsum Oz

English Translation by Mesut Şenol

DIONYSUS

ISBN- 978-1-913961-40-4
© Press Dionysus 2024

English Translation by Mesut Şenol
Cover art: Gülsüm Öz

Press Dionysus LTD, 167, Portland Road, N15 4SZ,
London
• e-mail: info@pressdionysus.com
• web: www.pressdionysus.com

ABOUT THE AUTHOR

Gülsüm Öz is a Turkish author who lives in Istanbul. She is a Novelist and screenwriter for films and tv series. She gained her first prize for her poem, Vatan (Home Land) when she was 13 years of age and later, worked as an editor with **Büyük Larousse** Publishers. She continues to write novels and short stories and screenplays and teaches writing at **Marmara Academy of Art.**

Literary works

"İltica" (Migration) 2009 GOA publishers

"Anneler Kızları ve Esrar" (Mothers, Their Daughters and Drugs) 2012 Astrea Publishers

'**Mübadele Aşkları**' (Love Affairs During the Great Exchange - between Türkiye and Greece in mid 1920s) 2016 SOLA Publishers "Love Amidst Population Exchange"(Mübadele Aşkları) was published by SOLA Publishing House in 2016. "Asylum", London: Press Dionysus, 2023.

Co-authored novels

"Tanıklarla 12 Eylül" (12th of September with Evidence)

"Söz kesmek Kına Yakmak" (Betrothal and Hena)

"Konan Göçen Kadınlar" (Migrant women)

Bülbülün Çilesi ('The Nightingale's Ordeal') A short story which won the Yahya Konbolat best short story award.

Screenwriting for TV series and the film industry

Co authored **Dullar Pansiyonu** (Widows Hostel), **Mahallenin**

Muhtarları (The Mukhtars Of The Neighbourhood), **Çiçek taksi** (Flower Taxi), and **Zoraki Koca** (A Husband By Force).

Also wrote the storyline of a TV film **'Her şey Oğlum için'** (Everything For My Son), and both the storyline and screenplay of **'Yengec Oyunu'** (Crab Game).

Her screenplay for, **'Bana söz ver Baba'** (Promise Me, Dad), received support from Turkiye's Department of Culture and Tourism.

Social Action Projects

Also known for her social action Projects, Gülsüm Öz started and managed full time, free of charge summer schools in the Borough of Şişli and with İstanbul Metropolitan Municipality. These projects provided sports and cultural activities for thousands of children. Her **House of Hope project** in Küçük Çekmece provided refuge for homeless, vulnerable children who lived in streets. İn the same district, she also set up the **'Küçük Çekmece Womens' Aid Centre'**.

In conjunction with **Cevko**, she started a **Recycling Project for solid waste**.

Membership of Organisations

(P.E.N) PEN Writers Association, (KYD) Women Writers Association, (FILMSAN) Film Artists Association, (SCREENWRITERS) Screenwriters Association, (BESAM) Science, Education and Social Research Center, (THSD) Public Health Association of Turkey.

This morning the mother was so tense… Even the fore-noon's sun filling the living room and the summer breeze blowing off the opened curtains would not soothe the young mother. It was not in her power somehow to forget about the day she gave birth to her daughter. The line between her two eyebrows looked like getting deeper and deeper; she was shut-tling before the tall dressing mirror at the entrance with her hands tightly crossed around her chest; her hair floating by its wind was whipping her cheeks yet she was not hearing an-ything else. The only sound she was getting was the splash coming out of bathroom. As if she was seeing her daughter who yielded her naked body to the warm water flow gushing from the shower behind the closed door.

Her daughter, who was glowing through the light of her youth, driving her mother out of her mind unexpectedly sing-ing energetically and joyfully almost all romantic songs, and now singing under the water with her silk voice, Christian Adam's "*Si Tu Savais Combien Je T'aime*", was going to cele-brate her birthday today. The steam rising from her daughter's very robust pearly body was floating from beneath the door and reaching the young woman who was striding through the hall so many times; and that steam was virtually tingling her hair roots and the gaps between her nails. Say that eighteen years had passed today since they placed her daughter on her lap. Young mother stared into space, and her lips were curled wailfully. The year baby Canan was born swam before young mother's eyes.

***

I did not want to remember that year at all but in no way I could dismiss it from my mind. Eighteen years ago I was getting prepared for my graduation night with a childish joy by going up the stairs of the public housing breathlessly since I was counting the days in order to marry my fiancé. I had finished my education which was a huge obstacle between my fiancé and my marriage. I was so much sure about the brightest route in front of me as was running towards my happiness orchard and having innocent feelings. All of my beautiful dreams were coming true one by one. Soon enough I was going to receive my diploma, to marry my beloved, and to travel to Thessaloniki. I was not going to have a baby for many years to come, and I was just planning to work. I was going to walk around proudly with the confidence of a woman who earns her money, and I would be free. I could have fulfilled my wishes without fear.

I just went to the hairdresser I stop by once in a blue moon… I had my hair buckled the way I wanted to for some time. My schoolmates were constantly complimenting me, and telling me that my honey-colored taffeta dress was reflecting back the summer lights encircling me with a corona of beauty. I had left the hairdresser cheerfully. I was going to Bebek from Beşiktaş by tram, and there at my school's farewell party we organized, I would be in fits, and then I would be keeping on the preparation for so many wonderful days by leaning on my fiancé's warm shoulder.

When I got out of the hairdresser and took a step in Şair Nedim Street, suddenly a car stopped by my side. A door was opened… A door was closed… A vortex, like a nightmare appeared in front of me, and a pitch-black fog rolled in around me… What a fog… Sticky, smudgy fog did not get up off me. What sort of sin should I have committed so that I found myself in hell while I was walking around the sunny gardens of paradise?

All of a sudden, a door was opened… A door was closed… I found a child on my lap… All of a sudden, a door was opened… A door was closed… I found a child on my lap…

***

The young mother who withdrew herself from her eighteen years old memory through his son's panicky call of *"Mom, I cannot find my math book"*, was still waiting at the corridor for her daughter's getting out of the bathroom. She was not giving a damn to his son's being unable to find his book. She has her mind on her daughter who was going to be nineteen today. She turned her face towards the door creaking coming from the bathroom side. Once the bathroom door with the Virgin Marry embossed stained glass was opened, the scent of daisy carried with the vapor cloud enveloped Fevziye who was restively walking down the floor at the corridor. At the very moment, her daughter stalked out of the bathroom, passed by her like a crazy wind. The mother felt that she was almost getting drowned by the water drops her daughter had left behind her.

After drying her hair and going to her room, Canan dropped at her feet her bathrobe which was large sized for her slim and delicate body. While her mind was lingering on the birthday party, her eyes were fixed at her tender body. As she was looking for her undies in a hurry to cover her nakedness and even her inner self, she gazed upon her image in the mirror. She was ashamed and blushed for seeing her maiden body without hiding anything. She trembled like a leaf since she did not put on her dress before leaving the bathroom.

When she was a small girl, she had her dreams about growing up in no time. After all, she would dream a lot. She would have constantly created happy and unhappy people in her own world. She would take note of them in her graph notebook, then she would act upon her writing. In the plays she was acting whenever possible, putting on her mother's high heels, she used to walk alone in full blast, sometimes in a bank, some other time in a school or at a hospital… There she used to see a small girl hiding for sure where the sun doesn't shine, and a small girl fearful of her mother and being blonde like her… After presenting a doll to her, she would take her under her wing, by immediately taking the mother of the girl to a hospital, as well as questioning her father why they were torturin this small blonde girl.

When she staged the plays she had written, she would impersonate both the mother and the small girl. In all of her stories, the mother's character would be sometimes good and bad some other times. The small and blonde girl was the one whose personality would never change. She was always sad… The small unhappy girl's story going badly would eventually find its right path through reading, learning, and experimenting and succeeding. The small blonde girl would dress the children of the mother she would be impersonating in the plays she had written with spotlessly clean clothes; she would go with them to the park, the movie theatre or other entertainment locations. And when the evening would come, she would cook tasty dishes to eat joyfully by the presence of their father, and then she would play the game of categories while frying chestnuts on the grill of the cast iron stove. In her stories she wrote, one of neighbor mothers would always be different. She was the mother who would generally pocketing the money she would take from her husband, and go to shopping after locking their children in the room to come back in the shank of the evening. When her husband would come back from work, he would bite her head off, and even beat her, nevertheless she would let it pass, and she would do the same thing the following day all over again. The small blonde girl would tell that neighbor, *"Did you hear that now here is a new law in force. The mother will be punished if they forget their children at home."*

Canan woke up from her childhood dreams. She was grown up since her childhood with great difficulty without realizing many of her dreams; her personality suffered some erosion, and she was hard-hit; nobody lent a helping hand to her for actualizing her dreams; at the age of 18 she was still keeping on fighting with the challenges of life. Let it be so; somehow one day her dreams would come true, and she would be tall in the saddle in front of her mother Fevziye Hanim; she would not tumble down no matter what her mother would do, and she would not run away from her. It would be easier right after she would be free from the conflict chain her mother put it around her neck. She would have her imagined dreams published, and everybody would be reading those books she would have written.

When Fevziye saw through the doorway her naked daughter standing in front of the mirror, she threw a very angry glance at her. It appeared to her that as if she was not seeing her daughter, rather her body of eighteen years earlier, the very young Fevziye. By taming her rage, she tried to figure out what was passing through her daughter's mind. Let's see what was today's plan of her devil daughter! She thought about the idea of jumping on her daughter like a panther and to lock her in her room after winding her daughter's hair around her hand.

In fact, Canan took notice of her mother's watching her through the doorway when she walked towards the dresser to take her underwear. She was sensing that her mother looking with that strange expression on her face, she would never comprehend why her mother was torturing herself. Even her breathing behind the door was enough for her to hit a sour note… For that very reason, she had organized her birthday party she was going to celebrate for the first time in the Prince Island to which her mother could not reach. Head to head with her beloved school mates… Far away from her mother. The young girl sighed by saying "Ahh, if only" … Ahhh, if only they put a ban on giving birth for the families who do not know how to raise children… Ahh, no woman who doesn't hold a motherhood license could not bear a child… Though her father was a good one but since the majority of her friends were complaining about their fathers, then if only the ones who don't acquire a fatherhood license could not become a father.

She put on first her underwear then her gauze tunic. Throwing a sidelong look at her mother seen in one moment and gone away in another in front of the mirror, and starting to coil her blonde hair applying curling iron she had made it lighter in color using daisy water, and with that hair reaching to her waistline, she panicked as soon as she heard her mother's intermittent hiccups. Sooner this utterance would turn into a crying sound…At the same time, she grew a gut-wrenching feeling

Fevziye who felt that she was noticed by her daughter pushed the door raginly:

"The dishes are not done; the beds are not made up… For what are you prinking yourself up?"

Canan didn't offer an answer. Even she was not contemplating a counter-attack, her mother was still grumbling:

"What on earth these clothes… What is the state of your hair…? It's like…"

Although she knew that her mother wanted to say "Like a prostitute", nevertheless she looked at her mother doggedly as if to say "Like what". She loosened the latch of the curling iron. One tress was dropped down her shoulder through the vapor cloud. The heat of the hot curling iron was roasting the surroundings. Canan was armed and ready for the duello. As if she wanted to openly say this word she heard frequently, she endeavored to blush her mother's face through her fierce looks. She was not her daughter Canan who conforms anymore. To begin with, she set her mind on rebelling. The books she had read had given her such a great power, and as soon as she revolted against injustice, life had immediately taken on great many colors. The young girl as yet a couple of days ago had given a kick to the jars of soft soap, thrown away the scrubbing brush in her hand onto the wall, and making her mind that she is her own master, not the slave of her family, her house nor her siblings.

She threw an overhead glance at her mother. Her mother wouldn't dare to touch her hair dropping down from her cheeks in the form of ringlets. What was the curling iron in her head for? She daydreamed that she glued the hot curling iron on her face for a moment while coiling her hair. For a moment, she fantasized that she left a mark on her mother's beautiful face in the memory of the day she was born so that her mother would never forget that day she would not recall at all. The young girl was startled by her own thinking. She got the shivers because of the things she had passed in her head. It would be best if she would be away from home in a hurry without making a scene. Escaping her mother's looks by closing her room's door, Canan remembered her mother screaming as she was putting on her wrangler blue jean wrapping her waist down tightly. She covered her ears with her hands… After begging so much, she had her father buy these pants. Her father was scolded by her mother since he paid tons of money for the pants. When would she be free from remembering the arguments she would be having with her mother for whatever issue she would like to deal even though she was not willing to do so? By taking off her hands from her ears, she looked at her reflection in the mirror with a smile on her face. She took a diary of yellowed pieces of paper and paper bags out of her crate in order to read it in the boat, and she jammed it into her bag.

Now Canan was going to the Island for the first time arbitrarily… The house was in disarray. Her siblings' beds were supposed to be made, things on the breakfast table were to be taken, and the dished were to be done. She knew that her mother would be going to a movie theatre or a tea garden instead of doing these chores, yet she would like to have her mother show an interest in her brother who was whining for not being able to find the math textbook. She was sorry for her brother; but she could not live her childhood since she always was sorry about them. The best thing to do was to close her ears to their complaints and go away immediately. To a faraway place… To a very faraway place… She was startled by this thought… Was it not that her mother had found her way like this? By shutting her ears to the crying of her children? But she had not such a right… If only she had not been married. Say she married, then it would have been better if she had not born a child. She looked at her out of the corner of her eyes. Her hands are on the sides of her waist and walking around with a strange expression on her face, her mother was waiting for an opportunity to argue with herself and to bark at someone instead of dealing with her son who was late for her school.

She was not trying to figure it out anymore that although her mother had an angel appearance and her submission towards others as well as her well intention up to a level of naivety, why her mother's personality was turning into a merciless, obstinate one against her. She had made her mind that there was no point in talking to her mother since she could not make a sense of her mother's approaches, sometimes laden with jealousy and violence, sometimes with excessive affection, some other times icy cold or as hot as the sun, and also with tears being shed painfully. Lately she was not giving any response whatever her mother told her, and she was not talking to her at all. She would have not talked to her mother very often even in her childhood. Like a slave, she would approach her mother in the vortex of a deep fear carrying her into some obligations she could not name.

She was not paying attention to her mother's words of

affection, her slander, her shouts, her begging and prostrating herself as well as her physical and oral attacks in order to make her talk to her, and she was not even looking at her face anymore. If only she was able to speak to her but it was impossible. The stress of not being able to talk to the mother at the same house was something unbearable yet there was nothing the young girl could do. Sigle-mindedly, while she was reaching out to her shoes, the shoulder bag seemingly to land on her back was in her mother's hand. She noticed again the expression of her mother circling around her, either to hug or kiss her, or killing her by strangling. She could not make out what was passing in her mother's mind. Her mother raised the bag in her hand as is to give a warning signal and ready to make the second move:

"You cannot go out," she was shouting at the top of her voice.

Having leant her back to the door, the young girl who could not tell whether she was hating or feeling sorry for her mother looking at her with a familiar strange flash in her eyes during such occasions, swiftly pushed her aside and took her bag to leap out. Out of breath, she left a woman behind as she was walking down the pier, a woman who was able to have her daughter doing everything she wanted her, and this time she was not calling the tune which was making her mother go crazy.

Being left alone after her daughter, Fevziye was not sure about what to do. Joylessness inside her was turning into a wrath. Her daughter who was pampering her back in the days, now had left her in this disarrayed home with children. Even having dolled herself up and hopping down the stairs with all liveliness of her youth, and walking away from her, and leaving her behind like an insect.

Fevziye heaved a sigh, by saying, "Fortunately this girl had not died" when Canan was a well-behaved girl. Her daughter had started from the age of seven to take care and manage the house and to look after her siblings. Fevziye used to drink her morning coffee at Kamuran's, then to go to Cinema Mehtap, to be followed her visit the Grand Bazaar, to visit Mahmutpasha, to come back home half an hour earlier than her husband after walking through the Egyptian Bazaar. Sometimes her feet would have been swollen because of too much walking, and she would have asked her daughter to prepare a lukewarm salted water to relieve tiredness of the day. She would have replied briefly, "I am done in" when her husband came and saw her feet inside a washbowl full with water. In similar situations her husband would have yelled at Canan, "Why don't you help your mother?" Fearing a lot of her mother's leading to disturbance, Canan wouldn't have uttered a word. After her father reprimanded her, her mother would have come near her and caress her hair without saying anything, then she would leave her silently in a manner of a guilty person.

Looking at already disappearing view of her daughter getting on the Island Boat and not being able to collect herself, Fevziye, raised her head sighing by saying "I know how to discipline her." She looked around. Her neighborhood had gone through so much transformation due to the migration from Anatolia. Tijen's and Behzat's families from the old neighbors were the only ones still living here. Nevertheless, slowly she was become friendly at once with them as well. Fevziye turned her head at the sky feeling a light breeze. Dark clouds were moving. The sky was rolling and roaring as if calling humans who destroy the nature to account. As Fevziye was lighting a cigarette at the threshold of the door and then puffing its smoke towards the poplar tree, next door neighbor Pervin from Bunyan who moved in this neighborhood around one year ago, sat on the sofa under the shadow of the climbing fragrant rose.

Pervin was neither an urbanite like her old neighbors nor a provincial woman like newly moved neighbors. She had only completed her elementary school education yet once she started talking, one would like to ask her about how many universities she had gone. She would have worn Bodrum flip-flops on her shoes, and put on a plain dress or a pair of jeans on her body, as well as a scarf around her neck. She would have held a daily newspaper called Cumhuriyet under her armpit, and she would have always carried a book and a ciga-rette in her hand. She kept reading and reading in order to fill the gap in her development and to reach her desired goal in that respect. Having placed the newspaper in her hand on the empty part of the table half full of flower vases:

"How about tea?" She called. Fevziye:

She threw away the butt of the cigarette in her hand into the waterhole inside the marble birdbath by saying, "Let me send away my son to the school". Pervin swayed the leaves of the basil in the vase with her hand. She was repeating this in every two minutes, and the scent of the sweet basil was scattering around. She glanced over the flowers one by one of which Fevziye having eyes only for them. It was such a great indulgence to enjoy drinking tea during hot days of the Summer in the shade of baby roses and honeysuckles which pervading all over the places. The garden was gorgeous with multi-colored geraniums although they were planted in the Vita oil and marmalade boxes, red earring flowers, lilac-color-ed hydrangeas which are standing on their branches. If tending well, the gardening was one of the best things Fevziye was good at, the other thing she excelled was to deal with her cats and dogs. She also liked very much to get about the places. She never huffed and puffed about going to Asiyan to listen to Zeki Muren, and to Tashlik Maksim to be present at the concert of Behiye Aksoy.

Fevziye, getting prepared for the tea drinking indulgence with her neighbor, was about to spend a nicer day than her daughter who was also about getting around and having fun. She got to the kitchen by hopping with her lily-white legs over the pajamas and nightgowns of her children. Soon she forgot about her daughter and the chores at home through her habitual psychological state oriented towards laughing instead of feeling sorry. After all she was not good at housework and cooking dishes, she was not laying her hands on them. The most she would do would be to deal with the untidiness in the house by stuffing the clutter into some holes, and when she was not able to find the socks, collars, underpants and shirts of the children, then she would go the Grand Bazaar to buy new ones. That's why even though they were earning more than other families, they were not making both ends meet. Possibly she had tucked away the math textbook her son was looking for and not finding it.

"Nothing will happen, go without the book" she said to her son.

"No way, the teacher gets upset… You seem to lose everything" he said to his mom by pulling her mother's skirt. Fevziye spoke to his son while caressing his head:

"You shouldn't have to repeat your examinations. Look, we willgo to Shile late because of you." Her mind was on her getting around. Today the teacher coming to their home to teach her son was going to conduct a group work in his house. Being unable to find the book, Fevziye having slipped just the notebook under his son's armpit and let him to get out of the house, raced to the kitchen to deal with the preparation.

After adding water into the tea kettle which had less water out of too much boiling on the cooker, she put glasses and breakfast meals the children had eaten some of them, on the tray non attentively. The cheese had some sour cherry traces on it since it was cut with the very forks to get that marrmalade. Bread crumbs had gummed up to the olives in the plate. She also put the scrambled eggs with garlic sausages which got firm in the pan, on the tray as it was. As she was putting the tray on the coffee table in the garden, her friend was swaying basils with her hand involuntarily, and with other hand she was reading the newspaper in a very serious manner. Pointing out to the newspaper Fevziye nudged Pervin.

"Release it from your hand… Have you come here to read the newspaper or to have a chat?

"Just a second Fevziye… Remember, Mehmet Ali Aybar founded the Socialist Party last month…"

"It's none of my business, my goodness…"

"Don't say it's none of my business. Had the youth who are being divided into hundreds of fractions become united, then the revolution would come within a short time."

"Please Pervin, do not start talking politics… I already feel blue."

"What's it to you? You get bored seldom, I hope there is nothing serious."

"Our daughter just went off…"

"I was about to ask where she is."

"She is not here… The slut shoved off… Today is her birthday… If only she was not born."

"Yeah, really… Today was the girl's birthday?"

"I've heard that she is going to celebrate it alone… she told her brother about it".

"Eeee… You had given a hard time to her last year on her birthday."

Canan recalled the day last year when her door was knocked hurriedly on Canan's birthday. As she opened the door, Fevziye jumped into the house as if she was going to explode with fury, and threw herself on the sofa and whimpered by saying, "Damn it!… I want to die" After a while, without asking what the issue was, Pervin wiped the tears on Fevziye's cheeks by her backhand and raising her head proudly exclaimed, "Call on neighbors… Tonight we are going to entertain ourselves." Fevziye's tears dropped in pain were replaced by that ill-tempered and greedy heedlessness. As opposed to these words, Pervin sensed that there was something odd going on in Fevziye's house. This must have to do with Canan but what?

Until last year, only Canan's brother's birthday was being celebrated. The young girl couldn't help but resent about this situation. Let alone celebrating her birthday, even talking about that day seemed to be a taboo. As if Canan was not born, and she was brought home by storks as happens in tales. If the records on her ID cart were not indicating that she was born on 15 June, and she is Fevziye's daughter, then even she would have had her doubts whether she was her daughter or not. Or else, did his father bring the daughter of another woman and marry her mother? Was Fevziye not her mother? If only it would have been the case, then she would go to find her real mother… With these mixed feelings, Canan had woken up early on her birthday last year. By holding the ID card in her hand against her father's face, "Whey always my brother's birthday is celebrated? Today is my birthday", she said. When her father was baffled what to say, Canan's suspicion had grown, and for a moment she expected her father to say" Fevziye is not your mother". When she realized that her father had nothing to say, she pushed her ID towards his face, she provoked her father to spill the beans about her birthday by saying, "Why?"

The man letting his affectionate looks escape like a guilty person from his daughter, got home that evening with a cake holding in his hand. Yet he was ready to be reprimanded by his wife. And with his concerned expression and cap in hand, Canan couldn't make a sense of his father's pathetic state, and she was now regretful why she had said "Where is my birthday". Seeing the cake box, her mother threw a long look at both her daughter and her husband as if this cake was not for her daughter but it was a poison for her. Fevziye was even frozen up for a long time on the very spot and couldn't find a word to utter. Then shaking herself, she had immediately left the house by winnowing her hair as if to declare to them "I will call you to account for it". Rather than criticizing her mother's strange behavior, her father had looked after her and kept his mouth shut.

It seems that her mother having gone to Pervin came back after a while with other neighbors as they burst into loud joyful laughter. The tea was brewed and the entertainment was started. There was something going on, yet all the fuss was not for her daughter's birthday, but for Fevziye. Already the young girl had forgotten that today was her birthday since she was serving for the guests, and she was exhausted for washing the empty glasses and plates. Her father had joined the entertainment alongside with their neighbors, and accompanied the song called "I cannot have the heart, you my beautiful magnolia" as he was eyeballing his wife… Long since her mother has cut the cake without telling that it was her birthday cake, and offered pieces to her neighbors, and the young girl in the meantime had not a chance even to have a piece of that cake, nor had she the opportunity to blow out the candle which was put aside somewhere. She was not also offered any gift for her birthday. As she was watching her mother singing on her father's shoulder some time, and her mother's head flashing with the blinks for revenge and radiating a proud expression as if she is a triumphant of a war, she felt that she hated her mother yet again. The young girl had reached her age of eighteen by carrying the appetizers to the feast table beginning from the evening till the dead of the night, and doing the dishes until she would collapse out of exhaustion.

By trying calm Fevziye down, Pervin said;

"I am not sure whether Canan was last year celebrating her birthday or was she acting as a cleaning lady to serve your entertainment? You make this girl suffer a lot."

Fevziye stalked out of the old wicker chair beneath the poplar tree.

"If only she was not born… Her ladyship is going to celebrate her birthday alone today. She doesn't let me forget about the day I gave birth to her: This girl is going to cause a trouble for me."

"I don't know what you are doing… Why do you torture this girl?"

"What! Do I torture her; do you think?"

"Yes… What's the problem with her going to the Island? She will go there for sure… They are young."

"Shut up for God's sake. Don't I have a deserving soul? I used to be young."

"You are a mother, a mother…"

"Do you think I wanted to become a mother… I did not want to be a mother."

"No good crying over spilt milk… You already got married and have children. Yes, it's not easy to be a mother. With good or bad grace, we have got responsibilities."

Fevziye took a look at Pervin. Since she was not an ideal housewife dedicating herself to housework like other neighbors, she could get along well with her, yet for some reason she was not letting her talk ill about Canan. Sarcastically, as if she fished around,

"Why didn't she invite you to her birthday?"

"Why would she? Am I one of her peers?"

"Actually… Since you get along well."

"Getting along is something… And this is something else… What shall I do among so many young people?"

Whereas Fevziye was failing to agree with her peers and with the people of the people advanced in years. Her best friends happened to be the young ones.

"You don't let us talk about this."

"Don't blow it out of proportion… After all the girl is going to celebrate her birthday."

"If only she was not born…"

"She is your daughter… Why do you talk like this?... Why does her being happy bother you?"

Pervin was mistaking by believing that Fevziye was hovering between being a mother to her children and enjoying her youth she never lived. The year she got pregnant for her daughter entered her head. As soon as she told herself "It was the spring of my life. I too had my eighteen years behind then", her lips trembled. She just held her tongue and froze… She didn't want to speak… She was not able to speak. Was she weeping inwardly? Fevziye's nose had turned red. She gulped. She appeared shaking off… Following a short period of silence, she started to recount.

***

That day was the last day of my internship for nursing. As Istanbul was assuming its silence among flickering lights, having dressed my nightgown, inside of my bed in my room of the public housing, I was thinking of my fiancé. My fiancé was almost a spit image of Tanju Okan who had come from Italy and started singing songs… Despite his not being famous, I had found one of his photos and put it on the wall of my room, and got off to sleep while looking at his photo.

It was a morning with a breeze of August. I got up early and prepared to the day promising to be filled with adventure and fun I had planned with my friends. I was full of joy. The gates of my happiness garden were wide open. I put on the necklace my fiancé gifted me around my neck. I headed out as I was hopping like a swallows with yellow throat, and I was also murmuring Frank Sinatra's song called "From the Bottom of my Heart" which I was carrying on and on.

I walked by hoping coquettishly on the cobblestone pavement to get the cinema. With my girlfriends we left the cinema by weeping openly as opposed to our expectation when we entered the cinema in a psychological state that we would die laughing. The father of my friend happened to be one of the employees of the film set. When we found out that the many of the scenes were censored and the whole movie was pared to a bone, we ran to the cinema go lend our support to the director Atif Yilmaz.

As we were moving silently towards Besiktas, we must have been so deeply affected by the fact that the heroes of the platonic love in the film called "Hiccup" played by Muzaffer Tema as Ferit, Nedret Guvenc as Nalan could not reunite, we kept on pulling at our nose and wiping our tears. All of a sudden, I looked at the open blue sky and the plane trees playing with the wind. As if all the living creatures in nature were hugging each other and making love. Girls and I took out our embroidered handkerchiefs at the same time and wiped the tears on our faces. This crying ceremony had lasted too long. Suddenly I stood around the girls. Out of the blue, I started laughing raucously for the state of the girls that they melted into tears and collapsed in sobs as if one of their relative had died and they were bidding farewell to the deceased by prayers by the head of that person's grave. I had formed such habits. I am always focused on laughing rather than crying. That day was one of our happiest and most beautiful days. We wouldn't waste our day by crying because Kerime Nadir killed someone in her novel. We hit the streets at the crack of dawn to have fun. What was the use of crying? The day was still young. This evening we were to go to the farewell party we organized together with our school mates. We were living the honeymoon of our life… It was the season of bright lights… I was about to get married soon, and then I would start working. Already I was doing my internship at Nisantasi Maternity Hospital.

My laughter brought other girls around. Again, giggling and walking arm in arm, we entered the zigzagging rout we love so much in between framed houses. I was about to leave my friends for a short time to go to the hairdresser in Besiktas to have my hair done. One of the girls asserted:

"Then let us go to Kambur's Garden."

"Hmmm, yours is there, isn't he?" I said sarcastically. All of them laughed with a provoking shyness. As they were heading for Akaretler, as always, I was ringing the doorbells of the apartments looking over my shoulder whether there were people descending upon the windows, and catching up my friends walking faster, and larking around the streets. We arrived in a square covered by huge plane trees after going through the passageway between two shops. All the tables in the garden were jam-packed. As the men were indulged playing games such as backgammon and chest, the girls with their heads down didn't seem to glance over them, yet they were struggling to look at cross-eyed to find out who was there and who was not there.

Now I was aware of the situation that the way they were acting had not to do with what they would behave naturally but how to the perform secret love affairs as opposed to the model mannerism they were taught. I was not sure whether it was the right thing to do, but I wasn't like them. I was living my life following my nose. That's why the elderly in my family were afraid of me, and maybe for this reason they were trying to get me married at an early age. What was there to be ashamed of or to hide. Smiling with joy, I talked to the first table:

"Uncle…" I said. Without raising his head, the man replied with a fatherly tone in his voice:

"Tell me. What is it?"

"Have you seen Samet?" I asked. The girls though were content with what I had done, still they told me softly by turning their back:

"Don't! Shut up! It's a shame." They moved away from me after whispering. The middle-aged man had an impish smile on his face as he was holding the dice in his palm he was about to throw:

"A little while ago, we had him go away after beating him in backgammon."

Thanking the old uncle, I informed my friends standing a few steps away.

"We are late. Yours had left here just a little while ago."

I was not curious anymore about why the girls who have more male friends than me, who are more knowledgeable than me about men and making love, were trying hard to appear more ladylike figure around other people. I had a feeling that they were happy to see me solving their many problems through my easygoing attitude. Though I didn't care what the other people think about me, I was aware that I was being loved at school and at the hospital I was doing my internship. Maybe I had that impression.

By bidding farewell to my friends and agreeing to meet in the evening, a honey colored taffeta dress on me, I entered the hairdresser's in Besiktas. I was full of joy. I wished to have my blonde curly hair buckled. Joking with the ladies at the hairdresser's, I described the model I wanted for my hair. I was full of beans like a five years old girl and asked about everything.

The woman hairdresser looked attentively at my hair while she was wrapping hair curler on another costumer's hair:

"Your hair got shortened. Who cut it?" she asked. She was trying to hide her discomfort with a sarcastic smile for my having another hairdresser touch my hair. She went on with a sheepish giggling.

"My hair was cut during engagement ceremony… My prospective father-in-law did it" I said.

"Oh… Is your father-in-law a barber?"

"Yes… Though he is not working anymore, yet she was one of the first hairdressers in Shile."

Her prospective father-in-law was not practicing his craft anymore. Already he was much well-off a person. He had brought up his only son very well, born after his two daughters. I was going to be the bride to his son freshly graduated from the faculty.

"I hope the best, when is the wedding?" the woman hairdresser asked.

"One month later… The paperwork is pending." I replied. My documents were to be posted for fifteen-twenty days. I also explained excitedly to the people at the hairdresser's that it would follow the marriage ceremony, the henna night, the wedding celebration, and then to move to Thessaloniki where my fiancé's relatives live.

In fact, I was not in a hurry for either wedding of marriage. I was going to marry one day anyway. I did not have a concern such as give over my fiancé to somebody else. I was sure that he was thinking the sun rises and sets on me. He made so much effort and pay so many visits to us in order to convince me to marry him. It's true that I played hard to get convinced on the way to marriage. Although many of my peers from Sile where my mother and majority of my relatives lived, got married and had children, I was desiring to enjoy my life and my bachelorhood to the full. Early on I used to say, "I don't want to get married, never". I was going to work at the hospital, to earn money, and with the money I was going to make, I would be dolling up and playing around. I had not such a problem to find a husband. The ideal age bracket of eighteen and twenty-eight was not suitable for me. One should get married at the age when it feels a right time.

But love is something with which reasoning would not work… Before getting engaged, whenever Ibrahim paid a visit, as if I did not want to see him, I would lock myself in my room, and peep through the keyhole. Actually, I couldn't get enough of looking at his very beautiful blue eyes and his light brown hair. He was tall and petite. I was thinking that he was a bit skinny but once we got married, I was going to have him put some weight through pastries and cookies I was going to cook. He had just graduated from the Engineering Department of the university. With his way of dressing and all mannerism, he could seduce girls. I was looking forward to his weekend visits. But again, I was hiding somewhere as if I did not want to see him and watch him admiringly. I figured it out much later why I was behaving towards Ibrahim like this although I was somebody who acts as is and lives by ear. I was running away from him because I did not want to get married. In time I fell in love with him so much and then I thought "Thank God I did not insist on refusing him." I was thinking this way not because he was an educated, well-off and handsome man but because now I loved him a lot. I had never flown high. It would be okay after my own heart whether he was poor or ugly. Actually my dear God had sent me very good fortunes. So many suitors wanted to marry me… As soon as I put on the engagement ring on my finger as part of this marriage adventure started with the insistence of my mother and relatives, I happened to love him as if a lightning struck me. I was about to faint out of happiness when he kissed me on my cheeks. On the days when my handsome fiancé was visiting me, I was actually full of life and waiting for his coming. In the beginning, Ibrahim had put up with my behavior of acting as if not expecting but waiting for him, not loving yet being in love in reality, consoling himself by thinking "She would love me when we get married." Now then we were discussing with each other how we would realize our Thessaloniki tour; our walk in Thessaloniki hand in hand, our cuddling up together in bed, and our waiting for those days to come in no time.

As woman hairdresser removed hair curlers, my blond hair dropped on my shoulder in ringlets. I took a look at myself in the mirror with a joyful smile. It was done exactly the way I wanted. I was feeling the admiring looks of the several women in the shop. They told me that I was already a beautiful woman not because I had my hair done. As beautiful as they can't keep their eyes off me. I had heard these words so many time all my life and took them for granted… I was conscious of my being tantalizingly elegant through my sleeveless dress wrapping my very thin waist and incitingly dropping down my thighs. On the last days of my bachelorhood, as much as my playing around, the things I did were a little bit exaggerated, let it be so. In fact, my mother was thinking that she got her comfort now that "I was out from her home", even thinking that my comfort would end once I got married, so that I could satisfy a desire. For this reason, she was not objecting to my dolling up and playing around. I guess, there was a more relaxed situation since my fiancé was thinking that in one month's time we would get married and then I would behave the way he wants. Moreover, for I wanted my fiancé jealous, I willfully exaggerate my love-cut dress, and still he was not interfering with my dressing and playing around. He was telling me that he loved me so much and he would pamper me after getting married. In our every meeting, he was telling me, "I got enchanted by your mysterious looks and proud expression when I see you for the first time. Yet you have got more than that. I was very sure then. When I get married to my fiancé who loves me a lot, there wouldn't be much difference in my life. Until having children though.

We had organized a wonderful party with my school mates. We were to celebrate our graduation, and we would be receiving our diplomas in a couple of weeks' time. Since our school was a nursing school, all the participants of the party were ladies. Maybe the head doctor would be attending and leaving after making a short introductory speech. Maybe he would not come and that speech would be made by the head nurse.

"Oh praise be" said one of the customers. When I took a look at the woman who made known her admiration by spitting on my face, I burst into laugh. This old lady resembling Neriman Koksal asked:

"Do you have an evil eye talisman?" in a serious manner.

"No" I said smiling like a small girl. The woman hurriedly searched for one in her bag:

"Come here".

After grasping one ringlet covering my eye and putting it on the side, I took a couple of steps towards the woman. In the hands of the lady, seemingly in her fifties, well-off and established one was an amulet. I gathered that she intended to put it on somewhere on me, and it was meaningless to object to it. I was sure that this lady of whose name was unknown to me, would like to put it on me obstinately. There was no need to upset her and prolong this issue too long. I reached out to the amulet in a joyful manner:

"I had one of those when I was small… Everybody and my mother would put it on in order to protect against evil." The woman pushed my hand,

"Why don't you put it on now?"

"I will… I will put it on at home" I said and extended my hand again to take the amulet

"I don't care if you do it at home. Come here."

It was obvious that this woman was a humane, cute, soft-hearted, philanthropist lady. But she was also an adamant person. Moreover, she had a very firm attitude like and army commandant.

"In fact, it needs to be put on your collar. It would be better if it is seen a bit. But apparently you don't want it for it would spoil your flamboyance" she said with a sharp look.

Yes… I did not want to have a blue glass bead to be seen dropping from the collar of my dress, yet I did not want to prolong it too much. I leaned against the wall. By zipping down my dress, she inserted her hand toward my front collar and put the amulet so neatly that it was not obvious from outside. I checked the amulet by my hand. It was just right over my chest. Pushing the Cumhuriyet newspaper on the coffee table as if inserting it into my eyes, the woman hairdresser said,

"Look… Did you see it? Wonderingly I looked at the newspaper which was slipped into my hand. Cumhuriyet newspaper had written a report full of praise of the Günseli Basar, who was the Miss Turkey and won the first place in the Miss Europe Contest organized a couple of years ago in Naples. The woman hairdresser:

"We had told you to apply for it but you did not. Had you won the contest, now you could have been that famous", she said.

Yes… In previous years, when I was not engaged, everyone told me to apply for the Miss Turkey Contest organized by Cumhuriyet Newspaper, yet my mother had made threats saying, "I would break your legs…"

The only concern of my mother was to get me married at once. Since I was not much keen on applying for the contest, I had not insisted on this issue.

It was time already to go to the party leaving the hairdresser. I was riding on the electric tram from Besiktas to get off in Bebek to meet with my friends. At the end of the party, my fiancé would have come to pick me up and drop me at the public housing. The woman hairdresser said carefully examining my face:

"Who knows, what would your children look like". With this such a beautiful girl and a very handsome guy talked about to whom their prospective children's hair and eyes would resemble… I was not thinking about having a baby yet, and wanting to enjoy my youth alongside with the marriage.

***

I did never look at the baby the doctor pulled out of my vagina with his blooded hands. I was brought to the hospital right after a mild pain started with a contraction in my uterus, and I had given birth through a push and vocalization of a sound of "Ahhh". I did not go through any difficulty during birth although the baby was overweight. Despite everything went well, I was not happy. The doctor was looking wonderingly at my face on which there was no expression of either an exultation or a sadness. Taking the baby from the hands of the nurse, he pointed it to my direction as if showing it in the mirror:

"Praise be; she is very healthy girl." He said. I did not give a look to the baby in the hands of the doctor. I had just found out that it was a girl. I was lying down with my legs open and having strange feelings that I was not ciphering out, as well as I was finding myself not caring about the baby and even the world. It was most probably that since I had my internship in a hospital, familiar hospital staff members were running around me and asking me if I needed anything. The nurse and the pediatrician who were taking very good care of myself and the baby, took the baby to clean her up. The pediatrician looked at my face with a smile:

"Let us wait until placenta would drop down by itself" he said.

To say "Do whatever you do" went through his mind. Maybe the pediatrician kept on murmuring something else. I was dreaming of Ibrahim's entrance and saying "Let take our daughter and head for Thessaloniki".

"I don't think the repair work is needed for the mouth of the uterus and inner parts of the vagina. I will check it out anyway... Well-done to you... You pushed very well. It has been such an easy birth," my doctor was saying things like that in a loud voice, and was either pricking up my ear or daydreaming. I guess since my fatherly doctor understood that I was not intending to chat, he was deep in conversation with the nurse while he was making preparations to clean up the inner parts of the uterus. They were talking about the firedamp explosion happened days ago in a mine in Zonguldak with four casualties of four mineworkers. As she heard about that one of the deceased was the brother-in-law of her nurse friend, I had unavoidably overheard what was being talked. I was saddened for the woman who became a widow at an early age and for the other who were also dead now. I dreamt of being one of the dead workers. Had I died at that very instant, I would have not suffered any pain, yet thinking of the possibility of dying got me the shivers all of a sudden. I was young; I was very attractive; I was full of life. What I wanted was not to die but to live my life the way I desire. I was a healthy woman. It was up to me to get rid of all the obstacles in order to have happy and joyful days in front of me. But how it would be possible with the baby. The job of a mother is to raise and care the baby, right? Suddenly I got out of this thought. What I wanted was not to care a baby but to wander in the countryside accompanied with my beloved and to jump rope.

***

I have been constantly praying for my beloved whom I love more than myself, now about to give birth to a healthy child and her birth being an easy one. I was happily overexcited. As I was pacing up and down the hospital's corridor, doctors were talking about the very recent establishment of the Union for the European Football Federations based in Basel,

Switzerland. I was involved in football closely and I was playing as right back at the neighborhood team and SSK amateurs league. For sure I was very happy to know that the UEFA was established. I was lending an ear to what was spoken and that alleviated the stress of fretting over the birth and I was distracted. At that moment I was told the good news that I had a daughter. To be honest, I wanted to have a boy baby. Let it be a girl. We would have more opportunities to have boy babies anyway. I ran into my baby immediately. As it was the same occurrence with the newly-born babies, the skin of our baby was pink white instead of being bluish red. Was it the appearance to me like every mother thinks her own gosling a swan. My baby was chubby. She was resembling her mother a bit, but if you ask my opinion, there would be no other creature as beautiful as her. Slowly I directed my eyes that were out on stalks towards my cute baby's closed hand. An undefinable warmth entered my body. A part of my blood and flesh was there sleeping innocently. I just wanted to embrace and take her to my bosom. Suddenly my mother's name occurred to me… Such a coincidence that the name of Fevziye's mother was the same of the name of my mother. For this reason, I was not going to have a problem with my yellow daisy. Given these beautiful feelings, and I was shaking all over out of happiness, the nurse asked me in a firm fashion to leave the room. Somehow lately the hospital staff was not treating me nicely.

***

While it was being mentioned as the pain chamber or the delivery room, I ended up having settled in the single service room of the maternity ward. Inside of my uterus, my vagina and my bloodstained perineum were all cleaned and there seemed to be no trace left from giving birth. If only my dripping breasts were dried. I had made my mind that I was resolute to remove all kinds of obstacles in order to lead a happy life from that moment on. I turned my head to see outside. On the street, some girls were skipping a rope, and some children were playing jackstones. It was the heart of June. While some women were holding a bed lining under a mulberry tree, two girls were climbing up to the top of that tree. Now what I wanted was to be in those girls' shoes, to watch the sky as I eat mulberry. I felt high with my prospective decision about the fight which was required to achieve happiness. Yet I was also concerned how to deal with a lot of problems I have been facing. I was supposed to keep my pecker up and to take no prisoners. In fact, in a while the nurse would be coming inside and having the baby sit on my lap before telling me "breast-feed now!". Her you go, the door was already opened. Gosh! The baby was not on her lap. The nurse said:

"Fevziye!"

I looked at her smiling as if to ask "What's up?" The nurse replied with a heavy heart:

"You will be discharged this evening" she said. I gestured:

I looked at her as if to say "What shall I do!" The nurse spoke to me:

"Haven't you prepared baby bundle?... There is no swaddle, no snap suit, nor a nappy!" She was talking with great effort as it was a shame on her while she was not trying to rub my nose in it. I smiled with a devil-may-care-attitude:

"No… I did not prepare it" I said.

"Why?"

"I have no idea."

"But how could it be. How would you not know about it… Where is your mother?"

"She was in Sile, but she might have gone to Ankara." I said. the nurse said:

"Anyway, let me go and find something suitable. In the meantime, you breastfeed the baby."

Breastfeeding!!! Hearing this word had made me upset. Unabashed realities were holding against me. Me on the other hand, was going to resist.

"The baby doesn't suck… Do not bring her in vain."

The nurse looked at my breasts overflowing from my nightgown. The milk had run down and wetted the chest part of the nightgown.

"You have plenty of milk… Why doesn't she suck?"

"She doesn't suck, you know."

The nurse approached towards my bed. She placed her thumb on my breast, and after putting her other fingers with her palm under my breast, she squeezed the nipple. Milk gushed.

"You are to hold the nipple like this and put it to the mouth of the baby."

"I am… She doesn't take."

"No way my dear. The baby is hungry… She is crying. Now I am going to bring the baby here with a nurse. She will show you how to breastfeed the baby. Even we can get to your home and help you. Whatever is needed, you can count on us, okay? Come on, you don't have to worry."

I did not utter a word. I was beyond caring. I was somehow seemingly in a state of not giving a damn even if my baby would die of hunger. The nurse went out of the room by saying:

"Let us find something to place the baby." In fact, I should have felt ashamed… I don't know why I did not prepare things for the baby. Maybe, it was because I was thinking that the baby could be a stillborn child… Even though I knew that the baby would be born either alive or dead, I had not made any preparations. I don't know whether I expected that somebody would make some preparations. Who was there from my side to do the job. I had only my mother. She was again in Ankara. She had gone there for election campaign work since she thought that there was much time before actual birth delivery. That said, the elections of May 2 were conducted and my mother's party had remained as an opposition party. Democratic Party had won the election, and Adnan Menderes had even formed the cabinet. Yet there was still no news about my mother. In fact, she should have known that the delivery was very near. My mother, whose skirt I always wanted to grab, I never wanted to leave her bosom, was just not beside me. Even she was near me, what would she have done for me? Maybe she would only buy swaddle and snap suits for the baby. I knew that my mother, who wanted to have me married and to get rid of me, would have left me to my fate.

Ten-fifteen minutes later, another nurse came in with the baby. The baby was crying. I didn't want to deal with a continuously crying baby, rather I wanted to climb up to the mulberry tree and to skip a rope. My eyes involuntarily deviated towards the pink and white face of the baby at who I had not taken a look by this moment. She had stared at my face with her eyes resembling her fathers as if she was calling me to account. Our eyes met. For some reason, she appeared to me not a baby but a monster who was scary through her poise. The day I went to the hairdresser's, came back to my memory. When I remembered that day, tears started flowing down from cheeks after the women at the hairdresser's were saying "Who knows, how a beautiful baby you are going to have". The baby who was born three days ago and I were crying together. The baby was crying out of hunger and myself because of the pain I suffered on that horrible day.

I did not want to remember that day but those terrible memories sitting at one corner of my head were beating my brains out every second. I was very young and as fresh as daisy. As soon as I took a couple of steps on the cobble stones of the side street on *Şair* Nedim Street from which I got out of the hairdresser's, a car approached and stop suddenly, and a man whom I didn't know jumped out of the car and dragged me into the car. Everything happened within seconds.

Whereas I had made a joyful and happy start to the day. As I was pacing around my gardens of happiness, I was so sure about the bright and very long road in front of me. Soon I was going to receive my diploma, to marry my beloved and go to Thessaloniki. I was not having a baby for many years. I had my hair done in ringlets the way I wished to have it for such a long time. I had got out the hairdresser's wiggly in a joyful manner wearing a shawl on my shoulder over my honey-colored taffeta dress. Soon I was going to meet with my friends, and to be in fits at the farewell party, then by leaning on the warm shoulder of my fiancé, I was going home and to make arrangements for so many nice days to come. It was a blue afternoon. The clouds flying around in the sky seemed to be kissing the sluggish stream of the Bosphorus. The warmish and gently blowing wind was playing with the magnolia in white bloom and tamarisks with small and pink flowers. A sweet fragrance from the other shore was spreading itself here on this side.

It was me to be dragged to the car… Nobody noticed my resistance to get on the car, my screams, my lying flat. While the man was trying not to hurt me inside the car, he was also pushing my head with one of his hand, and he was squeezing my arm with his another hand. I looked carefully at the man I thought I saw him for the first time. I seemed to know him from somewhere but from where. I was trying to figure out who he might be on the one hand and I was yelling at him on the other:

"Are you maniac!… Let me go!"

The man was trying to talk affectionately as he was watching my face admiringly and with great passion which was making me more fearful:

"Alright… Calm down… I will tell you"

Around ten minutes later, in front of four story building I was made got of the car into which I had forcefully dragged. I knew this place like the palm of my hand since I lived my childhood and youth in this area. By looking around and screaming, I was making all the efforts to escape his clutches. There was nobody around. Cicadas were silent and butterflies were not in sight. I was being dragged into the yard of a building somewhere near Şair Nedim Street in Beşiktaş. In the jet black backyard, mottled lilacs and mock oranges had wilted. The man was getting upset as I was kicking and stamping, and I was hearing of the sound of my heart. Down the stairs seemed to be scary. The sunlight was lost and my day had yielded to darkness.

I held on to the banister in force. I was both screaming and resisting to go down. But the man was so strong; he held me from armpits and swept me off my feet. He grappled me and had me go down two stories below by dragging. I was thrown into a one room and dark basement floor.

"What do you want from me? Who are you?" I was throwing a hissy fit. The man who locked the iron door from inside looked at me admiringly with a happy smile on his face since he had achieved his goal.

"I am Şahin" he said.

"What Şahin… Which Şahin?"

"I work at the hospital where you do your internship. At the gynecology clinic."

I remembered him when he told me his name. I had heard from one of my friends that a man called Şahin was in love with me. Yes, he had cut off me one time in the backyard of the hospital. "Let us talk" he had said to me. Getting angry about his brazen approach towards an engaged girl, after having looked daggers at him and made a sour face, I said: "What shall I talk to you. Are you crazy!" So I had snapped at him and gone away from there on that day. Later on I had not seen him and he had never disturbed me again. At the moment this man told his name, I searched a supporting element in the room against my desperation and fear. I was shaken all over like an orphaned child.

***

There was no other way except abducting her.

It was about the end of business day. Soon I would be going to my house which was very near where I work, I would be changing my clothes, and as always, I would go to Beyoğlu. As many of my peers had their families and their children they talk about proudly would be hopping from tea gardens to visiting their relatives and acquaintances, to be followed their making love with their wives whereas I would drink a couple of beers and be up all night with a woman named Ayşe or Fatma into whom I run into. Perhaps it must me my bad fate my mighty God deemed suitable for me while I had a great desire to have a family yet not being able to get it. At the age of fourteen I was talking about dropping out of school and getting married, becoming a father, now look at me, let alone being a father, even I had not met a girl I dreamt of. I had spent half of my life at my relatives in Beşiktaş, Istanbul where I left Giresun at the age of seven to go to school as it were. I had never gone to my village after completing my military service where I was visiting during summer months to collect hazelnut. I was not at all sure whether my mother who gave birth a child every year loved and missed me or not. After doing my military service, I had started working at the Maternity Hospital in Nişantaşı. I was making entries of patients, and after doctors' leaving the hospital, I was cleaning the room. Then I was heading straight to Beyoğlu boozers to amuse myself with women. I guess I had not saved any money even though I was over 30, since I had not met a girl with whom I could get married. As I was giving up hope to get married, I saw that girl of my dreams in the corridor of the hospital walking towards the public housing, taking her friend's arm. She looked like a yellow daisy with her blonde hair falling on her lily white face. The moment I saw her, I hesitated whether to go to Beyoğlu or not. I went crawling to my house to daydream about marriage with a strange feeling as if I would be testing my loyalty to her, had I gone to Beyoğlu then I thought I would be cheating on a girl I just saw a minute ago… The following days after having seen her, I neither went to any boozers nor did I mentioned the name of another woman.

In an evening, my best friend for life Salih from Giresun and I poured out of our grief to each other. I told him about my running across the girl who was in my dreams. I was wondering whether the girl would like to want me or not? Salih motivated me so much by saying, "What matters is that YOU want it. Then the following day I cut her off on her way. It's beyond my power to bottle up feelings. I told her all in a dither, "Let us talk." As soon as I said this, she hissed at me but I enjoyed it anyway. For sure she was not going to fall into my arms. The same day, by trying not to reveal my feelings, I fished around at the hospital to gather information about my only love.

I found out that the name of my yellow daisy is Fevziye. The following day, I took a nurse out who lived at the same public housing to hear more about her. If only I wouldn't go out with that nurse and if only I wouldn't come to know what she had to tell me. Fevziye was engaged a short time ago. My bright future was plunged into darkness at that very moment. The entire world was to come crashing around my ears. My mighty God had not envisaged happiness for me. The moment I thought I caught was getting vanished. I was off my oats. Lovesickness must be it! I was not able to go to work and I slept at home for many days. I was doing nothing but smoking. And I was weak. I wasn't able to move a muscle, and I just wanted to die this way. After months, I got very sick. I became acquainted with tuberculosis. I stayed in Süreyyapaşa Chest Diseases Hospital. My best friend Salih visiting me once a week was saddened seeing me like this and giving hope to me by saying, "You can't be sick in bed, a brave man would grab his lover."

So did I follow his advice. As soon as I was discharged from the hospital, I started following along Fevziye. She was sweeping me off my feet through her demeanor shining out joyfulness, and bright and breezy like a child. One day I tried to speak to her at the backyard of the hospital… She even did not reciprocate my salute and went away from me. I was eleven years older than her. As Salih was telling me, I was going to marry her regardless. I had no intention of having somebody else stealing her. If needed, I would do like the men in my village do and abduct my yellow daisy by holding a gun to her head. As it is the case for the girls of my village who got arranged marriage, Fevziye would love her husband one day although she had not seen him before at all. I was going to endear myself to her… Everything was going to be alright yet I needed to get a move on. I had heard that my yellow daisy was going to marry twenty days later. I was all of a tremble. I was going not to have somebody stealing her from me even if I had to abduct her from the wedding table.

I had to arrange a safe place to which I would take her before I abduct her. My friend Salih from Giresun offered the ground floor of his house. This basement floor in the Şair Nedim Street was exactly like I was looking for. That floor didn't have a view of outside and naturally it wasn't getting any sunlight. On the wall of the well of the building had a single window, and I had it reinforced with iron fencing. I was planning everything with Salih, and every time I was talking to him, my courage was grooving.

***

Now Fevziye was contemplating how to flee this single room worse than a jail cell, of which door and window were reinforced with iron fencing. Assuming a humble attitude, she said to him with a begging expression:

"I am engaged. I cannot marry you. The banns were published. Soon I am going to have my wedding ceremony". But her effort was in vain to convince him.

Şahin:

"When times arrives, I will organize a nice wedding event and feast."

"I am married."

"Not yet."

"I beg you, please let me go. I am no good to you."

"Will do. We would get married when the child would be born." Fevziye wanted to die as opposed to seeing his determination. Still trying to sing another tune:

"My fiancé would find you and make you jailed".

Şahin:

"It's better than living without you" said this time. He kept on talking like a suffering lover, by looking at her face affectionately:

"I love you so much. You will see how much happiness I will bring to you. I will pamper you. Believe me you are going to be very happy."

Fevziye took a look at the man disgustingly. She attacked the man with the empty beer bottles, who knows how long they were sitting on the table. Despite he didn't want, Şahin threw the girl onto the bed by slapping her down. Fevziye became pregnant on those days.

In the meantime, İbrahim became enraged. What an incident it was just right two weeks before he was going to marry his only love. Having broken his little finger because he punched on the wall, İbrahim was crying like a banshee at the new apartment his father bought for him in Şişli since he had planned to live there with Fevziye. He had decorated his house with high hopes… He had prepared so many surprises for his beloved… He had a Greek of Turkish nationality master make a special dresser with mirror at which Fevziye's eyes were on stalks inside a showcase of a shop.

İbrahim had eagerly decorated the house where he was going to live once he got married. He had taken pains even for the smallest detail by examining the magazines he had brought from Paris. Now with İbrahim with longer hair and beard locking himself in the house, his father hastily sold the house he had purchased it as a wedding gift for his son. The concern of the father was his suspicion of his son's hanging himself from a ceiling. Now İbrahim alongside with his fiancé were looking for Fevziye in every corner of Istanbul. Where was that outstanding beauty, Fevziye? They had spoken to her close girlfriends, and they had found the places she had gone and the persons she had seen, but in vain. In accordance with the police, they had traced the woman hairdresser, head doctor, yet there was nothing to indicate her whereabouts. Something had happened after she left the hairdresser's but what was it? As if his only love had gone to earth. Observing their desperate struggle, Şahin was laughing in the sleeve, and after work he was visiting the shop to buy something to eat before heading for home.

***

Now I was in a one-roomed and dark cell. Şahin was locking the iron door behind me when he was leaving for work in the mornings. In the room there were a make-shift counter, a table adjacent to the wall where a screen safe was installed; and a small and heavy tiger-legged tea table. Either this room was ready-furnished or the household goods were bought from a second-hand dealer. The inlaid iron bedstead with its bedsides stretching up to the ceiling was looking terrifying.

He had furnished the pretty flat which I saw only from outside. It had very nice balconies. He gave a hug and swept me of my feet when I told him that I was going to place vases with red geraniums. He also told me that that beautiful flat has got two child's rooms, and he wanted to have two kids. I did not have any hesitation what he was doing now. I was dead sure that he was looking for me everywhere. When I remember him, I couldn't stand anymore and cry aloud; I was throwing whatever I was getting hold of, to the wall, and I was punching the door in force.

I had waited for a miracle in this never catching the sun room for months. As I was having my hopes that somebody would be rescuing me, my belly was getting bigger and bigger rapidly. The room was bursting at the seams. The paper bag full of apples, was providing wonderful news from foreign countries and dark news from our own country. Was really everything going bad or else my ill-fate and my dark cell were causing the way I was thinking? As soon as Şahin leaves the flat every morning, I was carefully opening up the out of date newspaper, and reading one week or at most one-month old news items. I was even coming across some paper bags featuring the older dated news, but since I was not in this cell at those times, rather I was inside a real life, I wasn't looking at them.

I opened up the paper bag with the newspaper piece on it dated with a couple of months. The headline regarding the foreign news was about the discovery of the DNA molecule's structure. The news was explaining that DNAs are the molecules playing an important role in heredity since they copy themselves and transfer the life codes through their reproduction cells. The news was also asserting that DNAs can copy the bodies and characteristics of the living creatures. In this case, if a husband grew his suspicion about his wife, can easily find out through DNA testing whether the born child is his or not… Well, if a wife gets suspicions of her husband with blue eyes and curly hair whether her husband cheats on her or not, how would she find out about it? Would she be looking at every child with curly hair and blue eyes she sees on the road and saying, "How much does that child looks like my husband… I wonder if…" so that she needed to have him DNA tested? Alright, what is the benefit of the discovery of the DNA structure for me… Nothing… A big nothing… I heaved a sigh wishing if only I had made love with my fiancé before marriage. If only I would have been pregnant for his child. Had I known that I was going to be abducted, then I would certainly follow that path… What would have happened then? This man who abducted me, would have let me go by saying "you are not a virgin…" Once it was found out that I am not a virgin, then there would be no need to talk about a great love… If one day I would have escaped from this man, I wonder whether could I be also getting rid of what is inside my belly… And what if this man would become a trouble by not abandon the tie between the one inside my belly and himself… Even thinking about it was horrible… Should I say this to the man… The thing inside my belly was there before you abducted me… This time around I would have been faced with a question of how come a virgin could get pregnant… Like Virgin Mary… Could the fruits of what I suffered be blessed the way Virgin Mary lived through in case I would be escaping from this cell. Definitely I would get away from this prison… This ought not to continue like this… Well, what would happen afterwards? By putting myself in Virgin Mary's shoes, I started daydreaming. As much as I remember, my mother who is a staunch advocate of a good name, would not have allowed no one to talk ill about Virgin Mary. Her mother used to mention about her as a symbol of god's mercy and grace which was mentioned in all sacred books including the Koran. To my mother, Virgin Mary's eternal place was in the heaven. God created her on the top of all other women. Her baby Jesus had defended her mother when she was blamed with immodesty by saying, "I am God's prophet, be nice to my mother." How about the thing inside my belly…? Could it be saying that its mother has clean hands, and having her mother come together with her beloved fiancé? Daydreaming Virgin Mary episodes in a strange mood in my dark cell, smiling, I started waiting for the day when the thing inside my belly would be exonerating me.

***

İbrahim had not given up his hope. He kept on searching for Fevziye. His to-be mother-in-law was pining away under his very eyes. Having lost his first husband during the Gallipoli Battles and her second husband out of cirrhosis, his only son swallowed by having giant waves in Şile, this woman become hardened to so much pain, had been ceaselessly crying. This poor woman, whose village's almost all men being lost to the Gallipoli Battles, and some to fishing, acting like a nod and a wink, was clinging tightly to the fiancé of her lost daughter. She couldn't redeem herself since she was not able to take care of her daughter while she was dealing with party campaigning although she had entrusted her daughter with Nazire for whom she held high level of confidence. She was whimpering remorsefully by thinking that she did not provide a good motherhood to Fevziye. The moment Fevziye, whose father died when she was 6 months old, so she, the only orphan daughter had not ever seen her father's face, would be found, then she would not leave the side of her daughter even a second.

***

There was nothing throwing light on my dark room. Nobody was able to hear my voice and to rescue me. I shifted my gaze at other news items on the paper bag while daydreaming that the thing inside my belly was talking like the baby of Virgin Mary by saying, "I am the prophet of god. Be nice to my mother. Find her fiancé for her." At the depressing news of my country. The party for which Şahin was voting and providing a small contribution was in power. The parliament convened with the members of the party for which Şahin cast his vote, was forming a bad government even if it works miracles. I was making all the efforts not to judgmental while reading the news on the paper bag. But his party appeared to me a destructive one like himself rather than being a constructive organization. We were being ruled by a prime minister who was trying to chip away at all the great thing the previous government accomplished. Again, another bad news had affected me deeply. Myself and my country were expecting some troublesome days. Now the village institutes were being closed. How come such a beneficial institution would have been closed down while they were training thousands of teachers and carrying the light of science, education, arts to the remotest villages of the country! The reason for the closure was claimed to be… I couldn't believe what I was reading. Is it really true what I had read? According to the news; since the founding purpose of the village institutes was to replace the madrasah education with a modern system and to raise a group of intellectuals to the contrary of our manners and customs! It was also claimed that the village institutes were wiping the religious beliefs and building up a framework of thinking by promoting immorality, lack of national pride, materialism, and communism through a calculated and planned scheme… It was reported that the apparent target of the village institutes seemed to be education but their real objective had to be to raise atheists and communists. So and so, after declaring himself as "National Chief", İsmet *İnönü* had made the village institutes even more active in 1940… I threw away the piece of the newspaper. There was a stick in my craw to read the report full of slander for Hasan Âli Yücel who had a hand in raising so many educators who contributed to the development of agriculture.

Lying down on the couch for some time, I stared at the ceiling of which plaster had come off. What I was reading seemed to be a precursor of the bad things. I got up from the couch. I was standing in front of a window where I could only see a black wall. I wasn't anymore feeling the smell of dampness from the restroom on the narrow and small hallway. Every day I was trying hard to deal with the iron part of the window, yet I wasn't able to move it even an inch. Maybe I could have bent the iron part a bit but since I would not be able to gain enough room to escape, then most probably Şahin would find out about my intention, I would be scolded by him, he would beat me and the worst of all I would have caused him to take more drastic measures.

Seeing me read the paper bag newspapers, Şahin started bringing home a daily called "Istanbul Express". As much as I figure out from the headlines, this pro-Democratic Party newspaper was outright favoring Adnan Menderes. I still kept on reading the news on the paper bags out of boredom. Though the news was more tedious. In my dark cell, I was not able to hear any voice of a human being, nor a bird singing or a call for prayer. When I was born, then the call of prayer was in Turkish but today according to the news I read, from now on the call for prayer started to be performed in Arabic. On one of the paper bags it was reading, "For the people who don't know Arabic and their mother tongues is not Arabic, what would those people get from that call for prayer."

It was the last day of February. I was approximately five months pregnant It felt like I wasn't expecting the baby but the dark days ahead. My elder sister came back to my memory. My elder sister who doesn't love me at all. She was married for eight years and every child she delivered was stillborn. I wonder whether it was because she ate coal pieces while getting a craving during her pregnancy. I looked around in the room to see some coal but vigilant Şahin had piled wood instead of coal around the tin stove.

As soon as Şahin left the house, I leaned my head on the window's iron. Snow was piled up at the bottom of the wall space. I had no idea how the weather was like outside, warm or cold. Lately I felt that the weather was quite cold but I gathered from the newspaper which was brought home that life had stopped in Istanbul. The paper was reading that such a winter season happened to be lived for the first time in the last twenty-five years' time. I was not experiencing any winter or spring season; I was just reading about them. I had heard from my mother that there was such a winter twenty-five years ago. She was pregnant at that time for my elder sister… At that time the sea too was frozen like this time. Two days earlier Şahin was telling the walls that because of the snow storm, the staff members whose houses are faraway were not able to come to work. He had named the wall opposite of the kitchen bench "Fevziye". The opposite wall was called "Yellow Daisy". Since I was not paying any attention to what he had to say, he was talking to the wall to have me hear what he would like to tell me. "Are you hungry, Fevziye?" Do you want anything, Fevziye?", "What would I bring for you when I am on my way home, Fevziye?" He was speaking of all these words towards the wall as if to make me laugh using funny gestures. Once more, he was talking to the wall. The country was on the rack regarding wood and coal, but I shouldn't be worried. Since the smart guy, Şahin filled the woodshed, there wouldn't be a problem. "There was also bread shortage but the leftover bread from the hospital would be sufficient more than they would need…" So Şahin was informing the wall like this. I was spending my days by closing my eyes and grinding my teeth. I was reading the news covering perilous events in this winter, but I was also feeling very sorry that I wasn't able to experience them. So many happenings were being reported in the newspapers… I gulped when I thought that I could have been one of the people who walked across the frozen Istanbul Bosphorus because of the ice masses came from the Danube River. Would be the morning light dazzling my eyes and making my body warm when I got up one day in my dark cell? If only I would have woken in the first lights of the morning and seen the small ice hills on the Bosphorus. I took a look at the photos and read the news of the thousands of people who were curious about watching this wild beauty among this unique ice spectacle by the Bosphorus. I wondered whether my fiancé was among them. One by one, I looked at the photos in the news coverage of the newspapers including Gece Postası, Istanbul Ekspress, and Akşam on the paper bags I collected during last four-five days. I knew that he was not thinking of those icebergs but me, looking for me everywhere, nevertheless I was carefully examining the photos to spot my fiancé among the people flooded into Sarayburnu area.

Due to the heavy rain, life in Istanbul was paralyzed, and in the meantime, people had difficulty in getting around since putting chains on the tires of the busses was taking a lot of time. Even some drivers took advantage of the situation and raised the collective taxi fares... From the time I was in this cell on, people have had changed. Complaining about these opportunist drivers thinking only for their interest, I was looking at the snowflakes scattered on the baseboards of the wall.

At this very moment, I heard of meowing like a tender melody tone. When I looked out of the window, there was nothing to be seen except a black wall. But the meowing sound was getting more frequent. Suddenly I saw the cat writhing in the snow. That poor cat was struggling desperately like myself. It had fallen down from the road which I estimated six-seven meters high, into this cavity. How could I rescue it here where I was locked in badly. If only I would have removed the only faucet from its base, maybe then I would have half-open it a bit, and would jump onto the bottom of the wall. I never gave a thought of how would I get out of the wall to reach the road. What I wanted was to go away from this room at once and be by that poor cat. For the first time in months I had heard of a voice except Şahin's murmuring, and I had found a companion. Given the swelling in my belly, I needed to remove not only one iron bar but a couple of them. As I was having my first escape opportunity, my damn belly has come out as an obstacle. I wondered what this swelling might be preventing me from many things in my prime. Since I was not going to be able to incise my belly and take out what's there, then I had to succeed in removing several iron bars. Well… I had to start removing the faucet at home and with that shattering the connection point of the iron. It was still the early hours of the day. By the time Şahin would arrive, I could break not only the window but also its wall. I was going to escape from this prison. I was going to rescue myself and the poor cat from this quagmire. After having labored a lot I removed the brass faucet out of its place by hitting it repeatedly using a copper pan with which I wipe the egg dishes. This old faucet was bigger and thicker than a hammer. It would not present a big difficulty to sort the iron and the wall. I grabbed tightly the turn on/off switch of the faucet and started hitting the wall with all my power.

I didn't care in case the people upstairs would come to the door when they hear the noise. I had already shouted at the top of my voice every morning in front of the iron door which was locked behind me, and waited for months to have some people coming. Even a postman did not ring the bell for some reason. If only someone would come and call out to me. I had daydreamed for month to tell someone: "They abducted me and put me here. Please call the police immediately." But silence in front of the door was not broken except Şahin's arrival around five and his key's turning sound. I was constantly and will all my power hitting the iron. For I did not put the wood pieces to the stove Şahin was always lighting in the morning before he left for work, the heating stove had gone off, yet I had broken out into a sweat in the cold of February... There were only couple of hours to my liberation. I guess the poor cat was shrieking and meowing out of fear of banging sound. By standing on the coffee table, I took a look out of the window at the cat sitting down below. "Don't worry, don't cry anymore. In not time we both will escape from this prison" I said to the poor cat. "What is your name" I asked it. It was extremely difficult to make myself heard to the cat. Having jumped out of the coffee table I took a large piece from the cheese on the table which stands glued to the wall of the room, and again climbing on the coffee table and extending my arm through the window's iron, I called on the cat, "Here pussy pussy", and I threw out the piece of cheese towards its head. Yet, although the cat had smelled the cheese, still it was not able to find the cheese which was buried in the snow. I could crack open the iron and let my one leg be out. In fact, had I not been pregnant, I could have myself get out of this room. At the very moment when I was thinking how it would be if I would force my way out, by putting my two palms against the window and letting my two legs hang down, kicks were coming one after another from my belly. It was the first time I felt it this way. The thing inside me was kicking me continuously as if to say "Don't". I wasn't going to mind its kicking but letting my two legs hand down seemed difficult at the moment.

I went down from the coffee table and took the piece of

cheese from the table. Had I tied to a thread and swung it in my hand, then the cat could have caught it for certain. But since Şahin was thinking that I could do myself a mischief, he would not leave any thread of knife. I did not have any inclination to end my life even during the most terrible moment of my life. I was going to fight and rescue myself from this captive life. Firstly, by flexing the pillows out of shape, I threw the only two pillows at home on the snow between iron bars. Two pillows were fallen side by side. Then, I threw out the piece of cheese I had put on the thick paper bag which I folded on the pillow. I watched the poor cat for some time who didn't look at my side and ceasing its meowing was trying to eat the piece of cheese. My soul and body had some rest event to a little extent. I should have started grabbing the faucet and hitting the wall. I just froze at the moment when I heard a sound of meowing as I was coming down the coffee table. I smiled at the cat what turned its head towards me and stared at me with its honey-colored eyes. The cat shook itself and got rid of the snow glued to its hair, revealing white and yellow striped hair on its back. Had I not rescued it from there, it could have frozen and died till morning. I had already cut the connection of the iron with the wall. There was just a little work to do to get away from here with the cat. I took the faucet and climbed up the coffee table, and with all my force I started hitting the point where the upper iron bar was embedded. Since I was able to move the lower iron bar by hitting on its connection a bit more than two hours, understandably I would have needed as much time to move it the similar way. Let it be so… It was not still the noon time. There were so many hours before Şahin would be home. As I started hitting there and thinking that until his arrival, I would have been already on our way to Şile with the poor cat, suddenly I noticed that two hands grabbed my waist from behind. I had frozen with the faucet in my hand. Şahin put me down from the coffee table and faced towards me. I was so confused. I was dumbfounded not because of fear but out of puzzlement. How come he would have arrived here even before noon time? Well… During the first months of my pregnancy, he used to get home but he was not in the habit of it lately. Moreover, it was not even noon. While I was thinking all of these, Şahin looked at me wickedly and closed the window in a tearing hurry, "Did you think that you could run away. What's this all about!"

"Nooo… I wasn't going to run away" I said calmly. Now it's better luck next time, yet I had to rescue the cat outside.

***

Since being able to understand, Fevziye's baby was always calling her mother to account by saying "What kind of mother you are", contrary to the idea of exonerating her mother just like Virgin Mary's Jesus. Let us see how could her mother give an account for what she heard today! Leaving the hospital, to catch her course at Piri Paşa Junior High School, by taking her father's arm, Canan was walking towards the boats where she was going to embark on the Eyüp side of the Golden Horn to land by Hasköy.

Turning to her father Canan said;

"I don't know whether I could forgive my mother."

Canan had found out the incident caused by her mother when she was small at the age of twelve, and her lungs were x-rayed after the examination at the internal diseases policlinic.

"Come non… Why don't you tell me father… how did I return from the dead?"

"Your mother was feeding her cat she was holding in her arms."

"Was it Sarman?"

"Yes"

Since her mother was bringing a new one following the dead, cats and dogs were always present at home. Sarman was the name of her mother's first cat. Their current cats' names were Pamuk and Elizabeth… They had additionally a dog called Lili and more than ten cats named according to their physical states such as Tekir, Beyaz, Sıska, Arap.

"Then father, what happened?"

"Your mother could not make out whether you were hungry or you had a part of you body aching… Don't you remember?"

"No, father… Would I have asked you, if I had recalled it?"

"Correct… You were around 4… There you were … You had cried a lot. You did not let your mother feed her cat."

"Hey father… What a nonsense… Which one is important, the cat or the child?"

"How would I know my dear; your mother used to be like a child. One more thing, she was pregnant with Berkant. Well, Çınar was two years old. How could she have dealt with all of these?"

"Why do say so father. You always acknowledge her to be right. If I were…"

Canan dreamt of the rest in her head. She was going to show everyone how to raise a child once she grew up and became a mother. She would never fight with her husband in front of her children, and she would not let anyone beat her children. Not their teachers not her husband. She would have the people laying a finger on her child rot in jail. Canan would give love to her children, have them go to the best schools, support them to attend their hobbies such as music, painting, and other art fields.

However, she was finding about the reason for her regularly visiting the hospital to have a check-up since her childhood. Her father was explaining. Canan was paying close attention.

Fevziye was pregnant with her third child when Canan was four years old. Canan was crying as she was feeding her cat on her lap. Her father had named her after her grandmothers from both sides, and he had her birth certificate as soon as she was born. But her mother has not called her with her real name, and she once called her Canan. Then after a while her father too started call on Canan. All their neighbors and relatives knew that her name was Canan, and nobody was aware of her real name on her ID. Fevziye had given birth to her second child, a boy, and she had started calling him Çınar. Father saw the situation as an impossible case, then he had his newborn child after their two daughters be named with double forenames. So Çınar was Mahmut Çınar on his ID.

Three years old Canan was crying. Was she hungry? Or was she in pain, it was not clear. She was constantly crying. Putting the cat on her lap down the coffee table, Fevziye looked at her small girl as if to say " What now!". The girl kept quiet for a while out of fear. Then she started crying again. While looking out of the window Fevziye saw the neighor's son. He was going to the grocery store. The boy leant his head on the window as he was doing it as usual and looked inside. He liked Sarman a lot. Fevziye lifted Sarman from under its paws and held towards the window;

"Who is that... Is it your elder brother..." Fevziye was about to tell him what Sarman was doing since yesterday, how talented that cat was", Canan started crying again. Without turning back and looking at her daughter, Fevziye displayed the cat and said:

"Don't you know my cat's brother... it learnt how to open the door by jumping on the shelf..." Nobody would get surprised even this cat started speaking, to her opinion... Maybe one day Sarman would speak yet Canan was crying ceaselessly.

"Why is Canan crying?"

Looking at her daughter, Fevziye turned to the boy:

"She is doing it on purpose to draw attention... She is jealous of the cat and her sibling" she said. As if she was pouring out her grief to her peers. The child looked again inside the room with a serious face. Since he must have been saddened for the crying small girl, he said:

"That's pity... Aunt Fevziye... Send her to me here to play snowball."

It was a very harsh winter day and everywhere looked white. It was not as cold as the year Canan was born and then the sea was frozen, nevertheless this time around there was snow on the streets up to waist. Fevziye opened the door of the apartment which was on the first floor. Canan was out on the street with her house clothes along with the neighbor's son who was three years older than her. Kids were playing snowball. The boy tugged Canan to play snowball, but Canan was feeling cold and didn't want to play for one reason or another. She was standing on where she was. The boy got bored and went to play with his friends. It was snowing on Canan who was inside the snow up to her waist. Canan turned her head towards the window of their house... She could have gone to the house by herself but she did not move... She just stood up there. She was not crying anymore... What I would like to say that Canan was hurt and unhappy child, maybe she wanted to die...

Her mother remembered that she sent Canan out along with the neighbor's son when it got dark and her husband was home. They ran to the house of their neighbor's son. The little boy said:

"She did not play snowball. I then left her." The father rushed out like crazy to the place the boy indicated.

Was the boat careening on the way from Eyüp to Hasköy or was Canan recalling that moment she had not remembered by now? She hugged her father tightly. Her father asked:

"What happened?"

"I don't know... I just got the creeps..." Father and daughter kept quiet for a while. Then Canan:

"Well... How did you find me?" asked.

"I recognized your blonde hair scattered like sunflower on the lily white snow."

"You mean, I was inside the snow up to my neck, right?"

"More or less..."

"Thank God, I did not die, for God's sake."

"My whole world came crashing down around me when doctors told that I would not live long."

"I have nine lives in truths."

"It wasn't easy but you collected yourself in one year..."

"But my mother was not sorry for me."

"No… Your mother was also saddened."

"If she was sorry for me, then she should have cared for me.

"How come she would know what was going on… She must have thought that you were playing with the child."

After getting to the school, Canan attended two courses. While she was in the classroom, her father was chatting and waiting in the teachers' room until the end of the courses. Why was he waiting for her despite having so many things to do instead… Dropping her daughter off at home after school, her father went out for giving an injection. He was the man to do this job in the neighborhood. Working as a health officer at some factories was his second even his third job in order keep up with the household expenses and his wife's spending money like water. He was measuring blood pressure, and dress a wound. As soon as getting home, Canan shot out her chest x-ray to the face of her mother. Eating cake with her children, Fevziye was shocked.

"What kind of mother you are?" Canan was shouting. Fevziye replied:

"What happened now, you've gone crazy." Then Fevziye put the lemonade glass in her hand aside.

"I hate you" Canan yelled and turned up the volume of the radio full blast. Listening to the radio was the greatest fun for Canan whereas to turn it off was being her mother's biggest pleasure. On one occasion, when Canan did not turn down the volume of the radio, her mother had thrown away the radio from the window, and the radio fallen on the stones of the streets was torn to pieces although it kept on playing at the top of its voice. Canan repaired the crumbling but still running radio by employing her own methods so to speak. Now she wouldn't let her mother turn off the radio. If her mother would try to turn it off, then she would make a scene, and she would give a lesson to the woman who left her daughter on the street on a snowy day and got her frozen. Canan was not feeling sorry for herself but for what that little girl suffered. When she looked at the photos of her childhood, she was not able to see even a single joyful pose of little Canan. She had a photo when she was 6 months old, on which the tears on her cheeks were apparent. On the photo taken when she was 2 years old, she seemed to carry all the burden of the world on her shoulders as she was sitting on her father's lap. She appeared sad in all of her photos. This little girl was suffering a lot. Canan wanted a mother like the mothers of her friends. A mother taking care of her home and children, cooking dishes beside cakes, ironing and starching school collars. In the meantime, as if fear gripped her mother. Fevziye was telling herself that in the medical lung x-ray reports thrown on the table must underline the fact that perhaps her daughter was going to die, and therefore assuming that Canan was this much nervous about it. And Fevziye was not willing to give Canan a hard time because of this assumption. Desperate deep down inside, Fevziye was looking at her daughter's face as if it was the last time with a tearful expression. As to Canan, as if she took the signal of her win through resisting, she was fearlessly doing what she wanted to do. Her taking a tough stance did not last too long though.

When the father arrived in the evening, he told that Canan, who has gone through a medical checkup every year, was not very healthy without any trace left in her lungs. Fevziye was surprised. What was then her being up herself. It seemed that this little lady had found out and got upset that she froze on a winter day at a young age. This time Fevziye went crazy. She even didn't want to remember that day. Had her daughter died then she wouldn't have suffered much pain. After rescuing Canan from beneath the snow pile and taking her to the hospital, Şahin had come home and kicked the hell out of Fevziye. With his first punch, two grinder teeth were fallen on her palms. Before she raised her head, the following punches were hitting her face, her back or whatever part of her body. Fevziye had fainted in the middle of the room out of so much beating she had. Being drenched in blood due to beating, Şahin started wiping his beloved wife with gauze bandages with alcohol. Fevziye's cat Sarman had hidden down below the sofa.

Fevziye recalled the day she rescued Sarman from freezing. Şahing became enraged when he saw that Fevziye had broken the faucet and hit the iron rods of the window to crack open. He had walked all over her, thinking that his only love was about to escape.

***

"This is what, if you were not going to escape?"

Without making my being resolute to save the poor cat from freezing noticed, I turned to Şahin with a naïve and begging expression on my face. He had gone mad. The faucet I dislodged in his trembling hand out of nervousness, he pointed out to the window with its bottom rod was off.

"Ah what is this!" he shouted.

"I had heard a meowing. I checked... A cat."

"What cat are you talking about?"

"I just don't know. A poor cat was going to die there. I think it fell down." I said. Thinking I lied to him, Şahin went towards the window and came. I guess he couldn't have seen the cat. When he climbed up the coffee table over there and looked down, he turned his head towards me. He wore an expression of relief on his face. Taking advantage of an opportunity, with a hope:

Please, bring it here. Come on" I started begging. Şahin nodded his head to mean "okay" as he was leaving the faucet in his hand on the coffee table. By stretching his hand over my belly;

"Alright… Let me first light the stove, then I will go get it" he said.

The thing inside me started kicking but I didn't feel the need to tell Şahin about it. I had my mind on the cat. Şahin lit the tin stove quickly, and went out locking me in. I just ran by the window. I waited for long. Still Şahin was nowhere to be seen. Or else did he deceive me and went back to work. There was no way for him to go to work before getting this iron rod put back to its place securely. By heaving a sigh and saying if only he would have gone, I climbed up the coffee table and looked at the well of the building. I saw the cat sleeping on the pillow and leaning her head on the one bite of cheese. Or else was she frozen? In the meantime, I noticed that one ladder was being hung down. That was to say the road and the bottom of the wall was too high for Şahin to jump. I was living downright underground. I heard Şahin's voice. He was talking to a man. "Well done Salih. She would not do again. Anyway, if you hear a noise or something, them please let me know about it."

In this case, there was an informant in this apartment building but who could it be. Having seen Şahin's feet on the ladder, I came down from the coffee table. By pacing up and down in the tiny room, I contemplated over who might be the one letting Şahin know about the noise I had caused. As I was thinking of "At the most it could be the neighbor upstairs", I saw the poor cat Şahin held out from the window. I ran and grasped the cat. She was frightened. She didn't want to enter the room and pushing her back paws against the outside casing of the window. I took out and hugged the poor cat.

Şahin, who took the kitten from the well of the building and turning it to Fevziye, didn't return to work that day. He had his countryman living upstairs go the blacksmith. On that day, the window was covered with a whole black metal plate. Now with all of my hopes to escape were gone, I didn't leave the cat sitting on my lap, and I was crying by looking at my bosom friend. I named her "Sarman."

Sarman's eyes were hazel-colored like my eyes are. Her pupils were always wet as if she was aware of my calamity. She was in the lap of luxury in a cozy home but she was not happy. It was obvious that she was also separated from her mother… She was resting her hairy head on my chest with a sad expression on her face as if she was just about to shed tears. Now I wasn't crying and I was caressing her yellow and white fur by running my hand on hear back.

***

Maybe it's because Fevziye wasn't laying a finger on the chores, the room was as untidy as always. She did not do the bed at all. She was satisfying her hunger by eating cheese, olive, fruits etc. Şahin brought home, and she was not cooking a dish. As Şahin was coming home around five, she was washing the dishes and doing the laundry if any. She was putting the laundry such as towel, linen etc into a basin she had added soft soap earlier, and then she was going to the counter and there she was cooking easy dishes including pasta and eggs. After the dinner was over, she was washing the laundry she had wetted earlier. Since the room with very little ventilation and its window was covered with a metal panel, the dampness of the drying laundry on the chairs Şahin put around the stove was causing the plasters on the wall fall down, and the paint was getting blackened. Looking at the blackened walls, an idea occurred to Fevziye.

"Because of the walls are like this, who knows maybe the baby must be died of dampness. After all I have strange pains in my belly. Wouldn't it be necessary to be seen by a doctor?" she thought she would be killing two birds with one stone. She mentioned about that the baby was not kicking inside her belly.

"Nope… I saw recently it was moving inside your belly."

"But it is not doing it anymore. It has not moved for two days."

In haste for the possibility of the baby dying, Şahin went and touched the belly of his love. He kind of felt that the baby was alive for he was perceiving some warmth filling his palm yet he could not notice any wiggling. He had a midwife, a very close friend of him to call for the birth. Since she was working in a different hospital, he thought she would have not known Fevziye. He was anyway sure that she would not say anything about their situation to anybody. When cautioned, he could place his trust in her. He could have Fevziye and the baby checked by his friend midwife.

"You're right… I have a midwife friend. I will bring her along when I get home in the evening" he approached to Fevziye. "Ok, goodbye" he was also putting his hand on the belly of the woman. At that very moment the baby got so mobile, even its movements were noticeable from outside of her nightdress. As if he was feeling the baby's feet's sole inside him palm. Fevziye spoke as she was beating her belly:

"God damn it… Damn it" she started shouting. She was having hissy fit not because her lie was revealed but she lost the chance of being freed from this jail like place. In fact, it was going to be so much easier. She was about to ask the midwife when she came to call for police. Even she was going to report to the police that she was tortured here in this cell. Şahin said:

"Maybe you are upset about the fact that the baby is alive."

"Don't be ridiculous…" said Fevziye looking at her belly which caused her plans to be blown off course. Şahin changed his mind to bring his midwife friend home. But the walls of the room had grown dark out of airlessness and dampness. Şahin spoke of his worry for confining the baby and his beloved Fevziye in this place. He had no other choice. Fevziye was not listening to him and beating her own belly. The following morning Şahin started taking the dirty laundry by filling in a string bag to the hospital. Then he was bringing back the washed and ironed laundry home. As Fevziye was vigilant, Şahin was not naïve person. He was washing Fevziye's private laundry at home, and he was taking things such as linen, quilt cover, pillow, towel as well as his personal items to the laundry.

One morning when Şahin visited the touilet after having filled the laundry into a string bag, Fevziye wrapped the taffeta dress she had sewed for her graduation ceremony into a bed lining, she took out a towel from the swollen beg and threw it under the iron bed. As she mowed away a few steps, and then she took a look at the string bag; well, the dress was not seen from outside. In the meantime, the sound of flashing in the toilet was subsided. She collapsed on the chair beside the table and started buttering the toasted bread on the stove. Şahin had told her that this butter came from Giresun. Her aim was to draw the attention to the butter. She again began to talk about how delicious the butter was despite her initial reservation for it.

The following day all the laundry came back in the back washed and ironed. Şahin took out the taffeta dress and swang it toward Fevziye.

"Why did you put this?"

"I will dress it after the birthing. Why do you get your thing ironed only, why not mine as well?" said Fevziye. She was speaking desperately because of her plans were blown off course. Şahin was nervous.

"What do you have to do all day long? Instead of sitting idle till the evening, try to learn a bit ironing and cooking. After all the dirty laundry is going to be washed in this house from now on. I will not take them" he asserted with a soft voice.

"I will not learn… I will not find out how to do the house-work… I will not be your wife."

"Anyway… Don't be defiant now… You will learn things when you have your children" he was trying to show affection to Fevziye.

"I will not have my children… One day I will get rid of you and this one in my belly" she pushed the man.

Laughing up his sleeve, Şahin looked at Fevziye's belly which was about to deliver soon.

When Şahing went to work, Fevziye thought about bringing damage to the baby. Every rescue initiative was coming to nought because of the baby. But how could she do that. She had done everything for a miscarriage but all of her efforts did not bring about the desired outcome. The baby did not die even in this airless, dampness place. Had she hit her belly with the faucet then she herself might have died of bloodl loss. Moreover, she did not want to kill the baby anymore. She wanted to get rid of the baby, but she at the same time wanted to avoid becoming the murderer of the baby. How come nobody recognized her taffeta dress at the laundry.

The headnurse of the hospital got suspicious of Şahin's recent strange behavior and his having the laundry done at the launderette. After having a small scale investigation, she had found out talking to one of the caretakers that at one time Şahin was in love with Fevziye. By going down the laundry room, the head nurse felt out the workers there and in fact, and she heard from them that there was a taffeta dress amongs other laundry items; and when Şahin saw this dress there he was embarrassed. Even though Şahin was one of her staff member she liked, her gut feeling was telling her that if anything this man only would have abducted the girl. The head nurse called the police and that morning there was a surprise waiting for Şahin when he went to his work place. When he was heading towards the stairs after having signed the work report sheet, two policemen confronted him. Şahin was taken down the station.

As having her poor cat Sarman eat the mixture of egg and cheese, before noon time Fevziye heard of food steeps at the door and then the sound of key. She stayed stock-still with the duvetine dress she has had been wearing all the time since she did not put on the latest fashion maternity clothes. Şahin... His head down, in a state as if he cried, beaten, first Şahin then after him two policemen entered the room. Fevziye leapt up on-air. She pinched herself to believe it was the moment she was waiting for months not a dream. What she saw was reality, not a dream.

While the police did go out to wait at he door for her to get dressed inside, Fevziye threw a look at her honey-colored taffeta garment. Now into that dress only one arm of hers could fit. Despite her dislike, she put on one of the maternity dresses Şahin had bought. As she was getting dressed Şahin was telling her something in a haste.

"I told that you came to me willingly. Don't you dare press charges my yellow daisy. I love you so much. Whatever happens, I will spend the rest of my life with you. I cannot live without you." Not paying attention to what Şahin had to say, Fevziye was repeating the thought to herself "You will pay for kidnapping a girl" as she was pulling the skirt of the dress at both ends from her belly towards her legs. Even the 38 size shoes were not much too tight although she used to wear 37 size shoes before. This was because of her pregnancy as well as her swollen feet out of her immobility. As she was taking steps on her sole and running towards the door as if to say "I am ready", Şahin was making his rearguard action. "Look... I will kill you. Did you get it. You came to me willingly. Otherwise I will not let you live."

***

76

After months, Fevziye's fiancé gave up hope for his only love. His pending paperwork was already returned to him. He had shed tears by looking at the ID card of the girl he was in love with but life has gone on. He got a job and made new friends. He had tried to forget about his only love through meeting with his university mates and spending time together, yet it was impossible to forget. One day he was buried in the work, Fevziye's mother entered panting.

"İbram…İbram just come dear"

İbrahim looked at the old woman excitedly. He was still calling her "Mother".

"Mother… I hope nothing's wrong".

"Found… Fevziye is found"

Now his heart filled with the hope out of what Fevziye's mother told, İbrahim grabbed the old woman and leapt out of his office.

***

Wearing the shoes, I stomped on their heels, I got out of the iron door which had been locked behind me everyday. The police told me that I was going to be questioned. I had grasped more or less what happened. I think the moment had arrived that I would not see Şahin's face anymore. The iron door, metal plate window, dark and stinky room, barred bed were now left behind. I was climbing up the stairs by saying good bye where seven months ago I was being dragged down. Seeing his way from the police presence to come close to me, and looking at my face affectionately as well as his begging expression were something I didn't give a damn. As I was heaving a sigh to say "Your end has arrived", I took a deep breath when we got the the exterior door. My dark world had turned into a blue one. It was such a warm winter day. Did my eyes get dazzled because of the sun light I had longed for months or because I was thinking of my fabulous tomorrows? I looked out of the window of the police car. Even the tin houses in the Linden Creek (Ihlamur Deresi) seemed to my eyes like one corner of the paradise.

***

With bated breath, İbrahim had found out at the police station that his only fiancée was kidnapped forcibly from the street of the hairdresser, and the person who kidnapper her was working at the hospital. The man was denying that he kidnapped but all the investigation and pieces of evidence were pointing out to him. Soon Fevziye was about to get here and also her testimony to be taken. The joyful breezes inside İbrahim were progressively making him feel a thightness in the chest. Many questions started flying inside his head. For a moment his heart missed a beat. Why was his only fiancée kidnapped? Did something happen to her? For what purpose a girl about to get married soon would be kidnapped? Gradually, his heart started skipping a beat. His only wish was to find his fiancée as she was before and to have his lover with whom he did not unite, lean on his chest. Many bad thought were occurring to him but he was quickly abandoning those thoughts. If something happened bad, then Fevziye's mother would not have taken him up here. He had missed his Fevziye so much…. He started yearning and burning with the desire of holding her tightly once she entered from this door.

Following the foot steps of her at he police station the

door was opened slightly. First ther belly and then herself, Fevziye entered. İbrahim didn't see Fevziye but her belly. Having forgotten her being pregnant, Fevziye affectionately smiled and looked at İbrahim standing beside her mother. She wanted to fall into her only lover's arms. Whereas İbrahim was in shock in the face of Fevziye whom he wanted to take and embrace tight in his arms. He became rooted to the spot, and his looks were fixed at Fevziye's belly. Fevziye made an attempt to come one step closer to her fiancé but she stayed put once she saw him gesturing with his head as if to say "No" with a cold and insensitive demanour. Her lips which had turned pink through her smile curled up in pain. She took a serious look at her fiancé, İbrahim, he didn't seem like the one who loved so dearly but another person looking at a disgusting creature....

Where was her fiancé now who was claiming that he would not abandon regardless of whatever happened? What did Fevziye do wrong? When the old engaged people were stuck on the very spot, the police were asking many questions. Was Fevziye going to register a complaint againt this man who kidnapped her? Did her old fiancé want the woman who's almost due to give birth? Who impregnated Fevziye? Having heard the questions of the polise posed to Fevziye, "Tell us now... Did you run off with this man willingly...? Are you going to press charges...?" And İbrahim pulled himself together recovering from shock, and he put his hand in his pocket... Moreover, he handed Fevziye's ID card to Şahin and left the room at the double. Without making sense of what's going on, Fevziye took several steps towards the door. İbrahim was already gone out of sight. And what's more, he had delivered her ID card to Şahin, the man who made her life miserable. If he was going to give it to someone, why didn't he give it to her mother? Fevziye felt as if she was going to vomit and froze at the threshold of the door. Policeman repeated his question firmly. "Tell us now… Did you run off with this man willingly…? Are you going to press charges…?" Fevziye turned to the policeman with a resolute expression on her face:

"I did not run off with him… This man kidnapped me. He locked me in this cell. I am presseing charges." she said.

At that moment, Fevziye was annoyed ty İbrahim who let herself alone, but her only concern of the time being was to get rid of Şahin. The rest would be easier. It wasn't that important that her beloved İbrahim would not take her. Even he did, it was extremely difficult for her to forgive him after what he had done unless he would present a convincing reason for what he did. She was never desperate… A new start in life would not be difficult… She was only 19, in her prime. The policeman was bringing some fatherly suggestions as opposed the Fevziye's strong hearted and rebellious statement.

"Look my daughter. What would you gain if you press charges? Who would you mary with a child in your belly? Now look… Even your fiancé ran away. Who is going to father this baby? Is it easy to raise a child without a father? Think long and hard. If you press charges, Şahin will serve some time maybe. Well, what will happen to you then?"

"Let him be in prison… Let him stay there… He made my life miserable… Policeman, I am filing charges."

This time around Şahin was sheepfaced vis a vis Fevziye. He seemed to be like not a man who committed a crime, but walked softly and carried a big stick in front of Fevziye:

"Even if you press charges, I will come and find you when I left the prison. You are carrying my child in your belly. Come on, don't be stubborn. See, how happy we shall be. You can do whatever you want to me if I would not be making you live like a queen."

Fevziye got madder after hearing these words.

"Shut up… Don't speak. Nasty monster" she spat in his face. By turning a blind eye to her pain, the rape she endured, the trauma she had gone through and with an attiude of exonerating Şahin, and even getting them married, the policeman looked daggers at Fevziye and turned to her mother:

"Her mother… What do you have to say?"

This time around, her mother stepped in. Fevziye just took notice of her mother when she uttered the following words for her own comfort.

"This is up to her… Look at her being big with child. What would I say? Her fiancé too walked off."

"You're right ma'am. Is there any way other than to get her married with the father, given the circumstances?

"What can I say my dear policeman. I am set aback. I guess, there is no other way."

Fevziye felt as if she was going to lose her mind. She shouted in rage.

"There is one… There is another way out. Do not poke your nose into this, mother… I am pressing charges against this man Mr. Policeman."

The policeman gathered that he could not convince Fevziye, he asked Şahing to empty his pockets. Fevziye grabbed the key put on the table.

***

It was dark when I accompanied by my mother left the police station. The days were short and the nights were long. I was praying that Şahin would be dying of being beaten or going to prison without a possibility of leaving the prison. I was walking with my mother speaking and giving advices towards the old wooden house in Yıldız where I spent my childhood and youth. Were the streets changed a bit? As if they got dirth within the space of seven months. I caught the sight of the crowd who let me alone as I was being kidnapped and put inside a locked basement cell encircled with iron walls… Maybe everyone is looking at my belly. Everyone looks at me not recognizing the pain I suffered, but as is they confront me about a crime.

As we were heading home, suddenly Sarman came to my mind. I could not have left my cat I rescued in that cell. She was as quiet as a mouse. Although I had my tongue, but who did hear my screams… I mentioned about my poor cat to my mother walking alongside and dragging with me. Without paying any attention to her reprimanding as if I was going to commit crime one after another. Şahin for sure was going to the courthouse from the police station, and from there to the prison. That meant that the poor cat being alone home would have died of hunger… What was the fault of that innocent baby so that we would abandon her to die?

Ultimately I convinced my mother to take with the cat. We arrived in front of the apartment building on the *Şair* Nedim Street. By having a feeling that I would be locked behind a door after entering that cell, I handed in the key I took at the police station to my mother.

"Hey mother… Please go get that cat."

"I have enough of you. What would I say to you now… Everything is alright, and what's missing is a cat, ha!" she heeded for the stairs grumblingly. Even though my mother would be complaining about me, yet she would do generally what I wanted her to do. I looked up at the building. I turned my head towards the windows where nobody heard my shouts and screams on that day, when my bright day turned into a dark. Wearing a colored cotton kerchief, throwing one of her legs outside of the window, a woman was wiping the glasses quickly with a cloth in her hand. Obviously she was a cleaning woman… I immediately looked at the name tags beside the bell-button at the entrance of the building. There was no name written on our bell-button. On the one up button was written Salih Ketenci… The name of the man who extended the ladder when taking Sarman from the shaft. Without removing my hand, I pressed the button. I had to have a word or two with that man before getting to my mother. A woman's voice buzzed squeakily asking "who is that" from the megaphone. I asked her to send Salih to the door. "It's important… It has to do with Şahin" I said. Then I pressed the buttons of all the apartment building residents one by one. A few of them came to the megaphone and some descended upon the windows… As I was going to press the buttons again, my mother on the front, and that shag Salh came to the door on the double. I seemed to get cold feet for a moment but shouted hurriedly "Şahin is in prison… Now go get him rescued" and spat in his face and reached out to my cat. As he was wiping his face from hair to his cheek, he turned his head towards the window with the anger of being spat in his face by a woman to realize that there were so many women looking out of the windows. I was going to spit again in his face but since my mother threw the cat while trying to have me grab it. And I took my poor cat from the floor she was fallen and embraced her. In order not to have my mother grumble, I left the yard of the house on the double.

I was innocent, I didn't have any fault but I was walking beside my mother as if I was a criminal. Who did make me feel this way were the looks of primarily my fiancé İbrahim, the police and my mother as if I was an" evil-doer". My mother was carrying on her talk being on edge:

"Whatever you went through was because of your obstinacy. I told you not to walk on the streets alone. Yet you did... The man kidnapped you."

"No mother... Ibrahim was informed of all the places I went."

"Had you been patient until you get married, then all of these would not have happened to you."

"They would... Şahin was bothered his head about kidnapping me before I get married. He would have kidnapped me from the boarding house. This was his previous plan. Even he was not able to do something, he had contingency to abduct me from the marriage office. The man was working at the hospital I was working. He knew all the steps I had taken."

***

While going to the first grade of the high school, Canan found out that her father was secretly trailing after her. Her friend told Canan to look at the walls facing Piyer Loti slope, another corner of the school yard, the wall of the canteen by the Golden Horn. Canan didn't believe her ears... Why was her father following her? She took a look at the places where he could have followed her without getting noticed... And one day she saw her father; he was following her like a tief in the night. First she wanted to square up against him but then she abandoned that idea. Canan felt wretched. The worst was the fact that her father, whom she loved most in this world was not trusting her. In fact, she was doing something secretly but these actions were things like other families would have been proud of. She was sending essays to newspapers, and some of them were getting published. "*Raise in parliamentarians' salaries in five minutes*" was the headline of her news reporting published in the front page of Aydınlık Newspaper, and her father got it framed and hung it in his room after having seen that news. After all, the person who would be preventing her from writing she thought would not be her father but her mother instead. She did not trust her mother. Had she told that she was sending news reporting to the newspaper then her mother would have interfered and she would have not given permission using unimagined excuses, and this situation would have been another excuse to have her drop out from school.

As a matter of fact, it turned out to be that it was her mother who had her daughter to be followed.

"This girl is very weird in recent days. Just be a father and follow her." She had insisted. When Şahin asked "How weird", she replied, "I saw her reading communist magazines" with a big lie. "In case she reads those magazines, then she goes about for sure with communist men."

"She would be naturally go about. What's the harm in it?"

"What do you think will happen… You kidnapped me… Why not somebody would kidnap her."

Fevziye was kidnapped, raped, locked in the house, disconnected with the world, bore child one after another. Was it really she was being concerned about her daughter to be kidnapped or was she slandering her in order to remove her from school? Did she want to have everyone to suffer for the pains she has? Let every young girl be raped… Let every woman bear five to ten children… Let every woman bc beaten every day by their husbands… Let every woman not be backed by their families… Even her daughter… Or else was her mother feeding herself with the pains of others. It was not that obvious about the real interntion of Fevziye's putting too much pressure on her daughter but now Canan had a heavy heart as far as her mother and her father are concerned. Supposedly her mother wanted to confine her to home fearing that her really sprouted and beautiful girl would be kidnapped, and her father thinking that every man would be like himself, he was pressuring here daughter with a suspicion of someone's kidnapping her.

***

At the dinner table set in the evening of the day I was rescued from that cell, my mother, my aunts and I were sitting. There was a deep silence in the room. My aunts Nihal and Nazire who loved me so much were even looking at me as if I was guilty. I would consider myself to be freed from Şahin yet I was losing my appetite because of my relatives's accusing looks. Dropping the knife in her hand, aunt Nazire leant her elbows on the table and stared at me under her frowning eyebrows:

"It will never do… This child cannot live without having an ID card."

My aunt Nihal who was a teacher kept on enumerating

what kind of troubles a child without an ID card would suffer. Nobody was thinking about me. This baby kicking out inside my belly was being taken into considereation more than me and only its future was being discussed.

"You're not considering me at all. What's my fault?"

"The damage is done. We are talking about what could be done from now on. Either we will find a blind, lame man to marry you to register your child or you will marry Şahin to divorce him if you don't want to keep your marriage after the child registry is completed."

I didn't believe what I heard. They were talking about a blind, lame man. If you don't want Şahin, instead of him, a man blind, lame not someone like Tanju Okan, the singer… It turns out that ieverything would have been easier were my belly not swollen. I became more detesting the baby inside me. My aunts Nihal and Nazire were pittying me from time to time saying wods like "It's not Fevziye's fault", yet they were being reprimanded by my mother since they were giving heed to me.

"Since that vile man doesn't make the baby assume a name without marriage… You will marry him officially."

"No…"

Our talks went on until the dead of night.

Eventually my family heads decided to withdraw my complaint against Şahin, to have a shotgun wedding with him, to initiate the divorce procedures after the birthing and as soon as the ID card for the baby was issued, to have the baby raised by aunt Nazire, to start my work at the hospital.

The thing inside my belly was going to grow up in this wooden house where I started going to elementary school and

I had spent all of my childhood… Whenever I get this home, I have a mental picture of my childhood without a mother. The way I grew up without a mother, so now this thing inside my belly was going to live through the same thing.

With my black shool apron, my starched collar, I was standing in the large hall on the day I started going to the elementary school. One soldier had brought my schoolbag. Aunt Nazire was jockeying around me as if looking at a decorated and beautiful doll.

"Let me see… The ribbon on your hair seems to be a bit skewed."

"I don't care… Let it be so."

"Don't say let it be so… Now you are a schooled girl. You are going to study and become a doctor. You need to listen to advice."

Having kept telling me that the profession of being a doctor would suit me which is something I never dreamt of doing it, my aunt Nazire was trying to untie my ribbon and tie it again, and during that time I was making all the efforts to practive patience. Even though I had many opportunities many children lack, I wanted to to be by my mother in the village, in Şile.

"Why didn't my mother come."

"Why should she…?"

"How come shou would come… the fields need to be ploughed."

"Poor Fevziye"

We had just returned from Şile one week ago with my aunts Nazire and Nihal. We had gone to Beşiktaş for school but I wanted to go to school in Şile. My aunts who taught for years in our village in Şile, now living in the nice rooms of the stone house inherited from my father, wanted me to study in Istanbul. It was so much the better for my mother. This way she would have got rid of me, and she could go to Ankara very often.

"Whey don't I go to school in Şile?"

"Here education is better, that's why."

"Let it be so. I'd like to go to my mother."

"You are going to be late for school. Let God give you a clear mind."

The husband of aunt Nazire was the aide-de-camp of Cemal Gürsel. I extended my hand to the hand of the orderly standing by my side in a respectful manner. In fact, I loved İstanbul more provided that my mother would be by my side. But my mother would be either in Şile or in Ankara.

After having started going to school, I happened to see my mother less frequently. From now on, I was spending my school periods in Beşiktaş, and I was going to Şile during every summer holiday to be with my aunts and my mother, both working in the fields and go swimming lots of time. As if to make up to my mother, I was hoeing and watering the fields, and herding the animals. Perhaps like every child, I didn't want to leave the threshing floor. Nothing was much fun for me than riding on the threshing sled drawn by animals, falling from it and after wallowing in the bright yellow straws, being able to reride on the threshing sled. My aunt Nazire had taught me how to treat Şile gauze woven by my mother on the loom by stretching on the embroidery frame. Even as a small child, I was able to make wonderful tea sets, night dresses and blouses yet I wasn't bragging about it naturally. Since *Şile* girls are handed in the embroidery frames at the age of 5, I would have been considered even a late starter. After all, field, meadows and forest works were drawing much attention in me in comparison with doing embroidery work. I was cut for collecting chestnut, mushroom, linden, and thyme in the forest.

I wanted to be by my mother in *Şile* as soon as I finish my elementary school education. I said to my aunt Nazire:

"I don't want to go school."

"Why is that so"

"I will go to school if my mother comes here"

"Whether one's mother comes or not, the one who would like to go on studying, should certainly go to scbool. Consider your elder brothers Cahit and Nahit. They are in Ankara, far away from me. They put up with being away from their mother. Isn't it for their future?"

"Yes it is, though…"

At the time when I enrolled in the junior high school in Istanbul, the husband of aunt Nazire had moved to Ankara, and he rarely came back to Istanbul. Their sons, my elder brothers Cahit and Nahit were living with their father but since they were very fond of their mother, they were coming to Istanbul whenever possible. It was beyond my understanding at that time but then I realized that aunt Nazire got divorce, and we were told this: "Your brother-in-law in Ankara on duty". I had failed the class for two successive years. I was dismissed from the school. I had not gone to school for some time. My aunts Nihal and Nazire were trying to find a solution for my being able to continue my education. They had started searching for a nursing school, lasting 3 years on the junior high school level, and 4 years on the high school since they thought this girl did not have neither a stamina nor the will to become a doctor.

***

I was convinced for sitting at the wedding table with Şahin in order to have the thing in my belly can possess an ID card and not seeing his face from that moment on, nevertheless, our shotgun wedding ceremony was held as if two people in love were getting married. Şahin was very excited dressed in groom's costume and with his stylishly combed hair. His taking the flowers from my mother's hand, which I had thrown them into his face when Şahin handed those flowers in my hand, had doubled over my concern. I had a cream maternity dress with full skirt which was sewed by my aunt Nazire, and I hurriedly left the marriage office as soon as I signed the registry as if I was going to be kidnapped again… I got to the wooden house in Yıldız puffingly as it were. My aunts Nazire and Nihal did not come to the wedding conducted for the sake of formality. They did not want to see that man and make free with him. My aunts were very angry with the man who made my life miserable but why they did not make efforts to get him punished? There was something they did not share with me. When I got home, I found my aunt Nazire crying. She did not like to have me see her cry, and she locked herself in her room. But I could hear her sobbing whenever I pass by her room's door. I had my guess about her sadness being caused by the fact that her husband's being in Ankara and his coming back being reduced to zero. Short time ago, their sons had moved all their belongins to Ankara.

I had spent a year when everything happened like a nightmare one on the top of the other. After all, when thinking everything was over, my aunts Nihal and Nazire had a row with my mother because of me.

While my mother was saying, "Do not interfere with my daughter… I can take care of her. Of my grandchild as well…" my aunts were replying:

"Do what the hell you want." One month after this quarrel, my aunts Nazire and Nihal went to London. Two women I relied on so much were gone now. Nobody was left to back me except my mother. My mother had to be actively doing some party work for the general election to be conducted on 2 May. In fact, she said it was okay if she didn't work for these elections. She didn't want to leave me alone before delivering the baby. My elder sister who always envied me, just reminded that my birthing would coincide with the end of June. To her, there was no inconvenience for my mother's going to Ankara. In any case she would catch up with the birth, and she would be by my side… My mother left me with my elder sister and brother-in-law, and gone to Ankara.

We were bickering every day with my elder sister with whom I had not got along well since my childhood. She was married off with someone since she had a hissy fit to go to school… As if it was me forcing her to marry… I did not react to having my elder sister not being let go to school although she had a mind of a professor, and making her to get married at the age of four-teen, yet I was at that time still a small child. Now she was taking advantage of the sitatation I was in and she was talking without thinking…Had they sent her to school, and made me married as soon as I started menstruating, then they would not have been in trouble. Not my elder sister had a trick up her sleeve because of my being kidnapped, raped and got pregnant to scorn and reprimand me. After all, now my mother was not by my side who protected me since my childhood against my elder sister.

I couldn't revover from carrying pieces of wood from the forest. The one inside my belly was doing nothing but kicking, and it was not relieving me from these troubles by slipping between my legs, by being dropped in the forest, in the mountain or the hill.

Maybe the reason my elder sister was putting all the heavy work on my shoulder was the likelihood of the miscarriage. Having these thoughts in mind, intuitively I felt I needed to protect the baby from her. I was being so exhausted from carrying water from the fountain, drying balls of *Şile* gauze on the sand and bringing them home. Had I escaped from this place then I would have been deemed unrighteous where I was in fact in a rightful position. My son-in-law living in his wife's house was sorry for me but he had to keep his mouth shut for fear of my elder sister. I loved my poor and sheepish brother-in-law much more than my elder sister.

Eventually, I had labour pains in the evening when I escaped to my friend living in Beşiktaş since I was tired of the torturing of my elder sister.

For me not to spent the weekend at the hospital, one day after the birth, that was Friday, when I was discharged, my mother was not by my side. Şahin told me that my mother was informed about the birth and today she was coming to take me.

"Well, it's okay, but where is my mother now?"

"She should be on her way... In fact, she will come and take you from home..."

"From which home?"

"From Nişantaşı..."

With the baby, we entered the house in Nişantaşı which was rented by *Şahin.He* had rented a small apartment with one window looking up the road and the other to the garden, at the ground floor of a nice apartment building. Bu the apartment, the baby, and Şahin were not an interest to me. As soon as getting the ID card of the baby, I was going to divorce Şahin, and I was not going to see him until the end of my life. The baby wrapped in pink swaddling clothes was on Şahin's lap. He was looking at the baby so affectionately who pressed on his chest with one arm, and he was so tender with the baby as it were. On his other arm, a bag filled with several baby food cans and some gauze bandage was hanging. I thought about if only he would have taken the baby while getting divorced. Even let him take the baby and send it to his mother in Giresun. My aunts went away. Still there was no my mother around. Rather than having to deal with the baby alone, wouldn't it be nicer to have Şahin have the baby, I was thinking, and daydreaming of what I would be doing from this time on, I found myself shooting a glance at the windows and the door of the house. They were not ironed. Şahin pointed out the bed by looking at my face compassionately.

"You go lie down... Take some rest..."

I looked at the embroidered lining and the bed decorated with coverlets wonderingly. How was he able to buy all of these items considering he is a man? He was so excited as if he got married and had a child under normal circumstances. I sat on the edge of the bed. I had noticed the baby started whining only after Şahin took a side timid look and even sliding his looks towards my breasts while posing a question at the same time:

"She is hungry…"

I could have said: "What should I do?" Instead, "Isn't there her baby food?" I said.

Now he wasn't insisting "breast-feed". After childbirth, he wasn't thinking of having me prepare the baby food. I didn't have any intention of either preparing the baby food or dealing with the baby. As I was dreaming of the days I would be freed and get a job, Şahin opened the baby's diaper to change. By putting the dirty cloth aside, he washed the oilcloth. He was as practical and as adept as if he took care of ten children. "While the baby's bottom was getting some air, let me prepare her food in the meantime" he said and placing two pillows upon the baby's two sides, and he ran towards to kitchen after grabbing the baby bottle. These walls, covers which made me miserable were all rose-pink. If only instead of this room, my life would have in rose-pink color.

What could I see when I woke up to a noise and sat up in the bed… My mother leaning her suitcase against the wall, my elder sister, my brother-in-law descending on the bedhead, caressing the baby and talking with Şahin as if their daughter got married under normal circumstances and became a mother. My elder sister had been getting pregnant every year, but how on earth all the babies were dying in her belly before getting born, or even they were delivered, they would not have been alive after several days were passed. I was recalling all pregnancy cases of my elder sister. She was gnawing the coal pieces when she was pregnant. Why was that so? Still I have no idea why she was eating those coal pieces. I wonder whether babies in her belly were getting poisoned from that coal or not? My brother-in-law was very much willing to have his baby yet I wasn't that sure whether it was the case with my elder sister. Wonders never cease… My brother-in-law was making a vow at every time when my elder sister got pregnant, yet their baby was stillborn whereas I was giving birth to a cherub baby. After all, the eyes of my brother-in-law were not looking at me at all.

The baby they were caressing was commuting between him and my elder sister, saying "Tu tu praise be". On the other hand, I would have expected from my brother-in-law wiping the floor with Şahin by punching him, and saying "how come you would kidnap my sister-in-law. Beside it did not happen that way, they were as thick as thieves. After exchanging the pleasantry, Şahin went out to run some errands. My mother immediately opened her suitcase and flushed out things she brought. Perhaps she did not dope out whether the baby would be a boy or a girl, pants knitted with knitting needle, sweaters, snowwhite babygros, pajamas made of duvetine, they all looked sufficient enough to facilitate the baby' needs until the age of two. My mother was unfolding and showing some of them to me, holding them in her fingers

"Look at this jump suit. It is going to suit my grandchild very well".

"Okay, alright. Don't open them. Put them in the suitcase."

"Aaa!"

"Why did you bring all of them as if we are going to move in here?" I pushed my mother away.

I was frightened to death in case I would have to stay with this man. When Şahin entered the room with his all hands full carrying grocery, the son of the greengrocer placed a big watermelon, he was carrying, on the tiled ground, and then he left. My elder sister and my brother-in-law put the things Şahin brought on the table dexterously. The beers were poured and the watermelon was cut. The boiled chicken was settled in beside the rice. Salads and many deserts, primarily my favorite chocholate cake were occupying fully decorated table and even there was no room for bread. They all were joyfully enjoying themselves whereas I was brooding on my tomorrows. Everyone was acting as if I were his wife, and they were not taking into consideration that I was going to leave this house tomorrow, and after getting a job, I wasn't going to look after the child.

***

Everyone except Fevziye loved Şahin a lot. Her elder sister, her brother-in-law, and even her mother who returned to Şile just one week ago… Fevziye was determined not to do good to that man. "What an evil man! How come he managed to have everyone love him?" she murmured and got on the Üsküdar boat at Beşiktaş pier with her 40 days old baby on her lap. It was the middle of July and the weather was extremely hot. Her uptairs neighbor Necla in the new house in Nişantaşı had swaddled the baby. She had made a half swaddle since she thought her mother would be taking the baby by the shore. Canan's snowwhite chubby hands were clinging to her mother's hair. Fevziye sat on the deck with her baby. She struggled to free her hair from the tiny tiny fingers of the baby. Such a strength! She looked at the face of the baby she couldn't have opened her fingers. The baby was relaxed through the light of water on the deck and the mild breeze, and with her dimples on ther plump cheeks she was flashing a smile at the people and holding on the

97

mother's hair as if securing herself from falling. The boat had taken off leaving white foams behind and headed to Üsküdar.

"Please my child, watch out"an old man spoke indicating the baby.

Fevziye held her baby tightly. In fact, if only the baby slipped from her hands and fallen into these waters... Then both, the baby and Fevziye would have been saved. Fevziye went cold all over because of her own thought. The baby had made her life miserable but she could not harm her by herself.

There was such a great interest of the people around the baby in her sleeping innocently on her lap, and for that reason the baby was not able to go to sleep completely.

"It's too hot... Remove the swaddle" sad a woman sitting nearby. Even before waiting for Fevziye's response, she just slipped the swaddle from waist down and tucked it into the bag Fevziye had squeezed between her legs. The baby now was wearing only a thin bodysuit and the oilcloth over the bulging diaper between her perineum. Holding her baby on her lap and her basket in her hand, Fevziye got off at Üsküdar pier, and with an uneasiness of the feeling as if she was being hounded, she headed for the point where the busses for Şile stationed.

The bus was moving towards their village via the zigzagging route through the lush forests, deep blue sea shores. Before entering each of the villages, the mineratte of the mosque in that village was turtle heading as if to say welcome. The baby on Fevziye's lap was being held carelessly yet she was sound asleep as if she was being featherbedded. Fevziye had passed this road thousands of times since her childhood, but this time around she was doing it for the first time with a baby on her lap. Once the mosque's minarette of their village was seen from afar, she tought of putting the baby silently on the seat she sat and getting off the bus. She looked at the face of the baby. Not had the heart to do it. Yes… Had she not had a baby, her life would have been easier. But was it baby's own making? She held her baby tightly. By taking the baby in one hand and the basket in another, she went down the village coffeehouse. At first, the retired agriculture man who was spending whole day at the coffeehouse surrounded her

"Welcome daughter Fevziye"

"Thank you, uncle"

"Praise be, such a beauty"

"Where is her father. Didn't your husband come?"

"Okay, go get there … No wonder why your mother was cooking bagel in the oven."

Fevziye was walking toward home by smiling at the men of the village who were at the age of her father or grandfather and by giving short answers to their questions. It was for sure that her mother who cooked bagel in the stone oven had informed the villagers about her daughter's getting married and having a child. She wouldn't like this surprise. Yet, as soon as entering the village, she had felt the safety of mother's protection. When her mother fired the stone oven, for sure she must have cooked pastry with beet or mushroom beside bagel.

The locals at the fountain, farting Hatçe, lame Ayşe, the bride of hunchbacks exchanged glances:

"Fevziye got here, girl" she approached Fevziye.

"Hey Fevziye let me look at you… you look thin"

"No aunt Hatçe… I am just as I was"

"Eee... What are you doing... How are you... Where is your husband?"

When Fevziye arrived in front of the wooden gate opeining to the yard of their house after chatting with the neighbors in the village in haste, her mother was cleaning the leaves fallen on the mulberries collected on the bed lining spread over the wooden bay. Her childhood swam before her eyes. The yard they used to spread over with mulberry, grape, fig in large baskets in order to make dried layers of fruit pulp was again giving away the fragrance of the fresh fruits. Everty month one sort of fruit was being dried. She used to call the dried apple and plumb "kak". Fevziye's mother who heard the neighbors' saying "Fevziye got here, girls" went out to the yard. She had returned just one week ago from her daughter living in Istanbul. Joy, curiosity and apprehension weew blended on her face.

"Fevziye... Welcome my daughter" she immediately opened her arms to the baby.

"Thank you mother" she handed in the baby.

In front Fevziye, her mother behind her sat on the sofa by the bay window. It was evident through Fevziye's body gestures with her head down, and uneasiness in her behavior that her coming was boding somehow for something.

"What gives Fevziye. I hope nothing is wrong..."

Fevziye hemmed and hawed around as if she didn't not how to start talking. Then she said:

"Mother, I did make my mind in my way. To me, there is nothing wrong. You even will see, everything is going to be fine."

"What are you talking about Fevziye… Does your husband know that you came here?"

"No, mother… Don't keep saying your husband. That man doesn't interest me. I don't want to look after a child but work. I will divorce him. You had told me something, remember."

"What! May God give you a plain good sense."

"I will work. I would rent a house near the hospital. You will look after the child, mother."

"Stop right there. Tell me first what happened…" Her grandchild wriggling on her lap for a long time screamed at the end. Obviously, her diaper was full and she was hungry. While Fevziye was taking out the baby food box and the feeder from the basket, since her milk was dried for not breastfeeding, her mother opened the diaper of the baby. Even though it was the evening time, there was a scorching July heat. As the down part of the babywas put under the fountain in the garden by her grandmother, the baby first curled her lips with a shiver. As she was about to start crying, she got drowsy seemingly enjoying the bathing of her roasted bottom with cool-water without complaining.

The grandmother took her grandchild playing with the water again to the bay window.

"You rascall you" she said and dandled the baby several times. Forty days old baby, now with a clean diaper was going into orbit. The grandmother took out fro m the basket the only clean oilcloth and the bodysuit. After changing diaper, she put the bodysuit on the baby. Spreading the swaddle on the ground, she laid the baby over it.

"Oh my, how nice she is. Bable… babble." While looking cross-eyed at her daughter as if she wanted to soothe her daughter, she embraced and loved the baby. After finalizing swaddling, she looked for the lucky charm to pin.

"Where is the fishing hook?"

Preparing the baby food for the feeder, Fevziye was million miles away. She heard her mother at the second call.

"Where is the fishing hook of the baby?"

"Don't pin, let it rest."

"Is that so my daughter? God forbid, she could burst out of evil eye…" she just surged out into the house. She returned holding a trinket sack like a gold pouch. She pinned the fishing hook on which edge the amulet was hanging at the right up corner of the swaddle. She pawed at the baby's chubby hands.

"Grow up a little bit more. Your grandma will put golden bracelets on your wrists." She caressed the baby. As she was reaching out to the feeder in her daughter's hand:

"Do not take out this amulet once more" she cautioned Fevziye like she was lightly reprimanding her.

It occurred to Fevziye that there was a woman at the hairdresser when she was there to have her hair done for her graduation party. As she was putting on the amulet on the collar of her yellow taffeta dress on that day, she was telling herself;

"It would be nice if it is seen just a bit."

***

I suppose I had not lived through such a hot July. What a strange day it was. I had difficulty to breathe and got bored. I had told my friends that my small daughter Canan had reached her fortieth day. The ones who heard the news were coming to congratulate. But my heart was beating in distress as if it was going to stop. I wasn't listening to the people who wanted a photo of the baby or to pay a visit at home.

There was a strange troubling feeling inside me. I was suffering from the fear of losing my tender Fevziye and my baby I loved more than myself. Even though I did not reveal my feeling to them, I had that fear from the very first day. After all, I could not imagina a life without Fevziye. God forbid, the day I lose her, I would stick a bullet in my head. As I was thinking of all of these, my fear grew. I tried to move away from these horrible thoughts quickly. I wanted to make a surprise this evening to my yellow daisy and my small daughter who are in my head every second. Something different…. What could it be…? Nothing was making my yellow daisy happy. She did not accept me yet but as Salih was saying she would love me one day… I was waiting for that day patiently… Leaving my work early, I went to a friend's shop in Osmanbey and there I got them packed a nice suiting for my yellow daisy. I also bought a pink lamp for my tiny daughter from a small shop in Teşvikiye. I would even die just to make them happy. I ran to head for our house in Nişantaşı.

Neither my only wife nor my baby was home. I don't remember how I flew out to the enterance of the apartment building. By climbing up the stairs in twos, in trees, I asked the neighbors upstairs. I found out that Fevziye alongside with the baby went down the Beşiktaş shore. Well I knew about it… Today was the fortieth day of the baby… What drove me crazy was why they didn't return until this time. Had not had the fear inside me, I would have not worried about them even till the morning. I ran back home. The stroller neighbors had given to them was still in the hallway. Since she did not take the stroller, she must have gone somewhere far away. Now I was in a psychological state to do every uncontrollable crazy thing. Hurriedly, I pushed the dresses in de wardrope with my fingers. Well, but why any of Fevziye's dress was not missing. I regretted why I did not lock behind my forty days old baby and my wife, and I was about going mad. I had given my permission for the sake of my baby's fortieth day to be celebrated and I was fooled. She must have gone to Şile. I was going to pay her back. I should have given to my yellow centipede such a big intimidation so that she would not go for similar thing. When I arrived in Üsküdar, the evening bus had already taken off. I immediately found Salih. We ran to Beşiktaş, to the house of his friend who was a minibus driver. At the time we jumped in the car, the sun was about to set.

***

I had no idea what brought my palate back, or was it the beet pastry my mother cooked, or the smell of cumin near the sofa in the wooden bay window? Was it my dreams about my tomoorrows which made me smile? Or else, was it the air of my village I breathed in? Maybe the soul of my father sleeping in the graveyard over there? Or, this old swing on this pear tree? I don't know whether it is these non-stop singing cicadas…

I was so comfortable, so happy as I was eating the beet pastry my mother cooked, in the balcony my dear father built. This evening, even the baby who made my life miserable seemed to look cute to me. Millions of stars in the sky were presenting a musical show as if they were dancing. The insects were singing as is they are singing a lullaby, my baby was sleeping on cushion near me, and her grandmotherwas dancing attendance on her.

It was such a happy scene… Had a writer or a painter happened to pass by here on this pathway, how he or she would have painted a picture of what was seen, I wondered? With a gingham apron on her, an old grandmother butterfly singing conzonets. A sleeping baby butterfly holding a feeder in her chubby hands. A happy young butterfly arriving home whose hands are full… I don't know whether my beautiful dreams are short-lived or not, in fact, these dreams' realization was not that difficult. I suddenly turned to my mother. I was just about to say that I was going to file a diveoce suit, that I was going to get a job at the hospital, that I was going to rent an apartment near the hospital… In front of the yard a familiar minibus stopped. During the days I was constantly followed, when the baby had an ache, this was that minibus which took us to the hospital; now Şahin jumped out of this minibus. Without asking or saying anything he started to kick whatever comes in his way and break the glasses. As I was trying to protect my head and eyes from his kicks, my mother became moon-eyed:

"Stop my son" she was begging and trying to move away me from Şahin.

"Leave it mother… Let him kill me so that I would be saved" I said. I was preferring to die instead of begging him.

***

Despite all the beating, even a drop of tear was not flowing from Fevziye's eyes. While she was standing tall like this, Şahing was getting crazier and he was punching the woman as she was screaming and crying. Blood was flowing from Fevziye's nose the moment Fevziye was falling towards the sofa on her right hand without a murmur. A swelling was formed behind her ear, her eyebrows and lips were bruised. Her mother was hovering around her, and she was crying with frustration that she could not relieve her daughter from his groom's hands. The baby who woke up because of the noise was shouting and screaming. As if all of these happenings were normal events, Şahin turned to her mother-in-law and hissed out calmly:

"Mother, it's a tradition with us. Runaway girl is to be sent back to her husband. It just goes to show you something."

"We don't have such traditions. What we know is the man who lays a hand on the woman will give no joy."

"Look mother. There is no way for us to be separated except death. If she runs away again… I will not let her live."

"Are you a bandit… Get away" said the old lady but she cut it short thinking that his furious son in law might bring about so many troubles for her daughter. Şahin spoke by wagging his finger at her:

"Mother, do not pay heed to her anymore, alright?" He called on his friend in the minibus. His friend opened the door of the minibus. Şahin grabbed Fevziye from her waist and carried her to the minibus by dragging. Fevziye's mother embraced the baby and was in a state of not knowing what to do. She should not have abandoned her daughter alone like this. Trying to calm herself down:

"I had somebody make a bed and a duvet for the baby… Take them as well" after her words she walked towards the back room. She immediately made an effort to lift up the bottom part of the heavy wooden window without creating any noise. She could have jumped out of the window. It would have been good to have had her neighbor head for the gendarmerie, but it would have taken too long for her neighbor's ox-cart to reach Ağva in time where gendarmerie station was located. Well, she could have gathered her neihbors here not to let this man take here daughter. But Şahin was hard upon them. Here he was standing in the middle of the room. Getting rid of the thoughts of rescuing her daughter, grandmother pointed out to the bale filled with undergarments made of Şile gauze for the baby, batiste swaddles, crepe coverlets, wool beds, and duvet. After one or two moves, he put his back to the bale and carried it to the minibus. He looked at Fevziye he thrusted on the back seat. He reentered the yard to collect the baby. Her mother in law went out to the bay window.

"Shall I come with you?"

"Do not come mother, if you are going to spoil your daughter."

"Look at me… I did not give you my daughter to beat her to death. I would give you a rough time when I kick your door down with the police…"

Şahin did not utter a word. The old woman with the baby on her lap sat beside her daughter. At this very moment she succeded to be by her side… The coming day with the help of great God's mercy, she would go to the police, tell them everything and rescue her daughter from this man.

***

Sitting on the deck of the Island Boat moving on by leaving the foamy waters behind, Canan tried to straighten the torn pages of the notebook in her hand and then closed it.

On the Prince Island, Canan was celebrating her own birthday for the first time. Today she turned 19. Regardless of her efforts, she couldn't forget about her mother, sitting decrepitly on the door's threshold. All the more so, after she had read some of the passages on the pages, which held together until now, of the notebook she found in the attic… One of her talk with her mother flashed before her eyes. By throwing one of her columnar white legs on the coffeetable and the other on the chair, and without paying attention to her dressed slipped up to her hips, Fevziye blew smoke and turned to her daughter:

"You think that it's only you who suffered… You don't' know how much your mother suffered?"

"I don't' care… I am not the cause of your trouble. But you are the reason for my troubles."

"So are you my troubles."

"Seeing that your pregnancy was the cause of your troubles, why didn't you have an abortion or you would have given that child up for adoption."

"The abortion was not available. I could have not given up the child for adoption…"

"Why? Even the worst person would have taken better care than you…"

"Despite her mother being that bad, at least her mother would have been beside her."

"What!.. A mother like you, right?"

Canan was slowly making sense of the fact that why her mother hated women more than men considering the things happened to her mother, and why her name written in her ID card was refused by her mother.

Fevziye could not forgive her mother for not being by her side on her bad days, and her aunts for letting her be thrown on the Şahin's lap. Fevziye wanted to have her daughter cry all the time. She also wanted to wipe her daughter's tears. Secretly, she wanted her daughter to be in trouble all the time, and herself being by her daughter's side in times of need. She wanted her daughter to be fallen, and she herself wanted to hold her daughter and lift her to be on her feet... Oh my God... Such a terrible thought it was.

***

Running away with her forty days old baby to her mother's home, Fevziye was brought back to home in Nişantaşı in a welter of blood. The first thing Şahin did was to open the hospital bag and take out from it, things like some alchochol, tincture of iodine, cream, painkillers. As he was dressing the wounds of Fevziye, he had laid her on the bed, their mother was crying and jockeying around her daughter. She was again late to do good to her daughter yet she was consoling herself in thinking that it's better lose the saddle than the horse. She was taking the pledge to herself and murmuring to rescue Fevziye from the hands of this man.

Within a couple of days, Fevziye's wounds and bruises were gone. As a matter of fact, she seemed to have forgotten while she was playing with her cat that she was beaten earlier. As if it wasn't her who was beaten. Her mother was nunplussed seeing her daughter was playing with the cat like a child, tying a sausage ring to cat's tail and bursting into laughter for the comical state of the cat as the cat was circling around herself. How quickly she started to have forgotten what happened to her. She was not comprehending completely whether she should be happy or sad vis a vis her daughter's state on the one hand, and she was taking care of ther grandchild on the other.

109

If only she would not have witnessed that beating... She could have oved her son in law. The man was leaving the house for work and come back home with his hands full. He was waiting hand and foot for her to bring things including umbrella chochlate and pastrami his wife liked. During weekends, he was organizing picnics by the sea, cleaning and cooking bonitos he himself had caught. He was force-feeding Fevziye with a spoon in his hand since she was not eating much. He was bringing cloths to Fevziye even though she didn't want them at all, and he was asking Fevziye every morning before leaving the house whether she had anything she wanted to have. As soon as coming back from work he was bathing and feeding the baby. Since staying with them, the grandmother had not seen Fevziye having washed neither the laundry of the baby nor her husband's. After having completed all the house chores, her son in law was taking all of them to the shore, drinking one of two beers himself to become a little bit tipsy, and ordering tea for them. He was making a fuss over the baby sleeping in her stroller, and he was thrusting the feeder into her mouth. Whereas Fevziye was not concerened about whether the baby was hungry or not, and instead of sitting at the table like everyone else, she was perching on a stone by the shore like a seagull, with her palm full of sunflower seeds, she was also moving her toes inside the water and murmuring to herself something resembling a song.

Now, always being on his guard, Şahin was locking the door when he was leaving the house for work. One morning, Fevziye's mother seemingly being upset about their door locked behind them in order not to let Fevziye run away from home spoke to his son in law:

"But it's enough... Do not lock the door, my son in law. I am here by her side."

"Well… Anyway…" he stopped suddenly. Throwing a smile at ther mother in law indicating his trust in her:

"Alright. I don't want to lock it either. I am wrapped up in the house. What if there would be an emergency!"

"Right my son. Would it be right to lock the door behind a woman with a child?"

"Alright mother. You are here. You keep an eye on her."

"Okay son. Now, you have a nice working day."

Seeing off her son in law, when returned into the room, the grandmother saw that the baby was crying, her daughter was trying to fly the bubble she made out of the soap with which she was rubbing clothers while washing to her cat's direction instead of dealing with her child, and entertatining herself with the cat. In fact, she was not surprised. She got used to her daughter's self indulgence.

"The child is about to burst… Why don't you have a look?"

"She will shut up now."

"You are at fault Fevziye" she hugged the baby grumblingly.

"Oh my baby! Your half life has gone"

"Mother…"

"What?"

"The door is open, let's go…"

"Wait a minute… Don't rush it. Let him trust us a bit more… Somehow or other he would not lock us up. We couldn't go to Şile anyway… Ankara would not occur to him. Let us send a message to elder brother Cahit. Let him know about the situation, and see how he would react? After having investigate properly into where we would go and what we would do… In case he would find you in the place where you would run away, he would kill you for sure."

"We were going to the police…"

"It would have been better if we would have gone before your wounds were healed… The man is unwinking. He would not let us out before all the bruises are gone."

"It's not important… As soon as this door stays open, then let us go to the police and tell them I wanted to get a divorce, but when I left home, he came and found me, and took back by beating."

"What will the police do? They would say, he is your husband, he for sure could beat you… Let us not rush. Let us first send word to someone who would hide us in Ankara for a long time. Then we can buy our bus tickets."

"Oh mother… We would find a place."

"Be quiet… Listen to me. Don't worry, you will get rid of this man."

Fevziye seemed to be listening to her mother. Her mother was certain now seeing Fevziye's nodding her head indicating that she would not do anything crazy such as running away.

Şahin was the happiest man in the world. He wasn't locking the door behind her wife, now his only love was not attempting to run away. His workplace was so close to the house so that he was following them very frequently. He was also able to trust somebody for the care of his baby. His mother in law was taking good care of the baby. He was not blaming his wife for not knowing how to deal with house works. She was spoiled and went to school. Her mother had not taught her how to do house works but she would learn them anyhow. He was sure that she would become a better mother with the second child, and even more mature mother and hard-working woman with the fifth child of his love.

In fact, when her mother started planting in the flower bed in between the wrought iron of the window in order to gain trust of Şahin, Fevziye's nerves were shot with the fact that her mother was dragging her feet in terms of getting rid of this man, and one morning she secretly ran to the police station exiting from the open door. She told the policeman that she wanted to get a divorce from her husband, but her husband had beaten her where she was, then he brought her home. Firs the policeman replied by saying, "He is your husband. He would love you and beat you. ." But Fevziye insisted in her complaint. The policeman stood up and looked up and down Fevziye. Then he sat at his table by stroking his mustache with his hands, and while he was typing what she had to say, at one stage he pulled away his fingers from typrwriter's keys to put his hand on Fevziye's snowwhite legs. "Do not be upset, I can teach him a thing or two" he said. Fevziye got the creeps. She twitched to push the man's hand. Fevziye looked at the policeman with the mix of fear and repulsion. The man did not push forward not to scare Fevziye. Şahin was called to come to the station upon the young woman's complaint. The policeman started slapping in the face of Şahin in ordor to inigratiate himself with Fevziye. Fevziye looked at Şahin involuntarily. Şahin, who had ripped Fevziye in half, and knocked Fevziye's teeth out was now like a whipped dog. But great-bellied old policeman's grinning and looking at ther after each slap had displeased Fevziye. Fevziye's situation at the police station now had turned into something more desperate. If only she had paid heed to her mother and acted in a more planned fashion. What if now the policeman would put Şahin in jail and not let her go and try to take advantage of her, or else let both of them go by saying "Go, do what the hell you want…" She didn't want even to think what Şahin could do to her after having beaten by the policeman. As she was deliberating over this stalemate, the policeman hit hard Şahin's testicles. As crashing down agonisedly on his knees, Şahin was looking at the as if to say "I will make you pay back", and the policeman too was laying eyes on her to mean "How is it? Do you like it?" Fevziye could not cope with all of these and tumbled down.

***

Collapsed at the police station and then having opened her eyes at the hospital, Fevziye was shaken through two pieces of bad news. Her mother was not staying with her anymore since she ran away to the police station without letting her know, and she was pregnant again.

Her second child was a boy and her mother named him Çınar. Being herself thirteen months old, Canan had a baby brother now. When Canan was six years old, his father lived like a marked man. The number of people who nursed a grudge to Şahin who once kidnapped an engaged girl from the workplace and making her give birth every year grew gradually. Most important point was that even though he was a public employee, Şahin was involved in politics. The year when Canan was about to enroll in Nilüfer Hatun Elementary School in Valikonağı Street near their house, her father was transferred to Eyüp Hospital from Nişantaşı Hospital. Soon after they moved from the house in Nişantaşı to the house in Eyüp. Canan took her first step in education at the Emniyettepe Elementary in Eyüp-Silahtarağa. This new neighborhood they moved to was totally different compared to their previous place. After the neighborhood with its luxurious apartment buildings, fancy cake shops, now they had moved to a new neighborhood with wooden old houses' gardens and watermelon fields, as well as creeks at every step. When they got home for the first time, Canan was scared of the ants on the door's threshold and cried for days asking for their old house, and her father took her to the toy sellers market in Eyüp. This market made Canan love her new neighborhood. Though every child seeing that market would admire it. The shops lined along the street were full of colored peg tops, whistles, wooden cribs, wooden cars, whirligigs, and round-bottomed dolls. When they moved to Silahtarağa, there they didn't have so many rich neighbors as it was the case in their previous neighborhood, yet they wouldn't be considered poor either. Here the people were dressing like their neighors in the neighborhood they moved from, and stayed out. But when they went down to Eyüp, there were people as if they came from another country, women wearing chador, and men in baggy trousers, among others. Canan was considering them as tourist, and she was telling her father that they were "Black tourist". She was giving the name of "Yellow tourist" for the ones carrying a camera in their hands. At every turn her father was telling her that they were not tourists, they were Turks, yet she was not paying any attention to him and kept insisting to say "Black tourist" in her child's mind. Canan had obsessions as such. When not sitting right with her, she would have dug her heels in. She named the joker in rummikub game his father was playing with neighbor uncles in the neighborhood as "Replacement for Completion". Even though her father would have said "No, it's name is joker", still Canan would insist "No. Replacement for Completion".

Fevziye and the children got used to their new neighborhood and neighbors even they felt strange a bit. Fevziye freed her children to go to the street in such a countryside, virgin neighborhood similar to tales. Here things were different unlike say Beşiktaş shore they were walking down to it from Nişantaşı with some children in stroller, and some on foot. She didn't have to watch the children and to keep eye on them. After all, all children were running wild barefooted in the corn fields. Though Fevziye was not a mother making a great fuss over the children by Beşiktaş shore. She was even fed up with the kind but firm warning by many acquiantences since they were frequently seeing one another. They used to tell Fevziye that she was a young and attractive mother; and it was not easy to deal with so many children but these babies needed attention and love. Fevziye didn't want to hear this advice. She was sick and tired of listening to the same things. She used to shut her ears to the warnings not to have children fall in the sea, or to be run over by a car, such as "My daughter, why don't you hold your child by the hand", "Do not let the child go to the road".

For eight years, they were in this neighborhood made up of the old Istanbul folks, far away from the city hussle and bustle. When Çınar turned fourteen, her elder sister Canan had carved the date of her birthday nobody else remembered, inside the lid of the new fashion white formica dowry chest which was bought by her father the last year. Sweating his guts out in order to keep up with the expenses of his children and his wife, and as part of his job, being together with the doctors at the hospital, engineers at the factory, that is with the educated people, though Şahin was telling all his acquantences that "Having my daughter study is more important than the boys", still he had a dowry chest for his daughter and a classroom at home for his sons. He had turned one of the four room house with a big hallway into a classroom. He had a carpenter made these school desks exactly the same way in schools, a bit stooping, with cavities on surface to place pencils. As Fevziye was having the birthday party for his son on the large hallway of the house, Canan was standing before the chest and looking at the date she had carved before on the lid. Canan was going to throw in a gift, on every 15 June, on her birthday, which she knew but she didn't know that her mother's life fell apart on that very day.

When Çınar was born, his father sacrificed animal, and he gave gifts to everyone. But unfortunately his son was very mischievous. His father was making all the efforts for him to study, yet Çınar was repeating school years and barely grauduating upper grades. Perpahps that's why twice a week, French and Math teachers were coming home to give lessons to Çınar. At every turn when it comes to study, Çınar was driving his teacher crazy through his mischivious behavior; and in the meantime his mother was going to the Grandbazaar on the pretext of buying a dozen of socks or pastrami, thus was creating an extra opportunity for Çınar.

His questions like "My teacher, may I ask a question" were going on incessantly, and the teachers who came to teach Çınar were well deserving of the fee for the courses they gave to Canan. The returning mother was asking Çınar about what he had learned, and the boy was making up something, and in the evening when his father asked Çınar, his mother was telling Şahin before Çınar opened his mouth, she was painting in glowing colours what his son had learned during the course. And while his father was listening overjoyed, being aware of her dexterity, Canan was looking at her brother smilingly. Later on, a sociable and amusing man, the French language teacher draw his mother's attention, and she quit going for a ride on the course days. She prepared tea and cookies for them, and even though Çınar didn't like taking the course, she didn't care about it, and she spent time with them by playing check and some card games. And her husband paid money for the time they entertained themselves. Getting suspicious about Çınar's marks not getting any better had found out what was going on and he had changed teacher till the end of the school year. Eventually Çınar again had to repeat examinations.

French teacher of Çınar noticed indulgence in books, he brought a picture story book to her. Canan liked a lot that picture book entitled "Peter Rabbit" by English writer Beatrix Potter. Beating her breast, she pittied herself why she did not notice and read that book. Seeing Canan liked reading that book so much, when he came back next week, the teacher brought the biography of the writer and other story books. First, the happy family scene had drawn Canan's attention including pipe smoking father rabbit, mother rabbit wearing an apron and cooking dishes. She read the biography of the writer by heaving a sigh and telling herself if only we were a family like it. It was obvious that Çınar's French teacher had brought these books for Canan most especially recognizing her aptitude for writing and painting. Canan read the life of Beatrix Potter who not noly had written the stories but also drwawn the pictures of the heroes in the book, countless times. She also followed the story of Beatrix having written her story book secretly from her family and submitted it to the publishing house, and her struggle against her family. Sometimes she was full of hope and sometimes she was facing with the reality indicating to her that to be like her seemed to be impossible. She wasn't the only daughter of a very affluent family. She was a daughter of a multi-child-family gradually becoming even poorer. She wasn't sleeping like Beatrix Potter dressed in silk nighties, featherbedded, and going to sleep with the tales told by tutoresses. In order to have her mother and father sleep comfortably, she was sleeping until dawn rocking her last born sibling on the cushion put on her feet. Sometimes, when her father took the baby from her feet, then she could have drifted into a deep sleep. Despite all, there were many things Beatrix Potter and she had in common. She read that the writer was deprived of the love of her mother and father, and she was at the mercy of the tutoresses. The small girl had not lived her childhood, and she felt suffocated under his family excessive discipline. In this regard, knowing that her father loved her a lot caused her to think that she was lucky compared to the writer. Beatrix had written most of her stories with rabbit, by daydreaming at the summer resorts they had gone in the summer months. She too as the writer, was spending two months of the year – July and August – in Şile, and she was able there to dream of the stories to be lived in those natural venues to be part of the beautiful books. Like the English writer, she had the gift to draw very nice pictures. Even her elementary school teacher had explored her gift and said "Your daughter could become a painter", like the mother of the writer, Canan's mother had scolded, "To be a painter?" as if becoming a painter would mean to become a prostitute. Canan's mother was exaggerating this fact and making complaint to her father. By saying she couldn't recover from the house works and child care whereas her daughter going to school and entertaining herself with silly things such as painting, ballet, the piano, she was talking her husband's head off.

Not being able to be indifferent to Fevziye's inducements, her father could not help but going to school to say that his daughter could not attend ballet and music classes since she had to help her mother. In fact, when he told that he had sent her daughter to school just to have her learn a bit of math and a bit of reading and writing, nothing more, her teacher and the principal had reprehended him. Canan felt gratitude for her teachers for this thousands of times. As a matter of fact, her biggest change in this horrible life was to have very good teachers. Aside her mother's neglect, her wanting to oppose all the nice things she wanted to do was even worse for Canan. Beatrix's mother was also as indifferent like her mother. When Beatrix attempted to buy the ranch which was bought by land mafias and to be scheduled to be demolished by them, her mother being oblivious to her daugher's best selling books and her fame got suprised by asking, "Where are you going to find the money to buy that land". Thus, why not Canan would be working hard on the route of becoming a writer with her family not knowing anything about it.

The simplest way of getting her secretly written stories published was to attend a competition and rank in it... Canan... She turned to her graph notebook on which she wrote a true event that stroke her most... By completing this story, she could have sent it for the competition... But this was not something she could have done it in a hidden fashion. In order to complement what she wrote, she needed to do some research, and after finishing her writing, she had to copy the files. According the the Requirements of the Competition, she had to type or use stencil papers. For all of these, for sure, some amount of money was needed. She did not have huge amount of money in her bank account, so she had to share what she did with her father.

"Father."

"Tell me."

"I am going to apply for a competition."

"What kind of competition?"

"It is organized by Cumhuriyet Newspaper. The Competition for Yunus Nadi Prize"

"Well… I don't know. Go on for it"

"Really?"

"Yes but… Don't tell your mother about it"

"Why not father?"

"Well… We can let her know when we win."

"Alright."

"Before writing, I need to do some research, father."

"How come?"

"Could you buy an encyclopedia for me?"

"What kind of encyclopedia?"

"General knowledge encyclopedia."

"Okay… Don't ever tell your mother, right?"

In fact, she knew why her father responded like that. Still she asked her father to find out:

"Why so, father?"

"Don't ask why… I will buy the encyclopedia for Çınar. You can use it."

What she was sensing out of her father's behavior towards her was that her father was by her side like some of the things

121

were being bought for Çınar but in fact they were meant for her use, and sometimes her father's telling her mother that now she was taking Çınar to his friends' meeting. She was trying to find out the reason of his father's shying away from openly defending his daughter. Was it something to do with an issue of her father's kidnapping her mother, she was wondering.

Canan started getting prepared for the competition. Her writing was then to be typed on the stencil; she was writing on the graph notebook, and putting in in the chest, keeping the key around her neck all the time.

She recalled that around her age, her mother wanted to apply for a beauty contest organized by Cumhuriyet newspaper, yet her family did not allow her. Fevziye would have talked about it very frequently. She would have always cast in her teeth "My mother was never by my side, and if only she didn't impede me then I would have been in a different position now". Being only talented and beautiful was not enough. Even the bullheaded and anarchist Fevziye who fights against all types of pressure and oppression could not have attended the beauty contest, there must have been so many undiscovered and died beauties, writers, painters, singers, who knows. Setting her mind on becoming a writer, Canan took courage from just thinking back on the English writer. She was attaching importance to this competition in order to meet with her readers one day.

Canan was constantly writing at times she spared from her courses and works. She was also being saddened by the plunder of the wood and corn fields in their neighborhood. If only she had money like Beatrix to be able to buy these places before they were sold. It was impossible not to shed tears for the vibrantly streaming creeks, trees rooted in the mountains and hills to get dried. The migration waves had started to their neighborhood from Anatolia. Their old neighbors were selling their houses one by one and moving out from these places turned into a rubble. Every morning, neighborhood residents were waking up to look out of their windows to see houses, resembling a field of mushroom with their back to back white-washed walls instead of a pine grove, a wood, a strawberry field.

Now the waterfalls, creeks, vineyards and gardens were replaced in their own words, by the shelters of the poor people coming from Tunceli, Erzincan, and Sivas. The old neihgbors, the locals, aunts Kamuran, Müzeyyen, and uncles Behzat and aunt Semiha, uncle Behzat were now gone; and new names such as aunt Sırma, uncle Durmuş, aunt Nakış, and uncle Haydar became new neighbors. The pine groves where the Hıdırellez picnics were organized, and the creeks where the boat enjoyment was the case were now gone as well. The places they left as the vineyard or watermelon field as they went for sleep, would have turned into a grey small neighborhood in the morning. Led by some people, ganging together the villagers were able to build dozens of houses in one night.

Some of them were İlkay, Necmi, and Yusuf, and when they were wanted by the police, and when they were corned in this grey neighborhood they built in the direction of the poor people's benefit, nobody would have assisted them. By looking at the poor people living in the shanty town they had built with their hands:

"We engaged in the fight for you" while they shouted with their hands chained down and being dragged on the ground, by remembering that unsensibly callously watching poor people being uneducated, they were not going to judge them. Indeed, the people who were loking behind with fearful eyes were going to be upset but they were raising their children they brought from their village, land, traditions, and even escaping from feudist, without involving them with these kind of issues so that they would have thought they can't do anything to save those young people. And they would reside in the flats given by contructors because they traded their shanty houses, and every child would have had a flat as many as the cut pine tree.

The supporters for the chained young people who shouted "Workers and villagers hand in hand" had either a one room house, or being content, or maybe thinking that the state would not leave its citizens hungry and homeless, would have been the educated ones who were content with what they had and gradually becoming poorer.

It is not known wether Fevziye was trying befriend with the women who newly moved tot the neighborhood or to be able to chat with them, or else something seemed to be fun to her, nevertheless Canan didn't like her mother washed carpets on the roads, even on the main streets as her new neighbors did. Moreover, it was not only about washing the carpets... One end of the hose was on the road where it was connected into the faucet in the yard. The young girl was sick and tired of connecting the frequently coming of hose. Instead of putting water on the carpets, the mother was throwing water on the street dogs she soaped down and had their fur foamed, she was throwing the water up the top part of the acacia trees and even towards the windows of some houses. In fact, this was a new fun game for her mother. As she was playing with water, her wet clothes were sticking to her calves and breasts, creating an erotic scene. As the dogs were shaking themselves on the carpet, other women were turning their head as if they were nauseated.

Fevziye was not aware of the fact that the new neighbors were quite knowledgeable about how to beat the carpet, how to wash the wool in the creek, in their previous places; so they were doing their job perfectly and through whispering among themselves they were talking about how unskilfull Fevziye was. It was not something incorrect. The soil at the bottom of the trees Fevziye had watered from top was coming down the road to dirty the carpet she had spread on the road. After rinsing it with mudy water mixed with water and mud, two days later that carpet was thrown on the road again. At first, Canan found it strange that their newly moved neighbors were using all the roads as if those roads belonged to them. Actually, her mother's washing carpet on the roads and streets seemed a bit less strange to Canan. Their neighbors were using the streets not only for washing bed and carpets. The streets were like a wedding venue. The old neighbors would not have used the roads and strets except their registered houses and yards as if those places belonged to hem, and they did not put even a chair on the road not to disturb others.

New neighbors were celebrating their events such as wedding, circumcision, henna night, on the streets, putting chairs according to the number of the guests, with a flourish of trumpets. That meant, the roads built by the government had acquired new functions through the genius innovation of their newly migrated neighbors. Even the wedding saloons in the neighborhood saterted to fold up one by one… The weddings at the wedding saloons, and preparations at houses for the wedding, preparations at the tailor were now a thing of the past. Almond and liqueur, lemonade and cookies to be offered to guests at those saloons were replaced by the rice with meat cooked in the caldrons set on the streets and ayran. Orchestras on those saloons, dances accompanied by the music and tangos became history, and they were replaced by the people dancing horon day and night with the drum and the shrill pipe music… All of these had happened by themselves without anyone noticing this transformation… Grudually they resembled Fevziye, and Fevziye looked like them… As the newly moved neighor women started opening up, Fevziye began to get closed. It was not that extreme though… She closed part of arm, then some part of her leg. Slipdress was out, sleeveless dresses were in. That was followed elbow, arm, and mid calf dress instead of miniskirt. Without noticing these changes personally, and even though her way of dressing was altered, Fevziye's character has not modified. She was again unordinary, alive and kicking, cheerful, and marginal.

For a long time, Canan was not able to get used to their new neighbors. Moreover, new neighbors loved this young girl who was working her fingers to the bone, who was taking good care of her siblings better than her mother. Fevziye was extremely curious about what lately Canan was writing in her room even forgetting to undress her school uniform as she was closeting herself when she got home from school. She tried everything at all cost but she was not able to get the key of the chest. At last, on a day when her daughter was not home, she broke the lock of t he chest and found all what Canan had written. She even didn't bother to read them. Since her daughter locked them away here secretly, she must have written bad things. Though it would have not mattered whether they were good or bad. Instead of attending the house works, what on earth she had spent time with this nonsense? She must have made a strong complaint to her father and made him beat her. As if she was going to take revenge when her daughter was going to be beaten on the beatings she had taken in the past.

Being informed about what her daughter wrote was listening to his wife aback. In panic, Fevziye was talking about writing a novel would be equivalent to working in a brothel. She was mentioning things not written on those graph papers she tore. Love, sexuality, kissing, even communism… She was painting in glowing colors what her daughter was consumed with such things.

At that very moment, Şahin was frightened of Fevziye. He neither uttered a word to his wife nor made his feelings known. There was one thing he now knew. From now on, he shouldn't believe what Fevziye had to say to him about his daughter. Slowly he rose and went to his daughter's room. When he knocked the door, he knew that his wife was watching him by narrowing her eyes. Canan didn't open the door to her father. She wanted to die. Her mother had torn apart what she toiled to have written in twenty-five days' period. She was not going to speak to the woman, namely her mother until death. As Canan didn't open the door, her mother started grumbling. She kept saying that it was not a good idea to let her have her private room, and more, to have her father install a lock to her door was not something reasonable.

"Break this lock. Her everything is locked in this house" she shouted.

"She is now a young girl. She is entitled to have her room, her private things too. Do not interfere. That's enough. What do you want from this girl?"

"What will I ask her…? Had she harmed herself, we wouldn't have known about it."

Was she really worried about her daughter or was she changing her tune in order to pry more into her business, Şahin was wondering:

"She wouldn't harm herself… It would be enough if you don't interfere" he said.

Şahin startd to grasp how Fevziye was making this girl suffer, only after fifteen years. He did not see through the events of her daughter's being frozen, her being left on the street, and her being burnt by the boiling water of the kettle, what was going on. Today he realized the truth. Firstly, today he questioned himself, on a day he was frightened of Fevziye. The woman he thought would love him one day was still remembering the day he kidnapped her and she got pregnant. Who was the culprit? Was it Şahin who has been a mother and father to their children? Or, Fevziye who was kidnapped while she was engaged with her lover? Or else, were they the innocent children?

Knowing that his daughter had prepped herself for the competition with great eagerness, her father wanted to be a shot in the arm. He was telling her daughter that she could try to apply for the competition in the coming year, and he was following her with a fear of self-harming possibility of his never speaking daughter. Canan never thought of self-destruction. When she was up in the morning, her mother had gone to the grocery store. When at home, Pervin told her that her mother tore apart all of her writings. Pervin had thought for a long time what to say. She was saddened by Canan's efforts going down the drain, and she also was angry with Fevziye yet it would be meaningless to add fuel to the flame. The best thing to do would be to calm down Canan by implying to her that Fevziye too had gone through bad days:

"Your mother was forcibly closed to life… She cannot bear to see other people blend with life" she said.

"Yes… Even for her daughter."

"Unfortunately so"

"Well, should I suffer like this? Aren't I going to bring her to account?"

"Nothing will change now. This goes on like this."

"What are you talking about Pervin abla."

Pervin half-jokingly inserted her word between her hopeless smile:

"You will be freed when you get married. Though people like her would be as furius as not being able to accept that her daughter is having a union with her lover."

"Ah! Such a relief Pervin abla! What are you talking about? Maybe I should mary someone, I and nobody would love, is that so?"

"You should make efforts to make yourself happy, not herself."

"You're right. My mother is unable to stand her beloved cat's happiness. Poor animal is reprimanded when she goes out and come back, by my mother saying, "Who knows, with which cat you perched on the roof…"

Generally, the young women of t he newly moved neighbors had thrown away their embroidered headscarves and let their thick hair loosened. They also started to put on one-piece dress instead of their two or three layered ethnic loose robes. They had also taken off their wonderful inlaid broadcloth cardigans and socks not to wear them anymore and hung them on their walls as an item of decoration. The young ones among the men got rid of their regional dresses whereas the old ones kept wearing baggy trousers, a shirt on he tops and their collarless jackets. These people were previously staying away from the locals of the neighborhood and not giving replies to the ones who greeted them by saying "Welcome", now slowly they started to communicate with the neighbors. They were still not giving away in their talks what was going on within the family, yet they were exchanging pleasantry type of conversation.

The students of the best universities who were waging a struggle for the poor people had placed the grown-up sons of the migrated people with the nearby factories such as Türk Demir Döküm, Sungurlar, Rabak, and Vita. Now thanks to the newly mushroomed neighborhoods made of of shanty houses, the greenery had completely disappeared, due to the newly built factories, even the Golden Horn began to dry; and the stench started spreading from the creeks where the boat enjoyment was being indulged, and the hills from which the waterfalls were being watched.

***

Strange to say… Canan, who never went out to the street, was among the spectators. Just like everyone else, I too was watching the anarchists captured in our neighborhood. We were reading the news related to them. Since everyone calls them anarchist, I also call them likewise, but all of them are good kids. Anyway, these young people who rented our neighbor's house seemed certain to be anarchist, but what Canan who was not going out in public was doing here…? She was standing far from me and silently watching. Hundreds of policemen were running inside, outside of the house and even on the main street. As is we were watching a war movie. Some were even eating sunflower seeds, except Canan. Canan was extremely careful, too much saddened and rebellious as if she was about to jump over the policemen.

I didn' t like the police. Whenever I see a policeman, the policeman who did not punish the man having kidnapped me come back to my memory. Whenever I see a policeman, the policeman who put his hand on my legs when I took refuge at the police station swims before my eyes. As if the police do exist only to torture its people rather then protect them from evils. I also knew that my daughter did not like the police, but I had no idea about her reasoning. Did they also touch her legs? In the meantime, everyone was casually talking about the police operation:

"It's a shame on the people who rented out the house?"

"They're not anarchist. They are fighting for us."

"Aren't they afraid? What will happen to them if captured?"

"Their leader is called Yusuf Küpeli."

"You know, I overheard the police. They had dug a tunnel up to the street."

"Up to the street?"

"Sure, for escaping."

"Well, then they will not get caught. They would run away."

"Now the police enclosed every way out. Look, they were not able to get out of the house since this morning. Maybe they are inside the tunnel."

As I was listening to what was being talked, I recalled my

own tenants. I had rented the house of my uncle who moved to *Üsküdar* to the young people brought by the school principal in our neighborhood... I thought whether they would be anarchist as these anarchist police were trying to capture. The school principal Erol Bey with whom we visit each other as families had told us that the young tenant got a job here with his brother-in-law, his wife being pregnant, and soon they were expecting the birth and then to come here with the baby. Yet, in three months' time, hide or hair. Given this thought, I was shivered with fear. The worst thing, we would have lived an adventure like the one here. At that point, two anarchists were removed either from home or the tunnel, by being dragged among the police. As we found out later, they were *İlkay* Demir and Yusuf Küpeli. They were vigorousyly resisting while being between the policemen. They were also shouting so loudly. "We attempted this struggle for you. For the better days." Suddenly Canan stood up where she was. She ran uphill towards the house. As is she had something in mind to rescue these anarchists from the police. While looking after her, the front side of the house was stirred.

I turned my head toward home. Suddenly, I couldn't help looking at the curtains on the window. The curtains with red rose design. The curtains of the young people I rented the house of my uncle are similar. The same red rose design. I ran uphill. I got home out of breath. Canan wasn't home. At once, I looked at the window of the house next to our house. The curtains were removed. My curiosity grew even more. The curtains mounted in the morning were not there. The curtains which were the same as the curtains of the house where Yusuf Küpeli was apprehended were removed by Canan. This way, the young people who would be coming home downhill might become suspicious and not to get to their house. While I was thinking about these issues, dozens of steel-vested policemen encircled the house from inside and outside. Nobody was home… The police pitched camp there for days yet no one from those young people stopped by that house.

***

The newly moved neighbors whose children going to the same schools, shopping at the same grocery store started to socialize with the old locals of the neighborhood. But the old neighbors had for long gone after selling their house and gardens, and the ones still staying had put up their houses for sale one by one. There were two groups of respectful and charitable newly moved neighbors: one groups living in the newly formed small neighborhoods, and the other goups living the new neighbors of the old neighborhood. The ones who migrated from Anatolia and built new neighborhoods were sending word to the ones who migrated to Europe, and letting them know about the houses put on sale by the old neighbor in the old neighborhood. The houses put on sale were being bought by the Marks sent by the migrant workers in Germany. The migrant workers coming in Summer months from Germany were taking photos of their new houses they bought through sacrifizing an animal and decorating their new houses with double sets of furniture, thus turning them into a furniture store. Now, the doors of the sold old houses used to be open in the old days started being locked one by one.

Already having a fobia of so-called lock, Fevziye went ouf from the door she left wide open, to look for new doors to drink coffee. She wanted to be in rapport and socialize with her new neighbors. Accompanied with a dog she called *un-*

tenured walking by her side like a soldier, she knocked at the closed door of the house which was sold by Kamuran and now lived by Sırma. There was no sound reply from inside. Then she turned her head to the window. She saw the slight ripple of the the curtain with ethnic design towards the fringe. That meant, they saw her but they did not open the door. Wondering why was like that, she stopped by the grocery store and bought sunflower seeds. She returned home by eating the seeds in the bag. Knocking another new neighbor's door everyday, Fevziye was not being spoilt by them and in particular the women were looking at her as if she was a strange creature. Thinking that she could not live in this neighborhood, Fevziye too wanted to leave this neighborhodd but she was not able to convince her husband.

Her husband's respond to her asking was: "We cannot live in a flat anymore. What shall we leave for the children in the future. We don't have mansions, big houses. At least, do not make me sell this small plot of the land." In fact, this neighborhood was exactly the place where her husband would feel comfortable; actually when they first moved to this neighborhood, it was among very green woods, gurgling creeks and waterfalls which mesmerized them all, but later on Fevziye got bored of it whereas Şahin liked this forsaken place for its resemling an Anatolian villiage. His wife, being raised in a city, the woman he made her bear child but not being able to have her roll out dough should take lessons from the ones come from village. Moreover, had they lived in a flat in an affluent neighborhood, then he would not meet his ends with so many children, the demands of the children would change, and her wife would not be even finding time to come back home by going about the shores and summer resorts.

Now their daughter Canan, coming of a certain age to understand things did not want to live in this neighborhood. Whenever she asked her father about something to do with education, her father was saying, "Let us finish building the upper story, then we will deal with it." At this rate, she would not be able to enroll in Unkapanı Private Teaching Center, for which all of her classmates registered, and thus she couldn't get the marks at the university entry exams. She was scolded by her father when she asked him why still children and the upper story issues were preventing them from what they wanted. Their father was telling them that he was building the upper stories of the house by thinking of the future of the children whereas the children were screaming to say "We don't want the house." This was so because during the construction of this house, the children should have made great sacrifice.

During the first week of June, there was a tension both at their house and in their country. The tension at home was caused by an old neighbor's moving out from the neighborhood. This was all about everybody's moving out whereas Fevziye's inability to convince her husband to move out. In fact, Canan was the one who wanted to move out most, but since her mother did always do the reverse of what she wanted, then she was holding its desire inside. In the country though, everyday was witnessing a new event. Lastly, the change made in the Law for Labor Unions, was contraining the freedom to choose the labor union. It was the day of 15 June. She turned 15 on that day nobody remembered except herself. She placed the books given by her neighbor she was imagining as Ömer Ayna and the books of Beatrix Potter she presented to herself and the stories she wrote in the dowry chest her father installed a new lock on it. She closed and locked the chest and placed the key she passed through a ribbon around her neck. Additionally, she had a padlock of the chest, now the items inside the chest should be considered safe.

Gerçi babası her doğan çocuğuna İş Bankası'nda hesap açtırdığında ve arada sırada gidip çocuklarının hesabına az da olsa para yatırdığında bankadan verilen çeşitli İş Bankası kumbaralarının kilitlerini bile annesi parasız kaldığında kırıyordu. Almost every day she was broke. It was impossible to provide enough money for Fevziye. Even though she might have had so much money yet she in turn would have wanted to buy more things. The bank was probably fed up with giving piggy bank to them. Faltering between going or staying for a couple of years, their neighbor from Keşan had sold their house to the guestworkers in Germany. In the end they were also moving out. They organized a farewell party at Sabriye Hanım's vast garden adorned with flowers. Their previous old neighbors who had moved out earlier came to the party from Beşiktaş, Şişli, and Üsküdar. It was quite a joyful day. All of the small children were sitting in an order on the stairs leading to the summer cinema in the football field, and watching a movie for free. While the children were consuming sunflower seeds and watch the movie called "Clown" played by İsmail Dümbüllü, the young ones were talking about their new neighborhood, schools and friends in the shade of still surviving pine trees. Canan had prayed that the farewell party would not be held in their garden, and eventually her prayers were answered and it was organized in Sabriye Hanım's garden. This way she was freed from the burden of serving the guests all day long. Her father, mother and siblings were already gone, yet Canan had things to do at home. After finishing her works, she put on dark blue velvet dress of white satin with baby collar sewed by aunt Kamuran Hanım, and she got out of home after brushing her straight yellow hair. Before reaching aunt Sabriye Hanım, she saw her peers spread among pine trees. Canan was a young girl who had grown up without playing with her peers since she had not found time out of her book reading passion and the house chores she had to attend. Some of her childhood and youth friends were assuming that she was not joining them because she was reading books, and that's why they also considered her a little bit pretentious. In fact, while Canan was not finding time out of chores at home, her mother would skip rope, play hopscotch and tipcat with her girl friends. Seeing their childhood friend Canan was coming, her friends stoop up and met her. They also had heard from their families at home.

"Canan is a little bit odd… She reads books whereas her mother plays with us" as they were exchanging talks like this, and they had also heard more or less from their mothers that Canan in fact was working her fingers to the bone. First, Adil hugged Canan. They had grown together. They both loved each other a lot. Adil's family had bought a house in Beşiktaş, and they had moved out from this neighborhood. Canan had lots of things in common with Adil… Listening to music was their common passion. Adil handed in the latest forty-five record entitled "Mountains, Mountains" by Barış Manço. Canan pressed the record on her chest after thanking Adil, and one by one she cuddled her childhood friends she had missed since they moved out. She sat down at the bottom of a pine tree where they opened the space for her… Sunnily, they talked about their childhood. Behzat pointed out to the left side leading the waterfall where the creek streams. "We used to apply henna on our hands with stones" he said. Yes, sprinkling saliva or water on the green part of those stones, more saliva than water, then when it comes to a dark stiffness, they would rub on their palms, and they would have shown one another the following day to see which one turned out to be more beautiful. Though Canan was not able to attend those henna applying events, yet she was familiar with what her friends had to say since she used to carry water from that creek so many times. Sevtap and Mazhar painted in glowing colours about the mischief they did in school. Canan was among the gang who did all the mischief in the elementary school, and the leader of it as well. At that time, the foundation of the elementary school in their neighborhood was just being laid and even the construction barracks were not set up, Canan and her peers had to study in a school of another neighborhood. This was a burden for the families but it was an opportunity of joyful moments for Canan. While the young people were sharing their childhood memories, Canan cut her laughing short with an eye gesture of Sevtap. Her mother was poising over her.

"Canan!"

She looked at ther mother as if to say "What's up?"

"Get up and help your aunt Sabriye Hanım."

She again threw a look to her mother like asking "Why?"

"The woman got tired. Yoı are a young girl, aren't you?"

The young girl looked at ther friends as if to say "Sevtap, Nilay, Ayşegül, Vildan, they are here too!" Her mother spoke:

"They are considered as a guest… Come on, what are you waiting for" she started to raise her voice. The bottom of the pine tree was now occupied by her mother since Canan despairingly got ouf of that place not to make a scene. After a while, the jovial laughter was being resonating from the pine grove. The young people were shrieking with laughter at whatever Fevziye was telling them. Instead of helping Canan who was carrying in an out from the vine trellis in the yard of the garden where the adults were entertaining themselves, Canan's friends were accompanying the joyful laughter of their aunt Fevziye. Not taking offence at serving her neighbors she loved and shared a lot of things since her childhood, also considering them as her own family, Canan seemed to be happy with her sweet smile on her face, yet there she had something banging over her head. Why their neighbors, aunts Kamuran Hanım, Münevver Hanım, Fatma Hanım, Sabriye Hanım, and others, were not asking their daughters do an errand. Let alone they were not acting this way, why they were not saying anything about their best friend's, her mother's torturing her daughter? Whey they didn't say anything against her not allowing her daughter to study her courses, and why she made her take care of the children, and why she also made her the house works at the times they saw all of these happening? How come they would see it normal that while her daughter was taking care of children at home, and that grown-up woman was playing fiestones on the street?

As carrying the olive oil dishes their neighbors had cooked and brought one day earlier on a huge tray to the garden, Canan remembered that her uncle Faruk had wanted some ice a short while ago. Even her uncle Emin Bey had asked her to slice the melon. Yet Canan was coming up short for all the demanding jobs. Well, the mother of her friends too were doing something such as slicing the bread, serving the pasty but mostly the men were asking her things to do since she was young. As exiting from the door with a tray on her hand,

Canan turned to the host:

"Aunt Sabriye Hanım… If you call on Ayşegül to help, things will we quicker."

"No, don't call her at all."

"Why?"

"My baby… Why do I make my daughter work while I am alive and kicking?"

"But… I come short…"

"Why did you come my baby. Go to the side of your friends… You are young. You are going to laugh and have fun. This youth may not come again."

Canan was baffled what to say.

"But my mother …"

"Ah this Fevziye… She was supposed to do by herself. She did send you here, didn't she?"

Canan was having her guess about with which pretext her mother blew off her responsibility. Had she leave the tray and go to the side of her friends, her mother, not shying away from making a scene, would be saying some words and maybe embarrassing her. The best way was to finish the work quickly and then go there. As she was serving the cookies and pastries at the tables, she was hearing the following words since they were repeated since her childhood, "She is such a hard-working girl; she is such a model girl; so much intelligent… she turned more beautiful as she grew up… Brigitte Bardot can kiss her ass."

The following day, as the truck laden with the belongings of one of their neighbors she shared her childhood, Canan stared at their departure. It was a gut-wrenching feeling and she also felt that something had fallen away from her life. As she was waving her hand alongside with a couple of neighbors after the truck, her mother, forgetting about the departure of her friend of many many years and someone who shared so many things with, her mother was bouncing and going to the children playing the ball accompanied with her staff dog called "Princess". One of the remaining neighbors, Firdevs Hanım seemed to be hesitant to say something to Canan, nevertheless she suddenly turned to her and said:

"There is a prospective buyer for our house, Canan".

"Oh… Are you going to leave?"

"Yes… We found a large and nice flat in Üsküdar. We are going to move into that flat."

Firdevs pointed out with her head to the sofa in the garden as if she had something to tell Canan before she leaves. While they were walking together to head to the garden, the young girl looked enviably at Firdevs Hanım's large garden where there were trees of quinz, mulberry and pomegranade, and her house with its smoking chimney and red tiles. Was it only the house and its garden she took a look at?... She has been envious all along since her childhood for this family she loved a lot and for its happiness, for their constantly smiling joyful children. Although they were a well-off family, still they were so humble as if being rich is something they should feel ashamed. Moreover, even though her family was not as affuluent as they were and gradually getting poorer, and making the money fly, there were certain rules in Firdevs Hanım's home. While many children were complaining about these rules, Canan was wishing these rules would be observed in their house. In many households, primarily in Firdevs Hanım's house, even one drop of water would not be wasted, the pencil sharpener would not be used before the tip was not use up, and the torn socks would be patched, and the stale bread would be used in the dish of dry bread and broth.

On the contrary, in Canan's house, the socks, the pencils were being lost even before they were used, and months later they were to be found somewhere in the house in an unusable condition. Her mother would have gone to the grand bazaar for everything she could not find, and she would have bought pencils and socks in dozens. She would not prepare like her neighbors, tomato paste, sundried food made of curd, tomato and flour, jam, pickle. These food items would have been bought by her father in large tin boxes. While the delicious scent of strawberry, sour cherry and quinz jams was pervading the whole neighborhood, Canan's mother would have gone to the grocery store and buy the things she wanted by cash or if she didn't have money, she would have put them on the cuff. Fetching a sigh, Canan sat down on the sofa in the large backyard. She looked around. There was a frantic preparation for something. Did Firdevs Hanım bring her here to ask for help. There were freshly cut noodles on the snowwhite linens spread on the balcony. The dried mint leaves were dispersed on a large tray, waiting to be crumbled. She noticed that the charlady entered inside after throwing the carpets on the garden wall one by one. Say that today was the day the charlady was working. Pointing out to the carpets Firdevs said:

"I will have them washed and taken way… We would spread them in the new house."

Canan seemed to be crying her heart out. Maybe she would not be able to enter anymore this garden where she had many good and bad memories. She was feeling sad about their neighbor's leaving even though they had not been her supporter. "So, you are going to move into Üsküdar, right?" she said. Canan's beloved grandmother had a flat in Üsküdar. Canan was finding peace at her house… Every time they went to her house, her grandmother woud buy nuts for them and send them to the shore to swim. Had she been by her grandmother side with whom her mother did not get along well, she would have been over the moon.

As if it was a last ditch effort Canan told Firdevs Hanım, "If you insist by telling my father that we would be also moving out aunt Firdevs. By turning up her nose at her with a sour expression on her face:

"Your father would not move an inch from her, my daughter." It was kind of an indication of her not liking Canan's father.

Almost all of their neighbors in the neighborhood were liking Fevziye altnough she was not taking care of her children, not doing her home works. Canan was not able to make a sense of this situation. Sometimes she was explaning this to herself like this: When their neihgbors came to their house, her already joyful mother was setting up beautiful table with freshly cooked foods, and even the kettle on the table and cooker was always ready to serve the tea, and the halvas with walnut, pastiramis, liqueur with almond were being finished even before the children were tasting them, and everyone was having nice time with her mother's joyful laughter, and that's why they love her. Because her mother was not like other constructive but boring women who were locking themselves in the kitchen to prepare dishes for the guests, mostly labor intensive but cheaper recipes like ravioli, pastry with minced ground beef. And because of their hard working in the kitchen they were not able to participate in the fun, and waiting for the guests to leave as early as possible for finishing all the after party works to get up early to serve their children in the morning.

Unlike other fathers, her0 father was not voluptuous, and not up all night spending his time at raki tables. Her father was not liked by the neighbors for his working at several jobs, coming home exhausted, cooking dishes for children, and doing the laundry. Mostly Fevziye was invited even to the Rumeli Hisarı and Kemerburgaz parties, and already hard-working father would only be attending those events from time to time. Attending these and similar seasonal tours including Kilyos, Neşe Suyu, without getting prior permission from her father, upon her returning home, her mother was beaten by his father, nevertheless, she was not failing to go to the next pleasure trip. Canan had difficulty to understand her father, working like a guilty slave to meet the deficit to his children caused by his wife. Since her mother was not taking care of children, why they were making a baby. The young girl could not grasp the oddity in this issue in one way or another. She was recognizing the fact that her father loved her mother and all of his children. And also how he was struggling to make them all happy…

Her father was not having the guts to show that he had a strong liking for his daughter in order to close the gap of lovelessness since her mother alienated her daughter. One of the mistakes he had made was hiding the fact for a long time from the children that he kidnapped Fevziye… The most important of all was the fact that he was one of the psychological sources in the infrastructure of having the mother have mixed feelings of love and hatred towards her daughter.

While Fevziye was living in the dreams of Virgin Mary

and waiting for the day her daughter would be making her a heroine, her daughter was looking for a supporter to punish her mother. Before one of those several neighbors - still in the neighborhood - moving out, who were condoning her mother torturing her, she could have found out the answers to some of the questions in her head.

Canan;

"Aunt Firdevs Hanım... You are leaving here. Can I ask you something?"

"We are going... But we are not going far away my daughter. We will be in touch."

Canan was well aware of the fact that, in the first flush the visit paid regularly would be decreasing, the one who were gone would get used to their new neighbors, the ones who stayed behind would be having fifty times more new neighbors thanks to the endless migrations.

"Yes... But I'd like to ask anyway."

"Well, ask then."

"For so many years... Does it appear to you normal, I mean my mother's behavior towards me?"

Firdevs was surprised vis-à-vis this question but picked herself up quickly.

"No... It's not normal."

"Alright... Why don't' you then give advise to my mother? You both are good friends."

"What could I say?"

"You can tell her to treat her daughter well."

"Do you think we didn't?"

"You did tell her ha!"

"Yes."

"What did she say?"

Fevziye Hanım suddenly held her tongue as if she was afraid of letting a secret slip from her mouth.

"You now turne

d fifteen. You can ask your mother this question."

Canan should have her guess that she could not find out anything form their last remaining neighbors. In fact, they were treating their children like a baby. Occuring earlier to her but not attributing to their neighbors, Canan made her mind that these women having acted as an onlooker at what her mother did to her in her childhood, were as guilty as her mother. She was just about to tell her this point, at that very second the woman spilled the beans.

"If you want, you don't have to put up with your mother."

"If you want to be freed from these tortures.""

"In order to be freed from her, I need to study in a far away city... This time, my father..."

"But my daughter, you cannot be freed by studying."

"Should I kill myself? What else could I do?"

"Look... I have three sons. Be our bride of the one you want. Actually, I called on you to discuss about this topic."

Yes... To them, to have a young girl to be freed required her getting married. Who wouldn't want to have a bride like her, stong bodied, taking care and managing a house, looking after her sibblings. In case Canan was their bride to one of their sons, even the charlady occasionally coming to their house would not be needed. In fact, Canan liked the sons of Firdevs Hanım as well as the boys of her peers in the neighborhood. Adil in particular... Mazhar... Behzat. All of them were precious friends to Canan... The children of the neighborhood woud be walking to the far away school holding each other's hand. They overcame the snowy roads together. All of them grew up as siblings. She loved them so much yet marrying one of them had never crossed her mind.

Canan found out in the following days that another friend of her mother was thinking of her as a prospective bride for her son. "I heard of it from Firdevs. You didn't want to be her bride. I was so elated to hear it." When their neighbor talked to her like that, she had somewhat witnessed that she became a subject of negotiations among their old neighbor aunts.

"I am not going to marry... I will study" she chopped down in a dogmatized fashion.

One of the things puzzling Canan was, all of the neighbors in her neighborhood were not making as big an effort as her father in order to have their children study. The ones who would like to study were studying, the ones who did not want, were left alone, no one was insisting them to study. Most of her peers had fooled around and did not want to study after completing their junior high school education. Mosf of their families were in good shape economically. They in fact, didn't see the necessity to set aside money for their children's going to study further. The elementary school as well as the junior high school to which Canan was also going, had a full-time schooling, and even a nutrition package consisting of milk and biscuit was being given to students. During their gym and music classes, students were learning ballet and the piano, and they were not paying anything for these extra curriculum activities. Thus Canan was finding herself being lucky to study in schools like these ones. Maybe the most effective element in her solving so many problems was her beloved teachers. The name of her elementary school teacher was Veyis Şehirli. Teacher Veyis, not knowing in the beginning what Canan was living through at home, used to liken her as a Black Sea small boat. "Once she is submerged, once she floats" he used to say for the little girl. Her junior high school teachers, most of them were graduates of the Village Institute had made a positive impact on Canan's future.

They had listed her talents. For that matter, even she was just 11 years old, she had attended a competition at TRT since she was writing good short stories and poems, and she got the first place and appeared on television. At that time TRT was broadcasting from the studios of the Istanbul Technical University during certain hours, three days of the week. Her father had bought for her a red-dark blue check patterned wool two-piece dress and red shoes, taking her to Istanbul Technical Universty studios. In the neighborhood, only Firdevs Hanım had a television set. She had it brought from Germany. Saying Canan was going to appear on television, all neighbors were gathered at Firdevs Hanım's house. Canan kept on surprising the whole neighborhood through her experiences and things she accomplished. Earlier she had come first in the quiz program on the radio channel and received a prize.

***

There were so many children in the attached buildings which were build very recently. Şahin was coming up short in administering injection to those children. New neighbors were even calling him "Doctor Şahin", and when their family members got sick, they were calling on him rather than going to the hospital. The painkillers, vitamin and antibiotics given by Şahin were curing the sick children. Şahin's patients increased so much in number that he had to say, "Thank God, we did not move out from here ..." Old neighbors held no brief for Şahin as it were... But when it comes to new neighbors! They were always showing respect for Şahin as if he was a real doctor. Fevziye felt as if she fell from popular esteem...

They didn't like Fevziye that much. In addition to her husband's working like a slave at strangers' houses, and then coming home to iron the shirts of the children seemed strange to their new neighbors. They were not saying anything right to her face but for sure they were secretly blaming Fevziye for not being a proper housewife.

Fevziye realized that it's impossible, she told her story of how she was kidnapped to aunt Sırma who was one of her new neighbors and seemingly a half-wit woman, feigning madness as well. When Fevziye started telling her, starting with the words like "Don't be fooled by his appearance of a good man...", but to Fevziye's surprise, aunt Sırma was not amazed by her talk. "It's not a big deal... in our countryside, what happened to you happens almost to every young girl... very very normal." she had told Fevziye. Now it was Fevziye's turn to get surprised. More than getting surprised, her new neighbor's words had served her like a medicine... They were like cure for her deepened wound throughout years... What she had gone through was nothing compared to what happened to them... In the village of aunt Sırma, girls were being sold even they were still a baby for a couple of sheep, and some of the girls would have been raped by some relative, and then the raped girl would have been killed immediately by her elder brother, uncle or father...

"O oooh, you should go and see… in our village, the creeks are always full of corpses of girls…"

Fevziye seemed to be lost for words. She collected herself with the shame of feeling that other girls' suffering more than her made ease her distress. She liked the new neighbors more now. Fevziye would not move out from here. Her old neighbors were well and good but most of them got married with their loved ones. Fevziye was in pain as the melodies of happiness were rising from their houses roofs. Most of her friends were starting cooking even from the morning for their husbands arriving after their work. It was a labor of love for those women to prepare those appetizers, salads. How happly they were washing the socks and underpants of their husbands. How beautifly they made love and bore children to name them Biricik (Only One), and Aşkım (My Love). No wonder, their new neighbors were not pretending that they love their husbands, but they seemed to be holding high esteem for them.

Even so, the most colorful of Fevziye's newly acquainted neighbor was Pervin. While reading her newspaper in Fevziye's garden, the gate of the garden squeaked. A string bag in her hand, followed by several puppies and two poor kittens, Fevziye entered the garden. She arranged randomly the items from the string bag on the wooden table. Apart from the movie and tea days, she was frequently meeting with her new neighbor Pervin. In fact, she didn't like to constantly talk with Pervin about the recent history and politics, yet there was a special light in Pervin attracting her. Moreover, she knew that her daughter was talking to this lady very often, and her daughter's going to her with a pretext of borrowing books. There was something going on between her daughter and Pervin, but what was it? Again this morning her daughter and Pervin were whispering to each other, and as soon as her coming, they became as quiet as a mouse and her daughter immediately ran inside the house. Anyway, one day she would have found out all about the secrets they were having. After dividing into two of the bread freshly come out of the oven, she placed salami she made, and then sliced it and the cheese thinly. She pointed out to what she brought to Pervin, as if to say "eat whatever you want." She touched the kettle. Thinking that its hotness was okay, she poured tea into the glasses. She was not hearing the children inside, crying and fighting with each other, as she was heartily eating her sandvitch. She started excitedly sharing with Pervin an event she heard at the grocery store. She explained in detail that the girl did not commit a suicide, and according to traditions, as her brother was going to kill her, in order not to have him go to prison, she jumped out of the bridge.

Pervin listened to her friend for a while. She already knew the family of that poor girl, and was aware of what happened in reality. So indeed, that poor girl had jumped ouf othe half built viaduct in order not to have her brother go to prison. Her only offence was to want to marry a man whom his family didn't want. Her only guilt was she held out to her loved man. Pervin thought about Fevziye. How would have gone if Fevziye had married her loved one. Most likely, she would have been happy. She asked:

"Your fiance… That is to say. Your old fiance…. Did Şahin know about him?"

"Tell me about it… Sure, he knew."

Following a short period of silence;

"He turned out to be not a reliable man" Fevziye said.

"Who?"

"Old… That man happened to be my fiance. Do you know what offended me most? Okay, I was kidnapped, and he didn't want to marry me because I was pregnant… Why did he give my ID card to my rapist?"

Pervin raised an eyefrow. As she was heaving a sigh by repeating to herself "Oh poor", she wondered whether Fevziye should be hating all men given what happened to her. On the contrary, Fevziye liked all men, young and old alike, and she was getting along well with them. Even she was chasing the woman beggars knocking at her door, by saying, "Don't you feel ashamed begging. Why don't you work?", whereas it was a male beggar, then she was taking her time to listen to his pathetic life story. After inhaling her cigarette smoke over a gulp of tea, as if sensing what her friend was thinking, Fevziye spoke:

"The real culprit in this tragedy happens to be my mother who did not rescue me from the hands of Şahin. It was her who was not beside me during my difficult days."

Fevziye's looks were carrying so many meanings at the same time… Pain, grudge, hatred, love… All of them.

***

Being dead set on finding out what was going on between her daughter and Pervin, Fevziye was frequently visiting her friend. Pervin had a very interesting house. This three room flat was bought by her rich husband of her daughter, her son-in-law from Tunceli. When entered the house and passed the small hallway, a place built in fact as a sitting room was being reached… All four walls of the sitting room were fitted with library shelves. A table was placed in the small area in the middle of the huge sitting room. It looked not a house's guest room but as if the library of the Istanbul Governor's Office… A very large sitting room of only an elementary school graduate woman could have filled with books from wall to wall. Moreover, the books were not about romance but history and politics. Most of the neighbors who came from Anatolia had found Pervin's book passion odd. As they were making some remodeling in the house before moving in, they probably thought that a library was being built for the neighborhood. Pervin told her daughter who had bought this house that, she would only accept to move in this house with her daughter under one condition provided that "You should have the sitting room furnished with a library from wall to wall." So her daughter did her mother's bidding and had the sitting room filled with a wall-to-wall library.

Pervin from Bünyan looked carefully at her neighbor Fevziye. As she was alsa heaving a sigh for her unlived childhood;

"Like ours… the fate of all girls seems to be the same, even if there are different reasons, but the result is certain." she said.

It occurred to Fevziye that, her neighbor, being at the same age, had a daughter aged twenty-four, and two grandchildren from her daughter. Pervin became a mother at the age of just fifteen.

"Why did you have a child when you were still a child?"

"While I was shouting at the top of my voice saying I will study, I will become a doctor, they made me marry. As my peers were going to school, I had a real baby on my lap. A baby, I should have taken care of. Whereas I wanted to study like my peers… The baby I was holding in my one hand was sucking milk hungrily from my breast, I was reading a book in my other hand. They forced me to marry, but I never forwent reading books. That's why I wasn't able to show enough affection to my daughter. When I reached adulthood, I had a guilty conscience since I had not given love to my first child but to my other children. I had a sound grasp of the only trouble of my poor daughter she suffered since her infancy was to make me love her, through her having bought this house. Again, as if taking revenge on not being able to study, I was ashamed by realizing that this fury was still alive in me since I wanted to turn this place into a library."

Fevziye looked at the shelves filled with hundreds of books and encyclopedias;

"Have you read all of them?"

"Almost."

Pervin had read all of them, and still she was glued to the book.

"I will read until I die. You can take any book you wish. On the condition that you will bring it back.

"Noo…I don't like reading."

"It's apparent."

"Big freaking deal…"

"Don't say – big freaking deal – Fevziye. If people educated like you would say – big freaking deal –then we're busted."

In effect, Fevziye's educated side was now a thing of the past. She was a woman dealing with her cats, dogs and flowers; running around secretly and being beaten for this reason every morning and evening; not giving a damn to the worldly issues. As she was getting to know Pervin better, she liked her since she was not like her other housewife neighbors, yet there was something in her Fevziye didn't like. Maybe Fevziye didn't like her being a smart woman, knowing lots of things and being a political person. She was holding no brief for her being a pro-Karaoğlan like her mother, a responsible person for her ill-fate, and again like another responsible person of her ill-fate, her daughter, being a supportor of Deniz Gezmiş. Fevziye didn't like Pervin's bringing the topic always to politics. Here she had found a political topic to talk about.

"Look, when the politicians fall out with one another, then the terrorist organizations take advantage of this and attack."

"Yeah, tell me about it…" Fevziye replied casually. Pervin started explaining that quarrels between Ecevit and Demirel were playing into the hands of the enemies, and in recent months, unfortunate events increased.

As yet one week ago, simultaneously at both Istanbul Sirkeci Train Station and Yeşilköy Airport, at exactly the same time, time bombs were blown up, leaving 5 people dead and fourty-nine people wounded. The responsibility of the bombing incident was claimed by an Armenian terrorist organization called "28 May". While the Nationalist Front Government was in power, the Turkish Lira had been devaluated for nine times, 1 US Dollar's worth was equivalent of 17.50 Turkish Lira. The loss of the Turkish Lira against Dollar had reached 27 Percent. To Pervin, many members of the Republican People's Party (CHP), and Bülent Ecevit in particular were being attacked numbers of times

"Isn't that so? Didn't they killed Vize Mayor elected from CHP by beating? Didn't they attack Ecevit and all other CHP members in Niksar open-air meeting?"

Fevziye had her mind on other things… She asked naively… "Who did attack?"

"Ayy Fevziye… Aren't you reading even newspapers… Ecevit and his entourage were attacked in Erzincan… They still didn't get it to go nowhere using a brute force."

Fevziye's mind was in the teachers' lounge of the neighborhood school. Who knows, how joyfully they were laughing and having fun. She was frequenting there every day and drinking tea… She was supposed to get up and leave by telling Pervin that the school teachers, whom she was hosting them almost for every lunch, were getting her home for a lunch. But Pervin was talking twenty to the dozen.

"You… İzmir… You most probably believed the tale of Mehmet İsvan who was shut by the police by mistake at Çiğli Airport. Do you know how it happened?"

Fevziye stared into space but Pervin interpreted that look as "Tell me what happened?". Fevziye was someone to follow what was going on in this world, but the only concern she had at that moment was whether her daughter had stopped by the teachers' lounge at the neighborhood school. She wanted to talk to Pervin not about politics but her daughter… Whereas Pervin was explaining things frantically.

Pervin kept telling that the prime target was Ecevit, when Mehmet İsvan changed his place, instead of Ecevit, Mehmet İsvan got wounded, she didn't believe that the police shooting was by mistake since that weapon was of a special kind and taken out from the weapons depot secretly without any registration note. Fevziye was not listening to her neighbor as it were. Her aged mother too would not allow anyone to talk against Ecevit, nicknamed "Karaoğlan". Maybe because of ther mother's party involvement, Fevziye was thinking that her mother was neglecting her and that's why she was trying to be away from the political subjects. But since befriending Perving, something inside her had started to poke her… In fact, despite her appearance of having her head in the clouds, she had tried to follow the world event. But she had taken a dislike to politics since her mother's being leftist, who left her alone, and her husband's being rightist, as she hated him. Her mother would not ask her to which party she cast her vote but she was laughing inside seeing how her husband was trying to impose her vote being cast for a certain party. If only it would have been this easy to fool her. Previously voting for Democratic Party (DP), now her husband was voting for the Justice Party (AP), and he would not have anyone to talk against Çoban Sülü (Shepherd Süleyman). On every voting occasion, Fevziye was voting the opposite party to her the party her husband voted. Again, at 5 June General Elections held last month, after getting out of the folding screen, her husband asked her "Did you vote for AP, right?" and he gushed over her saying "Well done". She was laughing up her sleeve during this conversation. The party she voted for was CHP and became the first party with 213 deputies. If in case her husband were telling him to vote for CHP, then she could be voting for MSP, MHP, AP or DP, since her husband was an annoying person to her. Anyway, her husband would not become a leftist. The seeds for blossoming her political thoughts were planted by her friend Fevziye:

"Why are all assassinations against Ecevit? Why they are not plotted against Türkeş or Demirel?"

"That is so, okay… But who are doing this?" she asked.

"Who can it be! Fascists."

"Who is a fascist?"

"……"

"Is it Demirel?... or Türkeş...?" Fevziye insisted on her questioning.

"............"

"Tell me what a fascist mean"

After being silent for a while, Pervin spoke:

"Now I don't want to confuse you by explaining things superficially. In short, a fascist is somebody who resorts to violence, who is for setting up a system of oppression..."

While thinking of her husband's being someone who set up a system of oppression, who has tendency for violence, Fevziye asked Pervin;

"Is it Demirel?"

"What?"

"Who organized the assassination... Who?"

"Noo... No, it's not Demirel" Pervin said.

"Since his name was mentioned, should I tell you about the private letter Demirel sent to Ecevit recently?"

"A letter?"

"Yes... Demirel heard the information from the intelligence organization that during the open-air meeting in the Taksim Square, there will be an assassination attempt against Ecevit, and subsequently he wrote Evevit to warn him of the danger and be cautious about it."

"Really?"

"Yes... Then Ecevit talked on the radio at once... He made this letter public and he said he will go to the meeting. As you know, that CHP meeting was uneventful. The meeting was also attended by a very huge crowd.

Pervin told her that, what she did was not for doing a favor to Ecevit, and sje explained shortly the reason she was into these in her own way. Fevziye had started slowly to analyze the political side of her friend. Pervin was not voting for Demirel but for Ecevit. She didn't like Türkeş at all. What was baffling Fevziye was that Pervin was not allowing anybody to speak ill about the secret organizations. Even when she told her that her bullheaded daughter had attended May Day meeting at the Taksim Square two months ago, Pervin didn't react at all. And moreover, she had said:

"Well done to her… Your daughter is not an ordinary person." In fact, on that day she wasn't home but she didn't tell whether she was in the meeting or not. She could have found out from Pervin whether her daughter was a member of a secret organization. She should have had her father beat her daughter since she was one hundred percent sure that her daughter was a member of a secret organization. In order to collect information about her daughter, she should have visted Pervin frequently and pretended that she also had the similar political views. With an expression of being concerned about her daughter's life she said:

"Well, you are saying well done… Dozens of people died. What if something would have happened to her!"

"Eee… If you set your heart on something… Cowards die many times before their deaths, Fevziye"

"You don't say… She wouldn't have anything to do with an organization. Maybe she attended that meeting casually. Like a holiday… Worker's Day."

"It was already a holiday… It had started nicely. Thousands of people were celebrating the Worker's Day enthusiastically. Istanbul had not seen such a crowd since its early days. Songs were sung, and people danced."

"Have you too gone there?"

"Yes… I have."

"Aaaah… Why din't you tell me?"

"You didn't ask."

"Ah, tell me about it Pervin… Have you gone there with my daughter?"

"No… She attended inside DİSK - Labor Confederation line."

"Is she a member to DİSK?"

"I don't know … I didn't ask."

"Liar" saying to herself, Fevziye heaved a sigh.

After exclaiming "E eee!", Fevziye looked at Pervin.

"E eee or what… The meeting was going on in a festive air, and it lasted till the late hours since the crowd was enormous. When Kemal Türker was about to finalize his words, the sounds of gun shots were being heard. The direction of the coming gun shots was from the top of the Water Management Building and the different stories of the hotels at the square."

"Aaaah… Did they shoot even from the hotel rooms?"

"Sure… What we are talking about here… I saw opening fire from the upper stories of Etap Marmara Hotel with my own eyes."

While trying to gather information about her daughter from her neighbor, Fevziye, in the meantime, was getting saddened as she was listening to what Pervin had to say and repeating the words "What a pitty!"

"Thousands of so many enthusiastic people were trying to

escape in panic. The police were pushing the crowd towards the Kazancı Ramp. Even a big truck was parked at the head of that ramp. At the crowd squeezed there was opened fire but instead of dealing with the shooters, the police were attacking the crowd. Most of 34 people died at the head of Kazancı Ramp by being stuck because of the parked truck."

"It's a shame they died"

"Don't ask… What has been seen cannot be unseen… Believe me, the scenes haunt my dreams. I will never forget about that day."

Fevziye spoke as is she was sounding Pervin out:

"I guess our daughter doesn't care… In truth, I never see her being sad"

"She never smiles. How would you understand… Whether she is sad or cheerful."

"That's correct… She is sullen."

"Don't say like this… What do you want from this girl…? A aaah, you are a bit strange… Do not punish her for father's sake."

***

It was June 15. Canan had gathered with her high school mates in Büyükada, and in the meanwhile her mother who left home was trying to forget about her daughter's strange mood. In the past when she left home like this, she would feel remorse, and still because of her mother, she would not make herself comfortable and would come back home immediately. Now she had severed relations with her and grew indifferent. She didn't care what would have happened upon her return home. She would not be paying attention to whomever says anything, she would write her short stories or she would give a hand to her sibblings in doing their homeworks. Being thick-skinned was not her fault but her mother's…

Mother… or else… Was there any serious underlying reason for even her mother's being thick-skinned?

When she got home, her father was frying scrambled eggs with garlic sausages, and her mother was nowhere to be seen. She noticed that her father was on edge. She immediately rolled up her sleeves and ran to the kitchen:

"Do you know father… We celebrated today the birthday by coming together with Semiha."

Apparently her father knew about this. Neither being upset nor pleased, he was slicing the bread with a mired and hopeless expression. Canan was not expecting from her family such as a birthday celebration or a gift. It was enough for her not to restrict her freedom. Her brother Çınar, since he came of an age to be able to understand, had bought a gift wristwatch for her. She noticed that her father was looking cross-eyed at ther under his beetle brow. She at once turned on the faucet and started doing the dishes. The hardened sun soap was burning her hands. The rooms of the house were untidy and her brother was waiting for his dinner. To whereever her mother was gone, still she was not home when they sat at the dinner table. When arrived, she tossed about her cardigan and sitting at the dinner table as if nothing happened. At the very moment Şahin sprang from the table:

"Where were you until this time?"

"Today is the Mehtap movie theater day… Don't you know about it rather than asking every week?"

Fevziye was caring not a groat but her children were uneasy for a likely argument to turn into a fight, and they as always not able to eat comfortably. Yes, on certain days Fevziye used to go to the movie theather. She would not give a damn even though the house was in fire, in addition to her movie days at Mehtap and Sedir movie theathers, she would not delay going to tea parties alongside with her friends in Rumeli Hisarı and Çamlıca. Her children though were longing for a dinner to be enjoyed en famille.

As soon as her father sprang from the table in a tearing hurry, Canan took her sibblings to the room. As always they glued their ears to how their mother and father were arguing. They were accustomed to these kind of scenes. They knew that after a while her mother would be crying her heart out – as always – followed by her words of "You made my life miserable, you darkened my youth!", and then in a couple of hours' time, witnessing how they would make peace, locking themselves in their room, giggling and having their private moments. Regardless of what was going on, and despite her mother's making her suffer a lot, she could not stand her mother's being beaten, she was so upset, and she was despising her father in such situations.

The years of mother-daughter being not on speaking terms did not last too long. As coups rounded up the young and threw them into the torture chambers, the families embraced one another by realizing there could be even the worse happenings. It wasn't a time of being resentful, it was the time of solidarity. Fevziye's sense of solidarity was peculiar to her though. Since she adopted the principle of not being upset, she was able to shorten the ways to the First Section of the Police and Metris Prison, and to deaden the pains with her being joyful.

***

Being oblivious to her daughter's having read the notebook in the attic, Fevziye was telling her memories to Canan's 5-year-old son. Lately, Fevziye was accounting for the facts that… Her lover resembled to Tanju Okan a lot; when she was about to marry him, and his grandfather Şahin kidnapped her, but her old fiancé didn't live up to being a man with integrity since he handed her ID to Şahin; because she was pregnant, she had to marry Şahin, and then she would not escapre from him, in such a way as if she was reciting a tale to her grandson… Canan was aware of some memories through her evavesdropping on her mother, and for some other, she was having her guesses about what happened. But she was schocked when she found out that her mother was walking on the thin line of life and death, struggle many many times. What her father, she loved so much, had done.ç was not something to be forgiven. In spite of all these things, should these facts be considered mitigating circumstance for what her mother made her suffer. No… Her mother could not make herself be forgiven because her father kidnapped her. There were dozens of questions in the head of the young girl. Why didn't she divorce? Why did she give birth to a child?

Fevziye had tried to divorce but she could't succeed… She kept her promise to herself, and through her obstinate stance and having a strong personality, until hitting the age of seventy, she didn't show affection to her husband…When Şahin hit the age of 80, he was exhausted yet he was in love with Fevziye as much as the first day… He was saying to her, "Tell me, you are in love with me." He has made all the efforts to hear these words… Fevziye was replying to him out of consideration of his love for her, and his never lessening respect for her throughout all the years by saying:

"Big freaking deal… You say being in love. After all the years past" she was dodging her true answer.

Canan talked to a number of people to find out her mother's past… She was saddened for both her mother's not being able to have reunion with the man she loved and her father's being in love with her mother. She felt also sadness for herself and her sibblings being squeezed during these events. Never recovering from guilty conscience, her father had tried to provide motherhood and fatherhood for them. Everyone was right from their own perspectives. She forgave both her mother and her father. She did not waive the struggle she was making. She kept her promise and carried on writing. She cleared the deck to go abroad in order to collect information regarding her third novel.

***

Fevziye and her daughter Canan got off the cab and headed for the terminal building of Atatürk Airport. In fact, Canan knew that her mother had followed her not to see her off but to take advantage of the occasion to get about. Yet she did not have any intention to hurt her mother's feelings.

Her only concern was how her mother would be going back home from the airport. She was scared of the possibility that this woman to whom she couldn' stand back in the days would get hurt somehow.

"How will you go back. I will be wrapped up in you" Canan said. Raising her shoulder lightly, and being pleased by her daughter's interest in herself, Fevziye spoke:

"It's not a big deal, don't worry. I will go back the way we got here."

"Well. We got here together… Take a cab to go back."

"Anyhow… I am not going to fly from Yeşilköy to Eyüp…"

"Not that… I mean… Well… If you happen to run into an acquaintant, do not tag after." Get on a cab and be home before it gets dark."

"Alright"

"Look, just promise me… Times have changed, do not trust anyone. Just pick an airport cab and get home."

"Ayyy… You are going to miss the plane. I said the plane is about to take off".

"Do not forget mother… I will call you as soon as the plane lands."

Talking on the one hand, and handing in her small luggage to the counter on the other, Canan took her mother's arm and headed to the international departures. A joygul expression of 19-year-old child on her face as if she was not going to have enough of going about, her mother patted her daughter indicating to go to the gate, and turned her steps towards the cafe where motly young foreign customers were sitting. Even though there were not many of her peers being over 70 at the airport, she would have still found some of them to chat, yet she did not like to chat with the elderly people as if she was a young person herself. As a matter of fact, the years flew by, some had been born, some had died, many coups, many winters, many spring seasons were experienced, nevertheless, Fevziye had always remained as she was. She has not been getting on in years, and she was like as if she has not been a young woman either… She was not aware that her daughter was still there and looking at her. Now she was going to tell them many stories with cats and dogs, and struggles whether they went through them or not… How would she be taking part of the conversation with the young ones there regarding some historical events such as he Dardanells Battle… the First World War, the Second World War… etc. But she was going for sure befriend a young person… she was going to give her telephone number to him… and she was going to invite the persons she doesn't know to her house for a barbecue party.

For years, Canan had not been able to make sense of the mother's day. Until last year, Canan used to celebrate the mother's day with a heavy heart as if she had fulfilled a duty, by giving the gift either to her mother handed over by her father or the wild flowers her teachers made her collect. Last year for the first time Canan went to her mother's house in Eyüp to sincerely celebrate "the Mother's Day". Fevziye was in a sweet rush. But it was not because she saw her daughter. By gesturing the chair to her, "Make yourself comfortable," Fevzi-ye said to her daughter and ran to the market. Fevziye needed a secretary to answer the phone which never stopped ringing. So many people were congratulating Fevziye's "Mother's Day" … Canan got almost envious of this interest in her mother. Tons of people were calling her mother on the Mother's Day although her mother had not lifted a finger except giving birth to their children by just a light moaning of – ohhh- while Canan was pampering her child and dedicating herself to the child's future eduation, thoug her child was barely taking her seriously. Arnold from the Netherlands, the couple she hitchhiked with to get to the camp in Side from Antalya, Marji from the States, some people from the 68 Foundation she got to know during a Republic Meeting in Alsancak, İzmir, Dr.

Pervin Hanım from Edremit who was crazy about cats and dogs as well as her, all of them were congratulating her mother's day. As well as almost all teachers of the schools her children had gone to. The most interesting one amongst callers was the male couple who married abroad. The voice at the end of the line belonged to a male but his talk sounded more like a feminine voice. "I am Ahmet, from Bodrum-Önen." he said. "Could I speak to Fevziye." Fevziye had returned from Bodrum one month ago where she had stayed for five months... In other words, he was one of the friends she had made there. Canan told him that Fevziye was not in, she would be soon home, and whether he wanted to leave a message. The man on the line was being so talkative and sociable, Canan was hardly containing herself not to laugh while counting the olive oil dished she prepared in the previous evening.

"No. I am going to come for the barbecue party alongside with Edmund... I was going to ask her whether she has another request or not."

Canan put down the telephone by telling him that her mother would give him a call on her cellphone in case she has something to ask. Now she knew that the reason her mother hurriedly went to the market was not because she was preparing dishes for her... When Fevziye came back with the food packages, most of them fast food, including pastrami, sausage, American salad, hot spicy tomato dip, carrot with yoghurt:

"Your friend Ahmet called you" said Canan.

"Aha... Girl, was that Ahmet... Did they set off?" It was obvious that her mother's preparations were meant for them. She repeated to herself, "What is this – girl, was that Ahmet", then she talked the way her mother was able to hear: "Yes, Edmund will come as well." While putting the things she bought in their places with an impish smile, Fevziye spoke to her daughter:

"They are husband and wife" without giving any chance of her daughter's asking whether Edmund was a man or not.

"This is man to man marriage. Come look. In my cellphone there are their wedding photos. Look, how cute they are."

Not being able to have seen by now the photos of her mother's children and grandchildren in her mother's purse and her cellphone, Canan looked at the screen of the phone to see the persons she ddidn't know. Then she turned to her mother. She was still going on talking about some other people. That meant that she hardly said anything to her mother during her short visit of the short day. Using her hand to indicate a canister, Fevziye started talking: "Look, these olives were pressed by girl Ahmet... They will never forget about me when they prepared things like red pepper and sundried food made of curd, tomato and flour... Ah, how nice people they are, if only you get to know them... They are my close friends... Come on, postpone your things and stay... I get along well with them... I have a lot of fun... You to would have fun, hey girl, make yourself happy." While speaking, she was setting the table and haphazardly putting the dishes she had bought. "No way" said Canan... Looking at the exhilarated state of Fevziye with a wry smile, her daughter Canan had disappeared that day not because they had other appointments but to leave her mother to meet with her close friends she was getting along well.

Despite everything, her mother's being able to live this much of a colorful life was making Canan delighted. She had never had as colorful life as her mother had. She had never radiated around as much as her mother did. Even though she wanted, she could not be like her mother who let everything go because what she experienced, and it was her who tried to live her life as much as her heart's desire, who was oblivious to community's values, who was able to succeed to be happy through small things. Canan had become somebody who was afraid of her mother's disgracefull deeds, who cared about the value judgements of society, who tighthened up herself since her childhood for not being the way she wanted but for being a flawless person nobody could criticize her, and given her attitude described above, she had become a creeping—crud. She had not told her mother yet that some parts of her mother's life was included in her novel, yet her mother was aware of her daughter's writing a novel, and she was sensing from her asking questions about their past and her taking notes that all of these had to do with her. Previously though, she had insisted a lot on Canan by saying "Write about my life", but Canan had refused her mother's request stating "We would be disgraceful had I written it".

11 October 2009… With the announcement of the flight information, leaving her mother behind, Canan went through the last control after having looked at the boarding card in her hand and ran down to the boarding gate. Along with other passangers, she was taking a look out of te wide window of the hall they were lead to, at the parked planes on the apron. After a while, she headed into the plane in order to visit the historical artifacts exhibitied in England for her research works to be made for the new novel she was going to write. Recently she was either on the ground or in the sky… She had not buckled up her seatbelt yet. While she was looking around to see

whether they were waiting for a passenger, her eyes met with the sad looks of a young girl having the appearance of a Holywood star with her lit deep blue eyes resembling the sky. She was storing her hand bag in the overhead bin. Her brown hair dangling from her shoulders was dancing in between the fine curves of her very thin belly, as it were. Rather tall young girl lowered her head as if she became restive because of the admiring looks of the passengers, and took her seat by hunching her back, virtually trying to hide her beauty. Canan struggled to find out from where she might have come... As she was thinking that she must be either a model or an artist, and taking out some documents from her bag, something plumped down on her head. Her hand went to her shooting head. An elderly gentleman, holding a cane on his lap was constantly apologizing to her in a state of nearly crying. Poor man had dropped his cane as he was putting it in the overhead bin. It was her luck that it had landed on Canan's head. Canan was checking her head with her hand from time to time. There was no trace of blood but it was evident from the ecpression on her face that it was hurting. "These things happen" was her demeanor to soothe the elderly gentleman who felt discomfort and apologized ceaselessly, and she made him sit down. Already he had to take his seat since the announcement of the pilot was being heard, "Dear passengers... Time of flight is 14.30... flight altitude is 10.000 feet...", sharing the flight information with the passengers.

As the plane was taking off hassle-free, it was obvious seeing Canan's hand checking her hurting head that she was focused on her shooting head. Even she was making a grimace as if her pain was increasing. How come she wouldn't have! A swell first as big as a hazelnut had become bigger and bigger as if it would cover all of her head. At a loss, she wanted to make a move towards the stewardess but then she backed down. What use would be even she would report to her... They would not be able for sure to have a ct scan... Better still was not to think about the swelled head. Canan did so. She told herself, "Let me try to console myself thinking nothing worse happened to me." but this idea provoked evoking even bad things. She was trying to ease her pain by hoping that to reach London safe and sound without having the plane loosing the attitude, without experiencing a turbulence, without tilting to the right and left, without her engines going dead, without getting highjacked by a terrorist organization, without having to have toured five or ten times over London because of the thick fog, before the plane ran out of fuel, without hitting the mountains, and without having the pilot suffering a heart attack. She was sitting in the aisle seat and an English man was sitting beside her. He was about 40 years old. In the window seat was a Turkish man. He seemed to be a middle-aged businessman. Canan was surprised to see him not lifting his head from the book he was reading. Generally, the foreigneers would take out their books to read, yet the Englishman beside Canan had not taken any book out. Seeing Canan checking her head very often with her hand, the Englishman asked:

"Are you Okay?"

"Yes... I am fine" she replied in English. As if talking to this gentleman would ease the pain in her head, she stated her name enthusiastically. The English gentleman too introduced his name. After passing the acquaintance phase, they moved into a deep conversation... Mark was living in Istanbul. His wife was also an English. The name of their daughter was Rüya... While they were visiting Turkey years ago, they decided to grow old and die in this land since they were amazed by the country and the Turks.

Mark was speaking using inverted sentences and pausingly. They kept on conversation with his broken Turkish. The young man told her that his mother he had not seen for years living in Yorkshire was very sick, and he would be staying a couple of days in London before returning to Istanbul.

"In which neighborhood do you live?"

He made Canan surprised by saying, "In Yeniköy."

"How about you?"

"Me too"

"Really"

Canan explained where her house is located, so did the Englishman for his house.... Their houses were too close. They promised each other to meet in Istanbul. Mark seemed to be such a peculiar man kidding his acquantances... And for sure he was not failing to tell about what he did in Istanbul in such a sweet fashion as if he was one of Blacksea region's humorists. He used to be a postoffice employee in his country. He was serving as an English teacher at a university in Turkey. He kept on saying and thanking all organizations and institutions, "In my own country I would be made at most a post office employee but here in your country they treated me with great respect." Now he was in the phase of becoming an investigative journalist and writer. He told her that these days he started to write a book intented to give a teaching lesson to the people who thought wrong about Turkey and Turks... Whoops... Should Canan tell him that she is also a writer... Her neighbor from Yeniköy would then say, that's a hell of a coincidence… His wife had just graduated from a vocational high school in London and never worked, but in Istanbul she was teaching English.

Maybe because of Canan's look to mean, "How so?" he replied:

"Don't ever aspire to become a teacher in our country." half-jokingly. They had so much laugh… Saba Tümer was not a big deal seeing them. By all means, he knew that a Turk's becoming a teacher in his/her country is like getting blood out of a stone.

"No, no… I have not such an intention" said Canan.

He asked her through his broken Turkish the reason for her visiting London. She said she would be making research on the historical artifacts in museums and the asylum camps.

"Aha… I think the pieces our archeologists had stolen and exhibited here…"

The man was as sharp as a needle and he was presenting his thoughts with his added comments.

"Something like that."

"Which ones are you going research?"

"I will start with the Koran… The one got lost in 1990 from the Nurosmaniye Library collection…"

"Well yes… I had heard that 62 pages of it were in London. There is also something called casserole… the silver casseroles."

In fact, according to Canan's research, the casseroles belonging to the Lidia periods were in England. She was surprised to know that her fellow traveler was informed of all these things.

"You are quite knowledgable in this subject."

"But I didn't steal them."

Both of them burst into laughter. Canan mentioned about her being upset with the fact that more of our historical pieces were being exhibited every corner of the world.

She poured out her troubles by saying, "Unfortunately there is nobody to say stop our historical artifacts being smuggled to other countries and exhibited there or sold through auctions rather than having them exhibited in our country." Her fellow traveler smiled impishly:

"Your minister of culture... Recently he went to the British Museum in London."

"Yes"

"For sure he must have felt upset... He got emotional and was almost in tears."

He went into raptures in explaining to her that the minister got emotional seeing a grand mausoleum, and another magnificent tomb were tall in the saddle in a museum. He also spoke of Minister Günay's stating, "These pieces were being excavated in our country and now being exhibited here made me feel sad." Canan thought:

"Even if our minister could do nothing, then it means they got away with what they did."

They were so deep in conversation that Canan realized with the announcement made that they arrived in London. They buckled up their belt. Mark's hands were shaking and he impatiently wanted to get out of the plane... This was not because he was about to have a reunion with his mother or whether a matter of being impatient to see whether the plane was going to make a safe landing. He got tense, and his hands were a bit shaking.

"The most boring thing about these travels is waiting at the airport… I long for a joint so badly."

Canan smiled as if "I should have guessed":

"There is not much from now on. Be patient."

Canan and her English friend broke up to go through the passport control at Heatrow Airport. Mark, as it would be guessed, was at the passport control section not with more than a couple of people in line, whereas Canan was on a long line of the passport control for the passports of the poor countries. The girl she presumed to be a Hollywood star beauty young girl Canan had seen when boarding the airplane was just in front of her. She was speaking Turkish. Canan spoke to her:

"Hello."

"Hello."

As much as her being beauty, she seemed to be an educated person. There was a sadness in her eyes contrasting with this beauty. They kept on their conversation in the long line of the passport control asking questions where they came from, where they were heading etc. The young girl was living in Samatya when she comes to Istanbul. Suddenly she moved to tears… She couldn't go on. Canan kept quiet. After a short moment of silence, the young girl asked:

"You… Where do you live in Istanbul?"

"Yeniköy"

"Are you coming to London just for a travel… or is it for business" she continued.

"It's both travel and business... I will visit a couple of camps and museums for my new novel."

"Are you a writer"

"Ohh. I am trying to be. Why did you come to London"?

"For work".

Canan thought of the fact that when even the local people in this country could not find an employment, what kind of job this beautiful girl would geti

"Are you coming for the first time?"

"No. I had come here 9 years ago for my university education."

"Great... I think you must have been used to be here."

"Yes... It was difficult for me when I got here for the first time. I had stayed by a family as an au pair."

As the word au pair was mentioned, what was told about them occured to Canan. Generally, au pair was said to be the girls who seduced the man of the family, who broke up a home, who promoted to a house wife at the house she was a caretaker. But this girl didn't look to be one of those girls to break up a home. On the contrary, she appeared to be such a girl who could not give heed to the men who would be willing to break up a family for her. As Canan was thinking of such points, the young girl kept on speaking:

"When I got here for the first time, I was only 18... It was difficult then."

Adding 9 to 18, the girl's age was known. That meant she was now 27. Since there wouldn't be no wrinkles, crumpling and sagging, it didn't matter whether she was 18 or 28. The young girl standing in front of Canan looked a like a nursling suddenly wondered:

"Since you are a writer… Write about my life. You would win the Nobel Prize." This was one of those questions Canan hated most… "Sit and write your novel by yourself" passed through her mind… "Her life is a novel, ha… If you consider it, everyone's life makes a novel. Anyway…" After a huge sigh, Canan gave her response:

"Your life inspiring a novel doesn't solve anything… I think you are not aware of the things… There are too muc materials around to be a subject to novels… Especially in our country… there is no single day without events resembling nothing less than a dedective film, mafia films, crime fictions, and court movies. What is important here to write a novel is to have accumulated knowledge and experience, time, economic power and health… and then after you write it, you need to have possibilities of conducting advertisement, distribution and promotion. If you don't have that power, nobody would notice even though you might have authored the best works of the world. Lately by the way, in order to have your book being read a lot, actually being sold a lot, and receiving prizes, there are some other alternatives, as it is rumored… I don't want to talk about them since I am not much inclined to believe in them."

Being sorry about asking this question, and thinking as if she committed an offence, the young girl looked at canan attentively:

"I am sorry" Canan was not thinking that she acted rude. She has been buried under such questions. Everyone was sure about their life's deserving a novel, but the number of readers was very few. She was complainant of the fact that some people were looking at the writers with a reasoning of "they make money without working hard." Yet, being affected by the young girl's delicate and civilized attitude and thinking that she hurt her, Canan wanted as if to appease her and even to make it up to her:

"You are right… Everybody life makes a novel. My mother, my sibling and my friends tell me that their lives are like a novel, but there must me something driving me to write…"

"I get you… But mine is really an extremely rare life story."

She looked carefully at the face expression of the girl. The young girl didn't seem to be surprised, on the contrary she appeared quite serious. Gradually the joyful expression on her face was fading and her eyes were filling with tears.

Canan felt hot and cold all over for a long time. She started to wonder about her life story; what could have this young girl gone through given her beauty, her young age, and considering the short period of time that might have involved her life experiences. The tears ready to drop from the young girl's eyes made Canan feel that her life was full of many events enough to inspire more than a novel. The young girl suddenly spoke:

"My mother and I… My mother…" She was able just to utter these words.

Canan took a look at the young girl whose lips were trembling… Her mother… Mother… Yes, it is… She should have come up with the reasoning for the sorrowful eyes of the girl at this young age could be her mother… Wasn't her own big trouble at that age her mother, was it? Such a huge trouble… Thus, Canan had the cure for the girl. She should have to discuss about her mother Canan thought she should be blamed, and again Canan should let the girl free like a bird to land on spring branches so to speak.

"Why not… Let us meet one day. You would be first telling me in short what had you gone through. Should there be different and interesting happenings, then the stories having an impact on me would be authomatically put on paper."

"I am sure you will be affected"

"Alright then."

"Only my name… I am not brave enough at the moment to ask you to write my name as it is for the stories I am going to tell you… Maybe… Maybe in case my pain would have eased a bit. Then I might change my mind."

"Is it a pain?"

"Yes…"

"What was your name? Have you told me your name?".

"No, I haven't… You can call me Sevgi"

Now it was this girl of magnificent beauty's turn to go through the passport control. As Sevgi was holding out her passport, the officer was holding his breath and rooted to the spot in front of her beauty. Anyway, both of them went through the passport control hassle-free. When the young girl headed for the baggage claim section, Canan looked at the passport line and spoke to the girl:

"I don't have my luggage. I will exit immediately. Let me give you my phone number, if you will. Then we can talk," she said.

"Alright… In fact, in my luggage there are my diaries, but first I need to photocopy them to give you.

In Canan's head, the novel she wanted to write for a long

time was waiting. The subject of it was the asylum seekers from Anatolia whose paths crossed with the historical artifacts being exhibited in other countries. In fact, she didn't have time to leave the novel incomplete she had almost finished, and to set put down on paper the life of this both mysterious and pretty girl she saw her for the first time. To Canan, instead of meeting with the young girl and talking to her for hours, it would be easier for her to read her diaries at odd moments. As she was thinking that she must have written on her diareis all of what she had gone through, and even the memories she might have refrained from telling her.

"I can give two of them to you right away, but… After doing some photocopying, I could give both of them to you. Now I don't want to keep you waiting." the young girld told Canan.Meanwhile, she was writing down her telephone number on a pice of paper she took out from her hand bag.

"Alright… As you wish."

"Okay. This is my phone number. Keep in touch. First we need to talk. Then I will give you the photocopies of the diares." she said.

Since their telephones they used in Turkey were not operating here and since they did not insert the sim card of the county they were in, they exchanged their telephone number written on a pice of paper, after they shaked their hands, saying "see you soon", and the young girl headed towards the luggage claim area, and Canan wended her way to the exit gate.

Canan didn't mention to her sister living in London and a couple of her friends about this travel. Had she stayed by her friends of her sister, then it was for sure that because of the visitors and trips to be made insistently would be hindering her research.

She checked in the small and lovely hotel in Victoria she had booked earlier, and took a shower. At once she turned on her laptop and started to examine the research file. But she was not able to focus on her job. She had her mind on Sevgi's explanation telling about her story with full of pages. By closing her research file (except the smuggling of historical artifacts), she decided to read the unfinished chapters of her novel from cover to cover. As if there was something she didn't find in heart, and she seemed to be either not being able to devote herself to reading or not to like what she had written. She made her mind to go to sleep and to get up early to visit museums.

To go to the British Museum, she put on her blue-jeans and roll-necked sweater. As she was packing her rucksack, her telephone rang. The caller was Sevgi. She told Canan that since she was going to start working the following day, she had free time today and if Canan was interested in her diaries, they could meet today. Canan said that she was very busy and was about to go to the museum, yet she didn't want to give up seeing the diaries. When Sevgi replied by saying that they would meet at the museum, Canan answered with a "Yes", wearing a comfortable gesture on her face.

She spotted Sevgi among dozens of people in the large courtyard of the museum. As she approached a bit more, she also recognized Canan. Fleshy pink lips of the young girl with no make-up on her face whatsoever were curled with a slight smile. The sad look in her deep blue eyes shining like a gem was enchanting. Wearing low heel shoes, tightly cut overknee black dress, holding a bag and topcoat on his arm, she headed towards Canan. Through the decisive steps taken by her columnar legs, as if she appeared to be getting the upper hand as opposed to the columns of the centennial majestic museum. In all aspects, she looked like a noble princess. As if the sweet smile on her face, the light in her eyes, and her snow-white legs were not created to seduce but merely to watch a work piece God drew by his hand, without incurring damages. She extended her hand as if she was hugging her mother or elder sister. After exchanging pleasantries, she told that she had visited this museum earlier, and even she jotted down one of her memories in her diary.

Even though possessing all kinds of information related to the research into the novel, Canan took a free map of the museum and bought a booklet costing 5 pounds. They started chatting and touring the museum. As a matter of fact, Canan was supposed to pay another visit to this museum, and then to go to other museums which were on her list. But at the moment she grew her interes in the diaries she guessed to be inside Sevgi's hand bag rather then smuggled historical artifacts. She couldn't devote herself to her research due to thinking of what this young girl might have lived trough as she was getting to know more about her. Why do I waste my time now in that case, she thought, and turned to Sevgi…

"Let's sit down over a coffee." she said. They walked together towards the metro station.

Because Canan had a hearty breakfast before she left the hotel she didn't feel much hungry. But when Sevgi told that she didn't have breakfast, Canan thought quickly of a place not too luxury but a clean one where they could have their coffee and something to bite. Being a vegetarian, Sevgi suggested to go to a salad bar run by Brazilians at Covent Garden. Canan happily accepted this offer.

They got to Neal's Yard Salad Bar to which Canan had never been there before. The ambiance was fine. They got around the tables of the bar's wonderful, cozy and cordial atmosphere. After ordering their salad and freshly squeezed mixed fruit juice to the waiter, they looked at each other uninvitedly with an expression of sharing the similar fate. As Canan was looking unwillingly at the hand bag where she had her guess about Sevgi's diaries were, the telephone of the young girl rang. She quickly unzipped her bag and took out her telephone. Asking permission, she talked to the caller in English. The conversation was being overheard. While Sevgi was telling the caller that she met with Canan, and letting that person about where they were now, she looked in the pink. She didn't prolong her conversation and cut it short using kind words. Before Canan's asking:

"My boy friend... Kemal" she said with a happy expression.

Putting her telephone back into her bag, she took out the fotocopied and filed diares out. Both of them glued to the file on the table for a moment. Sbe probably wanted to speak out and secure something then to deliver the diaries to Canan but she seemed to be in a state of not knowing where to start her talk or maybe she didn't want to speak at all. Suddenly;

"Already everything is written here... If you would have something to ask while reading, you can call me... When you mention about me, it's okay to call me "Sevgi".

Canan nodded her head as if to say "alright" and pulled the file towards her. She produced one of her books to give to Sevgi as a gift. She wrote her heartfull love and feelings about the young girl and signed the page after the cover. The young girl reached out to the book with her hands. She looked at the cover intently.

"Have you read it?" Canan asked.

"No…" she replied with a timid expression.

"But I had heard about it. Even the local papers covered its news…"

"Yes…"

Suddenly the young girl became sad. Canan had realized when she read her diaries, how small sadness was caused by her not having read her book was pale in comparison with what the young girl had gon through. Sevgi was waging worse a war than the Second World War when her second book was published. She excitedly looked at the book in her hand, and;

"This evening I will immediately start reading" said enthusiastically. In the meantime, the waiter was bringing their ordered food and drinks to the table.

***

Having listened to some of the memories of the young girl, Canan found herself reading Sevgi's diaries as as son as she got to the hotel room. She was so much affected by her memories that she abandoned her research into the historical artifact exhibited in other countries, and she has already started writing about what the young girl lived through. As she was writing what Sevgi had to say to her, her sad voice tone was resonating in her ears like a wounded goldfinch. Canan was not lifting her fingers from the keysboard of the laptop.

SEVGİ'S DIARY

10 September 2000

My mother's name is Leman.

In a rainy winter morning; we met with Özge, Burak, and Semiha in the long line of waiting in front of the British Consulate in Beyoğlu, Istanbul. Actually I am extremely tense… What a nonsense. I felt as if we are not going to London to study by paying our fees, but instead we are getting there as if to eat their land.

As the smell of dampness at the Consulate yard encircled with stone walls was being felt even in the open air, my mother ran to the simit (Turkish street bagel) seller and threw one on my hand… At the moment I was slowly hissing out tomy mother that I had my breakfast just three hours ago, that simit was staying in between my fingers as if it was going to drop. My mother intervened the conversation with my newly acquainted friends by telling me that I could not find this sort of simit in London, and even she would put a couple of simit into my luggage. Then my mother headed quickly towards the fish market. I'd say I don't want to squabble with my mother at the last moment but my patience was wearing thin. As I wished that she would not bring new things. After she brought around ten oups of tea she took from the coffeehouse at the fish market and gave them away people around us, and she threw on my hand the a cup of hot tea with milk she had it made specially for me.

"I will not drink it" I said. She took no notice of it…. As I was thinking whether she didn't hear it or she pretented not to have heard it, she said:

"This simit will cry for the tea, look…" I was very tense. I replied rigidly:

"I will not eat simit either."

I had lost my temper for her baaying me in front of my friends. While I wanted to shout at the top of my voice, as if alleviating my mother's fault, Özge's father came up with a nylon bag in his hand. He also had bought so many things as if his children were out of a famine. Sandviches and ayran were laid on. Reflexly, our looks of my newly acquainted friends met. We were not different from each other. Then we didn't touch the food. I turned my look at the mother who were side-glancing at us as if we would die of hunger at the break of dawn had we not eaten them by noon.

I suddenly felt sad for seeing their pucker look they never took off from their children. The mixed expression of the happiness and separation was being reflected on their face for their sending their dearie children to kilometres away places, thinking that they would have a better future. While we were waiting in long line, those mothers and fathers, some are lecturers, professors, or painters, writers or CEOs, silently moved aside the walls through the warning of that person on duty who seemed to be an ignorant, uneducated person looking forward to his shift being over before his bottleeache started. At nine, the applicants for visa were being called on one by one to enter inside... As we were waiting for our turn, we started asking the people who were out of their interview what was going on inside... Now we were posing questions to everyone who completed their interview... "How did it go? What do they ask?" Even they all gave the same reply, we were anyway asking the same questions through a strange instinct...

At the very last minute we were preparing ourselves for the logical and illogical questions to be asked inside. I thought I hadn't taken the university exam as much as stressed as this time. The majority of persons I had met in this line wanted to to go Longon for education purposes. Except Semiha who was standing in line before me and called out a short time ago.

Semiha is about thirty-five, a quiet and introverted person. We have been here since the night. She told us that her mother died just seven months ago. They had decided alongside with her brother Burak to move into their elder brother in London. Being a newly graduate of his high school, Burak was going to continue his education in London. Semiha was also going to take care of the tree-year old daughter of her brother. It was not Mert's turn... All-night we had a conversation with Mert's driver on his behalf. When Mert was sound asleep in this warm bed, his driver had come into line on his behalf. In the morning, when the doors were opened, his driver recalled Mert. We wished good luck to Mert when he was going inside. Though I didn't think he needed any luck. He had enrolled at Oxford University for pursuing his Master's Degree. Already he had gone to London many times before. Now it was Özge's turn. We wished good luck to her too. Özge was going to Kingston University for her Master's Degree program. She doesn't come from a family as rich as Mert's family, yet her family is not like our family with a government employee background either. Her father is a renowned surgeon and mother is a painter. I liked her family. An intellectual family.

Semiha and Burak got out of the room. We immediately posed our question to them asking "How did it go?" Semiha had a smooth interview. His brother Burak seemed to be a bit tense. He argued with the visa officer. Semiha grinding away at her brother. "You are right, but... What's going to happen should they refuse your visa?" Burak didn't look regretful. He walked towards the door by taking masculine type of steps with an adolescent demeanor, "If I wanted to go to London, I could go sister... Then they would open the borders but I don't want it... If I cannot go through this way, then I would resort to other means." I wasn't in the mood of making of what Burak meant to say. Now it's my turn to be interviewed.

I was ushered inside a room. Two officers were sitting across the room... One is a Turk and the other is a British person. But the Turk, worse than the British, was scoping me out with a despotic expression.

"Why don't you study here?"

"In order to improve my English."

"Why? Cannot you accomplish it here?"

"For the last ten years, I studied German. That's why I wasn't able to improve my English."

"Is their any relative or acquantence of yours in England?"

"No, there isn't."

"Where will you stay?"

In fact, everthing was written down in the documents I had given to them. Information about where and with whom I will stay, how much money I would be spending, from where I would get the money, all of these. Nevertheless, they ask those questions again and again. They will examine my answers. To see whether I am trustworthy? Or not?

"I will stay by an English family as an au pair. The company arranged everything."

"Do you know the family?"

"No, I don't..." How would I know the family since I am going to London for the first time?" This would have been my reply to the question that I was about to speak out. But I kept quiet.

"Do you consider getting married?"

"I didn't get the question"

"This is a very simple question. Do you consider getting married?"

Oh dear! I had done my homework, but nobody had told me about the possibility of being asked such a question. What would be the appropriate answer, to say yes... or no... I am not considering it. Maybe it would sound to be rude had I said I never thought of getting there and finding and Englishman to mary him, and they might not issue a visa because of they may become irritated by such an answer.

"No... I don't have such a thought" I said.

The Turkish officer who was more royalist than the king riveted her presuming gaze on me. Had she been a male, then I would have thought that he had fallen in love with me and that's why his gaze was constantly on me. The interview was completed with lots of nonsense questions such as our house's deed transferred to me by my mother. I leapt out of the room without a backward glance. I felt humiliated so much, and I was hardly containing myself not to teach their place.

12 September 2000

Again, we are in front of the Consulate. With my mother you bet! I have my guess, how the Brithish find that mothers and fathers do not leave their adult children alone, strange. This time we came here to collect our passports. Withoug knowing whether they have visas issued or not. All of us seem to be tense. We are complaining being searched high and low at every turn, having cameras all over, the rudeness of the police and the harsh treatment of the officers there. We, the ones who attempted to *go abroad and our families as well as other visa applicants talk about the strange questions and our made-up answers. Making fun of the strange mimics of the face expressions of the author-ized officials who conducted the visa interviews, and nonsensi-cal characteristics of some of the questions they posed, and our bursting into laughter was just what the doctor ordered to our overstretched nerves.*

We talked about the tons of documents they demanded, their searching in every nook and cranny of our material and moral lives, and their being able to easily enter and leave our country. My parent's deeds, their property should be none of your business. Isn't it a shame! Isn't it nonsense! It's improp-er to have people go through kind of a humanity exam, does it seem appropriate for humanity. No wonder, I was taking part in all of these conversations, I had been having a side-long look at my mother with a concern of my mother's mak-ing me ashamed by her attitude of treating me like a baby, and from time to time I was pointing out to a farthest hillock: "Do not get tired mother. Look, there is a place over there. Go and sit there" I was telling my mother. Even though acknowledg-ing that it was impossible. And as if I didn't want her to move away, and as if I reminded her of checking whether my back oozed with sweat, she told me, " You are exposed to the wind... Come... Come and stand like this." I am getting bored. I am being impatient to go to a country to which my mother would never reach., as it were.

Placing aside the diary in which the memories were writ-ten, Canan recalled with a wry smile how she dreamt of hav-ing a mother in her childhood such as Sevgi's mother. She got into a depression because of her mother's lack of interest, and Sevgi sank into depression for having an excessive attention from her mother. Maybe in the end it was impossible to please the children. She took the diary in hand again by thinking that there should be a middle point in this issue.

We saw Mert in front of the Consulate holding his passport in his hand and getting in his poch brand car. I was just about to say we didn't have the courage to ask or Mert didn't feel the need to tell us, Mert opened the door of his car and he told us as he was getting behind the wheel with a half-smile:

"I hope we can meet in London."

Apparently he got his visa. My mother and I went through the questioning in the backyard. As soon as clearing the second obstacle, we would enter the waiting lounge.

Three p.m. afternoon. We were taken in. Özge was called. While her father and mother were waiting excitedly, Özge returned in a flash. You bet, my mother turned her gaze into the passport Özge was holding. She asked Özge on a tiptoe smile:

"Did you get your visa?"

Her mother replied in high spirits before Özge opened her mouth:

"Yes", and then she placed the passport in her hand bag as my mother was saying:

"Good luck with it my daughter", Semiha and her brother got out. My mother again asked with her nosy and excited manner:

"Did they issue the visa to you?" Semiha was very sad, whereas Burak was overeasy. As we were assuming that Semiha's visa request was refused, we soon found out that it was Burak to have failed to get his visa. Semiha was complaining about the fact that they refused to issue a visa to him although all

the paperwork was complete and all the payments were made, yet they didn't produce any justification in doing so. On top of that, while they didn't issue a visa to him, they were not going to give back the payment he had made. Apart from the lost money, being saddened by his brother's failure to get a visa, as well as puzzled and not knowing what to do, Semiha went out to call her elder brother who lived in London. I was gathering from my mother's moving lips that my mother was saying prayers to have me get my visa. Despite I loved my mother a lot, I was feeling suffocated because of her overfondness for me. Being her only possessin in life was overwhelming me. That's why I wanted to complete my education in London. Objecting to my going to London, and seeing my efforts to go abroad without her help, my mother had gone hurriedly to an au pair company, complied with all the requirements and enrolled me in a school. The company had found an English family whereby I would stay, and gave all the guarantees to my mother. I didn't receive any answer to my questions of how come she, as a literature teacher in a high school afforted to cover all of the expenses. In fact, I was not much inclined to go to London but on the prospect of my happiness was tipping the scales. Anyway, it's my turn. We are going inside.

13 September 2000

I took my visa issued passport in hand and placed it in the zipped compartment of my hand bag.

I was in front of my desktop computer which I was going to leave for my mother at the house in Samatya. My suitcases were staying in one corner of the living room…Though I had made a list of what I would pack in them, nevertheless I had not brough those items and placed them in the suitcases. My mother who would always bring even my water to me, was not for some reason helping me pack them.

"Come mother... I opened up a file in the computer. Let me show you how to use it."

On the box called Windows Messenger on the screen of the computer was written "Leman online". In the list of friends, my name was at the top, beneath of it several of my friends from school my mother got to know. I explained at great length to my mother how she could enter the Internet, how she could text chat with someboy by clicking the file icon where on the top, at the section of file, tools, actions, etc... I indicated to her where the game sites were.

"Do you know mother... If you get bored, you could play backgammon, rummikub here..."

My mother talked about the days of their gathering and playing rummikub from time to time with their friends when my father was alive.

In the evening of the same day, I had fun with my friends at the Guitar Bar in Beyoğlu all night long. When again would I be able to see my dearest friends... I was wondering whether I could be making friends like this? I thought of the possibility of my longing so much for Istanbul which has its İstiklal Avenue, which is living 24/7, full of joy and living city. I drank to excess under the influence of the feelings of getting orphaned from İstanbul and my friends through leading away from them for a while. Such things migh happen during special days once in a blue moon. "I shall miss you" was my words that I repeated while a couple of my friends carried me home. Since even my mother did not say a word for my miserable state like this, I gues everthing seemed to be alright.

15 September 2000

In the end, two suitcases were packed like sardines. Fortunately, we found out that meat and similar food were prohibited to enter the country. Otherwise, my mother would have filled the suitcase with meatball, pastrami, sausage and so many other foods that I cannot think of. Even so, the smell of the dried herbs which were allowed, was effused and permeated everywhere... The dried clove, cinnamon, mint, ginger, thyme, and dried fig were all placed in the suitcase waiting for their times to cure flu, stomach aches, constipation and many more illnesses.

My mother threw a glance at me as if to say "Do not dump them out; and I reciprocated her glance with mine as if to declare to my mother, "I will not use them anyway, you are placing them in vain."

20 September 2000

At the airport.

We are at the departure lounge. When my mother whipped around, she was holding a cup of coffee in her hand. More precisely, the content of the cup she was playing it off as milk was actually made up of three quarters with milk and the like which was apparent from its color and smell. She didn't care even to ask, would you like to drink, or I might have asked whether it was with milk, right? I am so full; I am sick at my stomach even as I look at the drink. "You drink it" I said even though I knew what her reply would be like... If she had desired it, she could have taken one for her... Even she had told me that she drank the whole kettle of tea when I was asleep, and she didn't want to eat anything anymore, I would have not believed her. She only didn't want to spend ten million for a cup of tea. In fact, even *though she didn't let it be known that she was under financial pressure, yet I was aware of it, I didn't want anything from her but to the last minute my mother laid so many foods in front of me as if it was her success to have me eat as much as I can. As a matter of fact, although we didn't have an income enough to go abroad for education, my mother had used her usual magical wand and made it happen. My friends who were in a better shape financially than us were surprised to see our success. I am used to it. Since my childhood, my mother never said "No" to my wishes. She used to have me take private lessons and go to a private school on the one hand, and she also used to take me to the ballet and the guitar courses on the other. I had gathered from my friends from the school I was going at that times that they were at sea during the summer months and in the mountains in the winter months, although we were not as well-off as they were, still my mother, a teacher, was so determined to make my wishes come true when it boiled down to my education... While I was gorging myself on the one hand, I was trying to change the subject in order not the listen to what my mother had to say on the other... But it was impossible... I felt suffocated. Even I am suffocating, my mother was talking my head off, saying things one after another.*

"Oh my daughter... Do not forget to eat vegetable and fruits"

"......................."

"Be careful with the family by them you are going to stay."

"......................."

"Do not trust anyone, even your father. These words were uttered for a reason."

Father...Instead of getting to know my father whom I lost

when I was 3 years old, only from his photos, now I would have loved not to be the only happiness of my mother. In order not to upset my mother at the last minute, I polished off the plates but my mother kept on talking twenty to the dozen.

"I know you don't like smoking, even you are getting sickish in the environment where the cigarette is smoken... They force you to get addicted. I know... They do this. Many of my students were seduced by their friends. Beware of it my dear daughter. Tthe element of friends is extremely important... do not ever be influenced."

"..."

"You are so beautiful... Watch yourself my daughter."

"...."

"I thought much of Özge. Her family seems to be fine... They are educated people. Keep in touch with her. Well... Semiha... She is not of the same age as you are but she is someone with good manners."

"...."

"Write all the of telephone numbers of your friends to me, okay? In case I cannot reach you, I would call them."

"...."

"Call me in case you need anything; you know now I can email you... send me an email ... Tell me about all of your time there. I will back you up all the time, alright?"

"..."

"Above all what matters is finishing your school successfully."

"..."

"Talk to British people as much as possible."

"..."

"Do not get bored for I speak all the eventualities. This is your third language, please take notice of it. Once you learnt it, you will speak better than them, alright?"

"…"

"Oh my daughter, do not walk alone in the parks."

"…"

"Do not go out when it gets dark."

"…"

"Do not stand close to the rails in metro. Let the metro get nearer, let the doors are open and let everyone get off."

While talking about all of these subjects, my mother for sure was giving examples of the situations she was explaining… Somebody's grandson was pushed onto the London metro by perverts… Harrassments in the parks, rapes and the more.

From time to time I was looking up to the notice board. There was still half an hour to enter. Suddenly I noticed Semiha. Her brother was standing by her side. She looked sad. I called her. She and her brother joined us at the table.

My mother asked curiously:

"In other words, you made your mind to go. How about your brother?"

Semiha was gulping something back:

"My elder brother said, 'You come first, in less than a month, I could have Burak come here'."

"Oh. Great. One month is not a big deal… Only a few days left."

His eyes being bright with desire, Burak turned to my mother.

"Sure, Aunt Leman. I also tell my elder sister the same thing, but..."

Semiha's lips were trembling.

Uh ah... I don't want to see this film again. I am not sure whether I should be happy or sad for finding a friend who would make me not to miss my mother... We began to walk to go through the passport control. Passports were controlled. Now I was looking at the section of the airport where no visitors were allowed. My dearie mother's eyes were glued to me, and her curved lips were trying to smile. When I embraced my mother, I felt to the bone that I started missing her even now. In order not to cry, I threw myself to the opposite side by wriggling myself out of her arms. Had I bowed my head, then I am sure that I would have seen my mother looking behind me amongst the people who also bended their head. By wearing a joyful expression on my face, I turned back. My mother was bent over between two persons and trying to see me through a narrow gap. I sent out the kiss I had dropped on my palms towards my mother. My mother was crying. Had I not set out on this journay, then she would have cried for her being in the way of my future... Thinking this way I consoled myself and called Semiha. Bursting into tears, Semiha was waving at her brother.

In the Plane

Kindly asking people sitting by our sides, Semiha and I sat side by side... We did not talk for some time. As our plane was mowing forward towards the clouds in the sky, I was looking down, my beloved İstanbul. The Küçükçekmece Lake merging with the deep blue Marmara Sea spreading around the grey buildings looked so beautiful. After a short silent moment, I turned to Semiha:

"Are you excited?"

"Yes... Sure"

"Come on... Don't be sad anymore."

"You're right but... Why I didn't come with Burak in one month's time?"

"Well... I would have been that way too. Rather than being so sad"

"Oh... My elder brother insisted a lot. My sister-in-law is going to get a job."

"They urgently want you to come in order to babaysit."

"Yes, my elder brother got married in London... To an English girl. Three years ago they had a daughter."

The conversation started to stress me... I had to change the subject right away but Semiha kept telling.

"They used to pay the babysitter one hundred fifty pounds a week... They will give that money to me. Burak will work part-time. Say he will make fifty, then we would earn two hundred fifty pounds a week. When you convert it into Turkish Lira, it totals around seven hundred million Turkish Lira a week. Monthly we would make three billion... Wouldn't it be enough?

"Hmm... I mean, I... had thought"

"Had we stayed in İstanbul, to earn even one billion a month let alone three billion, is impossible. We couldn't afford school expenses here. I applied for a number of jobs but none of them worked."

"Work... Where would you get it... All of my friends went abroad. There is no work available in Turkey anymore."

"Yes... By the way... he is not a stanger... In fact, I will take care of my cousin. We will also have our brother go to school."

Food service started... Being restles in my seat, assuming a joyful attitude, I asked Semiha:

"Shall we drink wine?"

Semiha nodded smiling. I reached out to the wine bottles.

"Alright. I'll take the red wine. They say they help form blood."

To keep pace with me, Semiha replied:

"Me too, I wil also take the red..." As we were sipping our wine and continue our chat, the stewardess disseminated a card. Semiha was trying to fill out the card aghastly.

"Why this card... Why only us?"

"For security." I said.

"For security?"

"Yes... They say it is for preventing migration and terror."

Au pair company had explained all of these before.

Heatrow Airport

Trying to protect our hurt dignity until getting to the airport, we came into line for passport control. Pointing out to the special passport control sections of foreigners, Europeans, and the US citizens:

"Why do they go through so quickly whereas we are still waiting?"

"For security."

We had waited in the passport line so much; I think the English family I would be going to meet must have started worrying about me.

Anyway, our turn came. There was no English-Turkish

translator. The officers were asking their questions in English. I understood and answered a little, but Semiha was stuck in there… I moved away a little bit from the suspicios gaze of the officer, and I noticed that Semiha was in hot water. The officer was about to send Semiha to the security room of the airport and to call the next person in line, I went by their side. I asked the officer in English:

"What's the problem sir?"

I could have bitten my tongue off… The officer started questioning me again. Nonsensical questions such as how long I have known this woman, why I was helping her. As if helping someone constituted a crime. Trying to smile instead of slapping on the man's face, I told him that I met Semiha at the airport, that we had a little bit of conversation, and Semiha was going to her elder brother in London as a guest. The man was not convinced. He said they would talk to Semiha's elder brother.

Oh my God… I had to keep my nerves under control… With a run, without even claiming my luggage, going to the upper story of the airport, I dialed the number Semiha gave me from a telephone box to call her elder brother. I told him that his sister was waiting at the passport control, the passport officer would like to talk to him. I also reminded him of what Semiha and I talked, and our replies to the passport officer. At that point, an announcement was made. I went down the baggage claim section and picked up my luggage.

Now I was not in a state of thinking about Semiha. Had I been a bit later then the family I was going to get to might not want to have me. I was already late though. In a haste, I showed the address in my hand to the person on duty… He directed me very calmly. I was supposed to get to the Piccadilly line. As my mother told me, I moved away a little bit and asked another person on duty. If he would also say the similar things, then I would trust what they had to say... Yes, the second person too told me the same thing. I was supposed to take Piccadilly line from Heatrow. I cued up at the entrance of the metro at the airport to buy a ticket. There was such a long line, I thought this would have taken me too long, so that I decided to take a cab. I got out of the airport.

I was looking for a cab... I was bargaining with the driver. How much to go to Haringay? Oh my God... No, nooo. They called it minicab. It was impossible to pay that much. I had to go back to the metro... Yeah... What a bad luck... Even at the first step you took in London. Where was the trolley I carried my suitcases on it... Offf, I would go crazy! I was dragging my suitcases again.

I got tense... As I was thinking of going fast to the metro, I saw Semiha and her elder brother. Hoping that they would see me and offer me to give a ride to the place I was going. I walked towards them. Semiha and her elder brother were in such a heated conversation that they were proceeding on their way, and it was impossible for them to see me. Semiha... If only you would raise your head, look around... No, nooo... I came close to them hurriedly. With a sweet smile, Semiha spoke:

"Aaaa... Sevgi. I thought you were gone. Oh. My elder brother. Serkan"

"Nice to meet you."

Her elder brother seemed to be a fresh-faced and gentleman person.

"I couldn't have gone yet. I looked for a cab but... I decided to go by metro."

Semiha looked at her elder brother. He took a look at his watch.

"Where were you going?"

"Haringay"

"Haringey?"

Uh oh... The man was not happy at all.

"At this hour... Those places... I mean they are not safe places. It's a neighborhood of London full of incidents.

Oh my... As I was thinking of how I would get there, now how I would find the house in the neighborhood where black people, Kurds, Arabs and Turks turned it into Texas' lawless character.

"As a matter of fact, through Piccadlly you would get there quickly" said Semiha's elder brother. Semiha was looking at her elder brother with a begging look.

"Oh. My elder brother... It was too late... Since it's not a safe place."

Her elder brother replied unwillingly.

"Though it's not on our way to where we are heading but... Let's give you a ride" he said.

Revealing how happy I was, I tagged behind them. On the sly, Semiha and I giggled like a schoolgirl and got in the car.

Following a short period of silence, Serkan wondered with a worried voice.

"Is the family you are going to stay by Turks?"

"No, they are British."

"There are not many British families in Haringey but maybe it might be a British family with a Nijerian heritage.

I didn't get what he meant...

"That means..."

If only you could have found a family near your school."

"I don't know... The company in İstanbul arranged the family. They said they are trustworthy." I said.

"........"

They kept quiet, and I went on.

"How would I know? Since the rents are too high in London, the company found such a solution. They will give my my weekly pocket money."

"That's fine then."

At last, being late for two hours, we got in front of the house where I would be staying

Taking my luggage, saying goodby to Semiha and Serkan, I pressed the doorbell.

Nobody opened the door. I turned my head to Serkan's car... They were waiting for my entering the house. Gluing her head to the glass of the car, Semiha was looking towards me.

Although I insistently rang the doorbell, no one opened the door. Starting to think that I was left alone in the middle of the street at this hour of the night, the door was opened with a pop. Oh my God. A huge black man, I caught his looks with difficulty, was standing up in front of me. I couldn't make sense of why he met me this tense and nervous way. Apologizing for being two hours late, I tried to smile. The man reminded me unkindly of the fact that I should not be late beginning with the first day, and I had shaken their confidence in me. He made the door wide-open and "come in" he said impolitely. Before I entered inside, I turned my head towards Semiha, and waited after seeing both of them got off the car and approached to us. Semiha's elder brother started speaking with the black man in a tense expression in English. He told him that I was entrusted to them, that I was their close relative, and in case any problem comes out, then he should call him. Then he handed in a piece of paper with his telephone number was written on. I felt secure thinking that it was best to have someone from my country.

As the black man was neglectfully taking the piece of paper extended to him, I thanked Semiha again and told her that we will meet. Not thinking to prolong the ceremony of farewell, the black man sort of pushed me inside and closed the door on our people.

Without looking at my face, the black man showed me my room upstairs and hightailed. I guess everyone in the house being even more appaling since it was filled with a foul smell of food, should have gone to bed... I had the pleasure of meeting with only Ferdinand, the head of the household in the first evening.

My room...

I feel even more in my room the strong smell. I opened the window slowly. I took a brief look at around. It seemed to me that everything I might need was there. But the dark blue patterned wallpaper and the floorcloth in the same color started to suffocate me. What a bad taste! Even though everything seemed to be in the right place, in my first night I was cast a pall upon me. On the single-bed, there was a heavy bed cover with ethnic design. A small and old television on the bedside table. A two-door old and dirty wardrobe. Even I did have no heart for taking out my nightie out of my suitcase and put it on. At the moment I was lifting the heavy cover with ethnic design, my telephone rang. It was not difficult for me to have a guess that it was my mother. Despite all of the problems I had gone through, I consoled myself thinking that I was away from her. If only she would have let me alone. With an excited voice she started asking me her questions one after another.

"How are you my daughter... Were you comfortable in the airplane... Have you eaten something. Then how did you get there... Was it comfortable? How was the English family like?"

"I am fine... The family... They are already asleep... I only met with Ferdinand. Good. Very good... My room? Looks very comfortable mother... What do I have here... Television, bed, wardrobe...I have everthing mother... I am full mother... Okay, okay... I will eat. Alright mother. Tomorrow I will buy prepaid card and then I will let you know the number... You... Cancel this... I know it is too much expensive. Tomorrow we can talk longer mother." Even though by giving short answers and making known that I wanted to hang up, our conversation went on and on.

I am not sure whether the heavy smell was gone or I got used to it, but since there was a torrential rain outside, I slowly closed the window. I needed to urinate, and I had to go to the bathroom. I started wriggling. I was pacing back and forth in the middle of my room. Now I was not going to wait for it. I opened the door of my room slowly and looked around for the bathroom. Anyway, I found it without a bumpy ride. It was very close to my room. After having locked the door of the toilet and going through, I shot a glance at the bathroom. The children's toys in the half filled water of the batchtube which was not very visible maybe because of its color caused by dirt or its being old, drew my attention. A yellow duck was looking at me as if to say

"Welcome." The plastic fish were spread out at the bottom of the bathtube as if they were asleep. A small boat was staying idle there as if it was going to take all them away. On the washbasin, there were tooth brushes, some of them inside of a glass and some of them staying outside of the glass. I knew that the house-hold was made up of three people, but there were five tooth brushes. Willy-nilly hung towels were not clean at all. Getting out of the bathroom I quietly entered my room. My first night was like a nightmare. I didn't like this room at all. I was get-ting suffocated. But the company had praised this family to the skies. I went to the bed without getting undressed. Even though I was exhausted, I was unable to get to sleep for a long time. The sound of the rain hitting the roof never ceased. I started crying again thinking that I had missed even now my sweet bed and quilt, and many other items at home. At the very moment that I had dozed off while I was crying and went into a deep sleep, I leapt up hearing a rattling sound. I sat crossed-legged on the bed. The rattling sound was not going away. It was not a mouse I had my guess... My door seemed to be scratched by someone as it were... As I was thinking whether I should go and open the door, the door was opened and closed. The ratling sound was gone and I hardly waited for morning, staying curious all along...

21 September

Following a night like a nightmare, I collected myself upon hearing the voices coming from downstairs and upstairs, and went down. Sulky Ferdinand was smoking cigarette in a huff. His wife approached to me smiling.

"Welcome... I amAmina" she said and kindly explained to

me that their daughter and themselves went to bed at ten o'cloak and that's why they were ubable to meet me. As I was talking the the mother, a smiling, cute and plump girl whose hair in plaits went down the stairs. Her name was Ellen. Before completing acquaintance phase with the daughter of the house, whom I was supposed to pick up from the school, hearing Ferdinand's imposing ringing voice, Amina straight off reached out her daughter'schoolbag and turned to me.

"A couple of days you need to come to the school with us. Today I will also get there after school, and you could learn the way as we come back home from school."

Sure... My first job should be to find out how to get to school. I just took my coat and sat at the rear of the car beside the girl. I was understanding some of the questions Amina asked, and I couldn't get some. I answered the woman's questions on the one hand, I was also looking at the places we were passion on the other. After the house we made a right turn and reached a turnout in front of a huge market. The name of the market was Yaşar Halim Supermarket. She told me that we would get across carefully and go through the traffic lights. By turning around the center point by car, we entered a parkway. Under something small and bridge-like thing, a weak and black water stream was flowing. A couple of swans were swimming in it. Things to bear in mind were the Market and the bridge. I gathered seeing the families were taking their children by holding their hands towards a hill. We came near a fenced, two story long and rectangle shaped building, sprawled on the ground. Pulling over the car by the road outside the school, Ferdinand waited for us to get off. As Amina, Ellen and I were walking towards the school, he lit his cigarette standing by the car. In front of the school was packed with the bright and breezy children and the adults.

There were children from almost every nation, yet the yellow head types of English were scarcely any. Amina introduced me to the teacher of Ellen. She told the teacher that from now on I would be picking up Ellen from school. I met the smiling teacher this way and after taking a look at the students entering inside in rows, we went out from the school yard. The parents or caretakers who had brought the children set off to come back in the evening. I was a bit surprised. This school was not like the schools I went to in Istanbul. As if it was a make-shift school. After all, we were not taken to school by our families except the first day of the school. There was a school service and it was quite comfortable. Why were these people being forced to hire an au pair just to take their children to school? Why they couldn't come toghether and hire a service car? This way it would have cost them less. I was going to make forty pounds a week. I would be a burden on them because of the rent, electricity, water, food – though I don't think I could eat – economically. Instead of this way, they could even send their children to school by a cab. We got there in ten minutes. The school is very close to home.

After having dropped the child in school, on our way back, I made them wait for five minutes in front of a market to buy a prepaid telephone card. The majority of the customers in the market were Turks. I felt that I was not in London, but in a neighborhood of the suburbia of Istanbul. I was just about to buy a ten-pound prepaid card, a helpful Turkish customer told me that the house telephone cards are way cheaper. He showmed me a card called "Yes Card." After dialing the number on the card, I was supposed to enter the number I was calling. Thanking him, I bought a yes card for three pounds. I got in the car of my new family waiting in front of the market. I showed the card in my hand to Amina. I asked whether I could use their home telephone with this card or not.

I watched their reaction to my very rightful request open-mouhtedly, as if I asked them to transfer the deed of their house to me. After a short silence, I got the permission provided that I was not supposed to busy the telephone too long. I had found out that using this card was not causing any extra charge to the house telephone. That meant that there was nothing for them to pay any money for my usage of that card. The car stopped in front of the house's garden. They gave me the key of the exterior door. They also cautioned me not to lose it. Smiling, Amina told me that there were foods in the refrigerator, and I had plenty of time to take a bath and to settle in my room comfortably. By engraving in my memory the hour of pick-up for their daughter, and the moment I got off the car, I saw the car darted out at the street from the yard.

I stood for a while in front of the red bricked house where I was going to live until my education was completed... In front of the semidetached houses, which seemed to be a product of the same factory, there were an equally small garden and a closed garage to the house only one car. As I noticed this morning, nobody was using the garage as it was, parking their car by the side of the garden wall and using their garage as a depot of trivial things. I looked around. I didn't like these houses resembling social house-dwellings but I had also realized that the exterior of the houses were cleaner than the interior, and the roofs were warming me inside. When I was entering inside by unlocking the door, a black next-door neighbor was going out to walk her dog. Smiling,

"Good morning" she said and turned her head. For sure the woman's saying "Good morning" to a total stranger was something a civil mannerism not to be surprised of. After I reciprocated her "Good morning" wish, I wanted to say something like,

"I think you are going to walk your dog," out of curtesy, expecting that the woman would like to talk with me... I wanted also tell her that I was also staying at this house. Yet the woman went away quickly. Maybe she didn't like to talk too much. I entered inside. The house was permeated with even the stronger smell than yesterday. I wanted to get out immediately but I had lots of things to do.

Swiftly I went up to my room and opened the window. I had to clean my room and get settled into it. The first day of the week my school was going to start. Firstly, I took off the quilt cover and hanged down the quilt from the window. The bed stuff was very important for me to have a good sleep. I took out all the pillows, linens. It was a nerve-breaking situation. In fact, at this very moment I wanted to be able to communicate on the Internet, to call everyone but it would be better if I made my telephone calls while these were being aired, done my laundry and got them dried. I folded down the quilt covers and the cover on the television and laid aside. I unpacked the suitcases. For a moment, the scent spreading from the suitcase made me feel that I was in my mother's house, as it were. I cannot put them inside, before cleaning the two-door wardrope. Running to the bathroom quickly, I poured hot water and plenty of detergent into the somewhat large plastic toy bucket that I thought it was small girl's item. All in sweat, I wiped the interior of the wardrope and left its doors open. Outside, the sky was cloudy and it was almost beginning to rain. After changing the water in the bucket, I wiped the drawers, the wooden parts of the bed and the wallpaper as much as I could have reached. I turned one of my brand-new tshirt into a dustcloth. Wiping things doesn't seem to end. I had lower back pain now. I am sneezing without stopping. I work hard by running here and there as it were. I rubbed down almost everywhere but doing it on the wall to wall carpet was the most difficult part. But I was disgusted to walk on it. No, no... I had to wipe the floor as well since I started this job. At that moment the doorbell rang... I checked the watch. It was yet twelve... Who might have come since I was supposed to pick Ellen up at four? I opened the door and was about to look down as I was walking towards the stairs. I heard Amina's voice.

"Sevgi, it's me..."

While climbing up the stairs with a timid smile, Amina spoke:

"I forgot my lunch at home out of the morning fuss. I will take it and go. How are you. Have you settled in?"

Holding a washrag in my hand,

"Thank you. I am." I said.

She looked at my face carefully.

"Are you really a Turk?"

"Yes."

"You don't look like the Turks here."

"Really?"

I said, "Yes."

Anyway, Amina went upstairs but didn't enter my room. As she was visiting the bathroom, obviously having seen the quilt I hanged down from the window, she reminded me of the fact that the quilt covers were clean and unused. I thanked her but I didn't tell her that I was going to use the quilt covers my mother put in my suitcase. She told me that the bathroom was a little bit untidey and asked me to put it in order. What? In fact, despite her having a smiling face, I was angry about her without revealing. At first, I was uneasy thinking that she came here to *check with me... Then her ordering me to do some jobs turned my stomach. In our agreement, the only requirement for me was to pick up their daughter from school. I told her that I would try to tidy up the bathroom, and I went to my room. While rubbing down the wall to wall carpet ambitiously, I figured out from the door's sound that Amina had gone. I looked from behind the tulle out of the window. Amina got out of the garden by walking. Apparently she was not brought here by her husband. She didn't take a cab either. I thought she was working somewhere near. I took off my shoes. I changed the water for five times when I was wiping the wall to wall carpet. Whenever I stepped on the carpet, a slushy sound was coming out. By hanging my dresses on the hangers in the wardrope, I spread two clean bedlinings one on the top of the other. I dropped off the items I was going to place in drawers onto the bed, and I put the suitcases on top of the wardrope. I moved the electric heater in the bathroom to my room and I turned on the heat to 70 degree Celcius. I had to have the carpet dried before they got back. Steaming with sweat I entered the bathroom without a delay. I hardly contained my-self not to vomit after having imagined the giant Ferdinand was taking a bath here in this bathtub. Summoning up my courage, I wiped the bathtub, the sink and floor stones with bleacher. After flushing out the bathtub, I turned on the hot water. Bringing my bathrobe and shampoo from my room, I entered again the bathroom.*

Taking this bath made me forget about all of my exhaustion. By sitting on the sweet smelling lining on my bed comfortably, I got dressed. Having my telephone card from my hand bag, I went out of my room. A very pleasant shampoo and detergent smell was spreading towards the corridor from the bathroom right across my room. I sneaked a peek at the room with its door left ajar. Apparently it was Ellen's room. That strong smell I got newly acquainted was in this room as well. Next room with its door closed to Ellen's must be her parent's bed room. That means, upstairs there were three bed rooms and one bathroom. Going down the stairs, there was a large but very untidy kitchen. Tea cups and the pots of the dishes from the night were on the counter without lids. The food remains and dirty plates had littered the sink full to the brim. I thought that probably the woman could not up to the requirements of the house works while also performing a job outside of the house. My mother too had worked in a job and also without delay she was able to do the house works. Obviosly not everyone could be as talented as my mother was. Moreover, my mother was always doing a second job at home, like editing and proofreading books.

I opened the refrigerator. In fact, since I didn't have breakfast, my stomach was rumbling but as soon as I saw the inside of the refrigerator, all my appetite was gone. Even the cut unions were put in the refrigerator without any cover. The smell of the broccoli and the smell of the strange meat with sauce were mishmashed as it were. I just closed the door of the refrigerator and entered the sitting room. On the left, the dark blue and artless seats looked very dirty. On the right, you could find everything on the rather large table. The item that turned my stomach most was the nail clippers. Newspapers, sleepers and some of the toys were thrown away somewhere over there. Although the surroundings didn't look very untidy, yet not clean either. As I was looking about the telephone, I saw a picture of the framed Kaaba. In that case, they must have been Muslim, I thought, and I reached out to the telephone. I dialed the numbers on the card. Then I dialed my number. Offf. I should have entered so many numbers... I was waiting. Answer machine! Anyhow, I succeded in ringing Özge's telephone half an hour later. Come *on! Oh well, my friend who I got to know in the visa queue picked up the phone.*

I let out a scream out of joy, "Özge! Me! Sevgi!" I started to tell her over the phone about what I had gone through since I got here. I told her that I even missed my mother a lot, whose attention was suffocating me, and I didn't like this family, and I was about to die out of exhaustion. First of all, she recorded my number. Then she told me that on Sunday we would meet at Victoria Station and then go to Mert's house to have a dinner together. In a clap, I had forgotten all of my troubles. After having finished my talk with Özge, I immediately called my mother. Gosh! Hearing my mother's voice has been such a great relief for me even though my mother bombarded me with thousands of questions. What a nice thing it was to hear your mother's voice. I gave her my new number. I told her that I was doing fine. I shared the information with her that on Sunday I would go about London and have a dinner at Mert's house. I gathered from the tone of my mother's voice that out conversation took a weight off her mind. As I was saying goodbye to my mother, I gritted my teeth not to cry. But as soon as I put down the telephone, I couldn't help but crying sobbingly. Even in the first week, I had missed my mother so much.

Pulling myself together, I called the elder brother of Semiha at once. Semiha picked up the phone. Her niece happened to be very sweet girl. She loved her a lot. Semiha also told me that her English sister-in-law seemed to be a good person. They wondered about me. They were afraid of the man's trying to eat me. I relieved Semiha by saying to me that no one can eat me in this world. We just laughed. After feeding her niece, she had her go to sleep and went for cleaning. She talked about the intidiness of the house yet she didn't allow anyone to speak ill of her sister-in-law.

"What could the woman do, she works from morning till night... There is now a child."

She told me that in case her elder brother would allow her, then she would come. We all were going to meet at ten on Sunday at Victoria Statin's north gate. I had still two-hour credit in my card to make calls. It was fine that this yes card was cheaper but since there was no home phone when you were out, I still needed to buy mobile phone prepaid card. I went up to my room.

Offf, I feel terribly cold. I was hungry and everywhere was still damp. I put on the jumper my mother knitted, my warm socks and my winter sleepers. While walking in Istanbul just wearing a sleeveless blouse, to put on dresses one top on another bored me frankly. I placed my underclothes and socks into the drawers. Putting on the pillow cover and the cover onto the quilt I prepared my bed. My room smelled so pleasant. I forgot the smell of the house. Now I was wondereing where to put my bits and pieces. My cosmetics, hairclips, my books, my beanies, medicines my mother filled in bottled just in case, napkin, bath glove, shampoo, dental materials, a couple of family photos, and most important of all, my shoes and boots. As I was pondering on what to do with these items, our people arrived. Letting the window open, I went down. A very strong rain had already started. We left the house to pick up the girl from school.

24 September

It's now my fourth day since my arrival. Today at four, I will pick Ellen up alone. The family would not come with me anymore. I had known the road between home and the school in one day. Even finding out the Haringay neighborhood didn't appear too difficult to me. I didn't have any trouble since in every neighborhood there are a coffee-house, a market, a second hand *shop, a church, a pub, a children park, a tesco, and a doner kebap shop at every step. After all, the majority of the shops in this neighborhood belonged to Turks. You could see the Turkish advertising everywhere. It was impossible to feel here that you were in England. In reality, I was in one of İstanbul's suburbia. Most of them came from Maraş. Everyone spoke Turkish. Most of the women from Maraş didn't know how to speak English altnhough they had lived here for around twenty years. The men on the other hand could speak some broken English. Generally, the women looked not very pleasing with their patterned skirts sweeping the floow, and wearing long cardigans over their skirts as well as sleepers on their feet. For so many years they didn't benefit from civilization so to speak. Even so, I liked to talk with them. These people who were complaining about their country were not happy here at all. As if they were grumbling in the gizzard to buy a house in Turkey in no time and to return to their land after setting up a business in their native country... When they got rich and attempted to go back to their country, they encountered always some obstacles. They had always some excuses to postpone their moving into their own country: Let the children finish their school; let the children have their own houses; let the children get married; let the grandchildren go to school here, etc. I made a sense of their dilemma of the guest workers facing with these obstacles all the time and only consoling themselves by looking the photos of the houses they bought in the country they had been missing, by watching the furniture inside their houses through cameras, after having watched those videos myself...*

Since I was not eating at home, generally I took pita doner from Ali Baba at the corner. Here the doner meat was not like in Turkey. In Turkey the most bulk of the food was made of bread whereas here the meat was more than bread. I guess here the meat was cheap, and that's why the meat pieces keep being dropped from pita. As to the evening meal, I buy this and that, and nibble on them in my room.

In mornings, I only drank a cup of tea. My mother should never know about what I do here. Even on the first day, I forgot about the daily requirements of the foods measuring the need of taking vitamins, protein, starch, and iron. Had I told my mother about the state of this house and the family, I was sure, my mother would have died out of grief.

This morning there was a note dropped on the counter in the kitchen.

"Hi Sevgi. After Ellen arrives from school, please warm up the rice in the refrigerator, and give some yoghurt beside it. Give her an apple when she finishes her meal please. I will be at home at six at the latest. Amina."

We haven't talked about doing all of these as far as my work contract was concerned. But warming up the rice was not a big deal. It would not tire me.

I couldn't help looking at the picture in the bright dark blue frame beside the table. I focused on their sad looks matching up with our chat last evening with Amina. They were an English family with a Nigerian heritage. Ferdinand was born in London. When having come to London from the North Nigeria, Amina was fourteen years old. Their being poor continued in this country too. Even though both of them worked under difficult conditions, still they were barely able to feed themselves. When Amina was telling me that she loved her husband Ferdinand a lot, and she got used to his nervous temparement, I felt that she was frank. They had arguments and even fights between them. Once, when Ferdinand landed a punch and cracked her *head open, they performed eight stitches. The state protected Amina and Ellen. They had to stay in a women's shelter under very difficult conditions. Still she had met secretly with here husband. Ellen was just two years old at that time. When Amina, who was subjected to violence from her husband, did use violence against her daughter, and subsequently the state wanted to take Ellen away from her mother... Amina, who had intimately lived violence throughout her life for thousands of years as if violence was coded in her genes, had feared a lot. If she wanted to beat her daughter, she resorted to this by doing it secretly in bathrooms. That was to say that Ferdinand never gave up beating Amina, and Amina did not forgo beating Ellen at all. One year later they sent them to a one-room house on a temporary basis. Last year, the municipality had given them this house. This house was going to be Amina's. Over a morning coffee, Amina told that, now they were getting along living in this house without paying any rent, that she was working illegally at a dry cleaning shop, and the state had put her and her daughter on a salary. It was all evident from her state that Amina suffered a lot. Even though she felt more secure, she was extremely carefull vis-à-vis her husband. I would be sensing a primitive cunning side, wouldn't I? I haven't talked to Ferdinand even a single word. A nerveous, unhappy and a bit mysterious personality.*

My room smelled very nice but it seemed to be a little bit untidy. My novity was inside a box on the floor. The carpets look like dried. Putting the electric heater that I had used a couple of hours a day back to its old place, in a little while I would go pick up Ellen. At a minimum, I had to iron the shirt I was considering to put on Sunday. I was excited for I was going to start my school on Monday. I wondered whether I would be feeling myself living in London by getting away from this neighborhood and people. Af-

ter hanging up the shirt I ironed, I put on my coat and went out.

The children lined up in front of the school were being handed in to their relatives or authorized persons by their classroom teachers. It was my turn. I got the girl, and we set off to get home. Behaving nicely by her parents, Ellen was trying to give to whim thousands of times and made me go crazy, I tought. Today was our first day. I was making an effort to be patient by thinking maybe this was because of that. I extended my hand smiling. Ellen did not hold my hand in a huff.

"Nice! My father used to take me by car" she said.

As Ellen who didn't extend her hand and myself were walking on the parkway, I was trying to explain to her that her parents had to work, and that's why they wanted me to come to their house, but she was not paying attention to what I had to say.

"You English is very bad... I don't understand you" that was a shock to me. By jımping from the wall instead of going through the gate of a building complex, she made my hair stand on end. She even attempted to climb up the trees after throwing away her school bag in the garden of that building complex. I was waiting patiently but what if her family would be checking to see whether she got home in time or not. I'd like to drag in her by force but what if her father was following us secretly on this first day. Thank God, she ended her whim in the garden.

She goes on walking without taking her school bag. I swiftly took the bag and approached to her. I grabbed her hand with anger. We passed by the locations where there were no vehicles. We were going to go through the traffic lights. She was in a hissy fit for letting go of her hand. I hardly contained her. Oh my God, what kind of a child she was. I was unable to cope with her. She wanted to go through the traffic lights by herself. No, I would not let go of her hand and I would drag in her but the cameras would be capturing our scene to be perceived as if I was kidnapping her. By kneeling down in front of the girl, I was explaining to to her that now it was too early for her to go through the traffic lights alone by herself but one day I would be giving her permission to do the way she wanted.

Ellen disobeyed me and tried to run away from me. Now passerby people were looking at us. Keeping my nerves under control and wearing a smile on my face, I squeezed her hand hard inside my palm and walked forcibly together across the road. The light was almost turning red, but the girl didn't want to walk. Tugging her away I had her cross the other side. This time she stuck around the Yaşar Halim Market. She said she had money and she wanted to buy a chewing gum. Anyway, we bought ther chewing gum. But this time around she insisted upon her not entering the house. I just took out my cellphone and told her that I was going to call her father. Ellen stopped suddenly. Sensing that the girl was looking at me with fearful eyes and trying to figure out whether I was going to call her father in earnest. I dialed my number and pretended that I was talking to her father.

"Hi Ferdinand... I was going to talk to you about Ellen."

Pulling at my hand and with a lickspittling manner,

"Alright... I wil not do it again." She said. I made it clear through my gesture that I was going to end my talk to her father."

"To you... Well... We got home from school. Ellen is a very nice girl. I was going to tell you about it" I said ungenuinely.

Ellen's relieved expression changed back to its old version as soon as I hung up the phone, yet she did not resist entering the house.

The moment Ellen entered the house, as she was climbing up on a stool to grab a chocolate box, she toppled all the spice boxes. I was about to die. It was half past four. It lasted fourty minutes for us to cover ten-minute walk. There were still one and half an hour for her mother to come. I wonder whether I should lock this girl behind her room. I hoped it was just the first day syndrome. The telephone of the house rang when I was thinking that otherwise this was something I cannot bear this way at all. As I guessed, it was Amina. She had been calling us for the last ten minutes. Why were we so late? She was worried. I told her that Ellen caused some problems and I could tell her when she arrived. She immediately wanted to have her daughter to talk. I hand in the phone to Ellen... The first thing she said to her mother was,

"Sevgi pushed me."

A troubled girl, and a liar as well. I was moon-eyed. Had I quit on my first day, I had nowhere to go. I didn't want to hear the lies Ellen had to say to her mother. This small girl seemed to me like a huge monster. She extended the handset to me with a sullen face. Her mother wanted to talk to me. As I was expecting that her mother was going to be upset with me, on the contrary, the woman offered her apology to me.

"I am sorry... Ellen will get used to you, don't worry about it." I sat my heart at rest. Why did Amina talk like that? I think no one had to put up with her. When I hung up the phone, Ellen was unwrapping the chololate with a great appitite. I pulled the chocolate from her hand swiftly. I heated the rice, undeterred by her crying, kicking and stamping. I put the rice with some yoghurt on the table. After all, I had to have her to clean the spices fallen on the ground but my softheartedness didn't let me do so. And while she was eating away the rice, I cleaned the floor.

This one hour seemed to be such a long time to me... It lingered too long. I gave Ellen one chocolate and an apple. I told her that she needed to change her dress yet Ellen seemed to be determined not to do so. I told her that I would take back the chocholate from her hand as a punishment, but before I had the opportunity to take it back, I gathered from the sound of the key on the exterior door that her mother arrived. It was half past five. Perhaps it was the first day, she had come home early. The moment she entered, Amina looked at the chocolate in her daughter's hand. It was no use for Ellen trying to hide the chololate by taking it behind her back. Amina's gaze turned to me.

"Why did you give it?"

"I didn't. She took it by herself."

If only I didn't say it. Crash. Amina boxed small girl's cheek. I didn't know what to do, what to say. I looked at this girl and I felt sadness, although she turned my last one and half hour into a hell. Despite her mother's five finger's trace was on her cheek, not even a single tear dropped from Ellen's eyes. I felt blue.

"If my job is finished, then I'd like to up to my room." I said.

Tossing out her hand back to one corner and her overcoat to another, Amina had already started to cook for her husband.

"Had she done the same thing while coming from school, please call me" she said as she was peeling an onion.

"Okay. I wil call."

In a manner of getting used to be beaten, Ellen had gone to the living room and turned on the television. Once the music of the teletubby, a children TV series, echoed in the house, a pain inside me was increased.

As I was going up the stairs, Amina called out from my behind.

"I cannot find the spices"

I was stuck on the stairs. Had I told her that your daughter toppled them while grabbing chocolate, then the girl would be slapped again.

"Me... Well... I am just going to buy from the market in corner right now" I said. Amine looked at me intently. I thought she got it that it was her daughter's mischief. After she nodded her head as if to say "Alright", then I put on my shoes on the door stone. Wiping her hands on her dress, she took out money from her purse.

First, I hesitated to take the two-pound note she put on the counter. Thinking that I was going to meet with my friends this weekend and also that I didn't receive my weekly wage, I reached out to the money.

There was everthing you look for at Yaşar Halim market. The girl at the ounter asked how I was doing. She told me that I was patient enough to survive for five days but she didn't expect me not to stand any further, and the fact that this family had changed au pairs once a month or even once a week.

When I entered the house and left the spices on the counter, Amina threw on my hand my weekly wages of fourty pounds. Even though she gave the money to me as if to say "it's too much" despite what I put so much blood and sweat into my work and made a face for it, still I kindly thanked her and went up to my room.

I took out the fruit juice and croissant I bought at the market. I turned on the old small television. There was only the BBC channel available. The set didn't show other channels. On TV, the film called "Protest" was being introduced through its teaser. I had watched it before but it was one of the films that I could watch again and again. Mathieu Kassovitz shot this film in 1995. This was a French film, depicting a section of three young people's life who lived in the ghettos of Paris. One of the young people was a Jew, Vinz; the second one was a black, Hubert; and the third one was from Africa with roots in Europe, that was pied-noir Said. This film was shot on the story of these three friends; since having made referrals to racisim and social class disparities, the film had created a tremendous impression both in France and in the world. Deciding to watch the film in English this time, bringing this and that to nibble by the side of my bed, I settled to enjoy watching it. One of the things remained in my mind when I watched the film earlier was its being shot in black & white, and the second one was its music arrangements. Above all, listening to that short song sung by the Jamaican singer would be quite a pleasurable thing for me.

25 September

As soon as the alarm I set up for eight o'cloak went off, I jumped out of the bed. I had heart some rattling sounds in the night, but since I was so tired, I couldn't get up and try to find out what it was, and I had gone to sleep. Today is my day off, and even though there was no place to go, still I wanted to go out of this house… There are some sounds coming from downstairs. Apparently wife and husband were in an argument. I was just about to go down, I heard that there were some things broken, and Ellen and Amina started crying as well. Silently I shrank in my room. I was waiting to see the end of the argument, now having turned into a fight. I was not thinking of staying in this house at all. I gathered that someone went ouf of the house since the exterior door was slammed harshly and the glasses of all windows clanked. I looked from behind the tulle. Ferdinand was flouncing out to walk towards his car. I went down. Ellen was in the living room watching television, and her mother was collecting the broken glasses by crying. Thinking that the poor woman could collect herself hearing me, I pretended to caugh and approached to her. I noticed that in the meantime Amina wiped her tears with the back of her hand. I told her that I would be back home late. I also added that tomorrow I would be meeting with my friends. Without looking at my face, Amina said.

"Have a nice day"

As a mere formality, I turned to Ellen and said

"Good bye."

I was not expecting her to reply. While Ellen was zapping even without turning her head, I surged out of the house. I took a deep breath.

Since I was going to meet with my friends in Victoria tomorrow, then it would be wise for me to go about those locations today so that tomorrow I would be at ease without my knees knock together. I went to Yaşar Halim super market and asked shop assistant Leyla how to get to Victoria. I took note of the directions. She sold me one-day-travel card. She told me that by that card I would travel as many times as I wish all day long. I thanked her and went out.

By one bus, I got to Victoria Station. There was no such a Nort Gate. Incredibly complicated. Inside of it resembles a huge shopping center. There were all of the things you might be looking for. I cannot finish going about this place. I entered into a Vodafone shope. I purchased a new SIM card for my mobile phone, and started walking for fun with a guidebook in my hand. For I felt for the first time being in London for the last five days, I was skipping rejoicingly. I was very happy because I *was far away from the bad electricity of the house. The historical stone buildings, fancy pubs, cafes made me so exhilarated.*

Multicoloered begoinias decorating the narrow balconies specifically constructed for the flower, even geraniums shedding of flowers, and fuchsias looked so appealing. I walked withoug knowing where I was heading. I had plenty of time until the evening. I was at a crossroads. Where to go, I wondered. I looked around. I kept on walking in the direction of Kings Road. Everywhere seemed nice. I witnessed that here the true English people reside. This was way different than the Harringay neighborhood where the family lives by whom I was staying. I caught my breath in front of an elegant café-bar like place right by the Slona Square before entering Chelsea from Kings Road. Seeing the people's having their breakfast hungrily at the tables in front of the door, the sweet smell of the coffee motivated me. I entered the place. Having a look around, you could readily see that this place was one of the expensive ones. I went on walking. I was walking on the Kings Road Street. Whereever I turned my gaze, I was seeing the elegant people were stopping by the world-famous stores. I thought that maybe this was one of the exclusive neighborhood of London. In the end, having my cappicino at a spit-and-sawdust café, I asked the location of the British Museum. I found out that it was five minutes away from the Oxford Street. Very near where I was.

Touring the museum took many many hours. Here there were hundreds of artifacts belonging to the Anatolian civilizations. As I was looking at them admiringly, I started talking to a middle-aged English man.

"Are you Turk" he wondered.

"Yes." I replied.

"I toured your country. Very beautiful."

"Thank you."

There was a short period of silence. I had lost myself in the ethnic designs of a magnificent palace gate.

"This gate should be exhibited in your country" he said.

"Yes... But even its being exhibited here made me emotional" I said.

As I was getting ready to say "Have a nice day", he introduced himself. His name is Joshua... I also introduced myself hurriedly and told him that I had to leave now. He was about to part.

"Do you have time to have a coffee?" he asked.

"Thank you, I am afraid, I don't. I just came from Turkey. And..."

Before I finished my words, Joshua spoke wonderingly.

"I got it... You don't have time. This is my phone number. When you have time, call me if you want."

By thanking, I got his phone number and I went out from the museum before finishing my tour. Joshua was not insisting. He was a polite man. He didn't bother me at all, but instead of drinking coffee, I wanted to go about the places to see and to get to know London better.

Passing by many shopping centers, magnificent churches and historical buildings, I got back to the Slone Square Station. First through the Circle Line, and then Jubile Line I reached Regent's Park. I was amazed by incredibly pretty cafes. While I as walking amongst the greenery, I ate the sandvich I took out from my bag and sat in a coffeehouse to drink a cup of coffee. Having other people's eyes on me wherever I go since my childhood had always been a bothering situation for me. I guess for that reason, I wanted to be an ugly girl all the time. After having drunk my coffee, I was walking inside the park when I came across a mosque. A mosque... I approached to the yard of the mosque standing invitingly by all its grandeur located inside one of the most beautiful parks of London. How could I explain, I got so much emotional! I asked a woman over there.

"Is this a mosque?"

"Yes"

"Well... May I enter?"

"Sure" she said and looked at me carefully.

"Here is the place where Muslims worship"

"Yes, I know" I replied.

"Are you a Muslim?"

I nodded as if to say "Yes".

For some reason the woman was dumbfounded... After a short period of silence, I turned to the woman.

"How nice. Having your municipality building such a mosque in such a beautiful park."

"No. The actual realization of this mosque... Cat Stevens... Do you know him?"

"Yes... Yes."

"He is called now Yusuf İslam."

"Yes, building this mosque was only possible thanks to Yusuf İslam."

Even though it was twenty after five, it got dark. I walked toward the metro station. I had so much fun throughout the day that even I was not feeling the pain of my swollen feet caused by walking for so long,

On my way back home in metro I observed the people in my car discreetly. It was evident from the passengers that I was out of London and heading to a location where the slum dwellers lived. There were more than twenty people in the car. Many of them were from Pakistan, India, and Sudan. Also two passengers were seemingly Turks from the Eastern part of the country. Taking out my diary, I looked into my finances. I noticed that I was instinctively careful with my spending as if someone had whispered into my ears that I had to be prudent in this country. I had spent only fifteen pounds. Coffees, sandvich and travelling money. After getting off from the station, I bought one banana and a small bottle of milk.

I was dragging my heels as I was approaching to the house. How could I be happy with this family where violence was running rampant. Here mother's smack on her daughter swam before my eyes. Event though she was driving me crazy, I noticed that I was sad for the small black girl while I was looking the door's key inside my bag. Since I was in this house, I had seen her father looking babies in the eyes of his daughter even for once. Even though there was a speckle of love in this man on the needle, it must have been dead for long. I wondered whether I was lucky to have grown lacking a father... I slowly opened the door by thinking that how patient my mother has been towards me. I just wished that everyone had gone to sleep, but I heard the sound coming from the television. They were not in bed. Since they were also taking off their shoes within the house, I took my boots in my hand and headed to the stairs. I turned my head and said

"Good night!"

With a joyful and as frisky as a pup manner Amina got out of the living room,

"Welcome. How did your day go?" she wondered.

Thanking and saying that it went well, without prolonging the conversation I went up to my room.

The balmy impression was given to me by my sweet smelling room after the gloomy atmosphere of the house.

After gorging myself on the banana and milk, I put on my pajamas I watched a documentary about the animal world on television, I heard that Amina and Ferdinand went into the next door giggling. For some reason this bothered me a lot. Maybe having lived for years with my mother at a house without a man made me become a person so sensitive. Not needing to shut my ears in order not to listen to what was coming next, my eyelids started feeling heavy. I slept like a log and I just woke up in the small hours and straightened up in my bed when I heard the footsteps coming from the corridor in front of the opposing door. The footsteps stopped by Ellen's door. The similar sounds I had heard before. As if a tief was walking inside the house trying not to make a noise. The door of the Ellen's room was opened slowly. I felt my heart was missing a beat. Someone was going to hurt the small girl. Quietly I went down from my bed. Making all efforts not to make any noice, I swiftly thought about what to do. The best thing I though would be to call the girl's family without a delay. By putting my phone on silent, I started dialing the number. Their phone was wringing downstairs. I would hear its ringing even from upstairs amd the ones sleeping in the next room would not... It's so hard to believe that at this moment a murderer, a tief or a rapist was in girl's room. I had to jump in no time to the next door and I should have alarmed everyone.

In a swift move, I opened the door of my room and knocked

at the next door. No... As if they were dead... Nobody opened the door. As my heart was beating fast, I threw a side-glance towards Ellen's room Its door was ajar but the lights were not on. But a faint light is oozing from the side of the balcony to the spot where I was. The only balcony in this house was in the small girl's room. By deliberating everything in seconds, I dived into the room of the wife and husband. I called "Amina." Amina straightened up in the bed. Her husband was not beside her. I told her excitedly "There is someone in Ellen's room." Amina was very calm. She said, "He might have gone to her room to cover her. That's right... Since the father was not in the bed... What about that light oozing from the balcony? Thinking that the light might have come from outside, and I was heading for my room while I was apolagizing to Amina for making her wake up, I came face to face with Ferdinand. When I saw him so suddenly in front of me, I was almost going to die at that very spot. As I was going to enter my room after explaining to him shortly why I woke him up, what I thought what was going on and apologizing to him, my eyes moved to the side of the small girl's door. The door was closed but the oozing light was not seen anymore. I went to my room and took a deep breath. I was angry at myself for getting so much excited in vain. But still I couldn't set my heart at rest. There was something strange going on. Every night, the slowly opened door, the rattling sounds coming from the next door... And the light oozing from the balcony which I noticed just this night. I just ran to the window of my room and turned my head towards the balcony of the next room. There was no lamp or electricity post with the light hitting the balcony from outside.

26 September

Despite getting to know my friends very recently, I was so excited as if I was going to met with my bosom friends. There were sounds coming from downstairs. I raised my head and told the household,

"Good morning."

Amina replied.

"Good morning."

"May I hop in the shower?" I asked their permission and went into the bathroom.

As if there was a war in this bathroom. From here to Sunday. Again, there was a puddle at the bottom of the bathtub. Having pumped the bathtub, I sprinkled the hot water. I took a shower by standing inside the bathtub without taking of my sleepers. After getting out of the bathtub, I washed my feet under the faucet and got out of there.

I went down after putting on the dresses I had ironed earlier. Amina and Ellen were having their breakfast. Exhanging good morning pleasantries, Ferdinand went out of the living room when I was wearing my shoes which I had brought them carrying in my hand. As I said "Goon morning" to him, I was hurriedly heading for the door to get out, Ferdinand asked me,

"Where to go?"

"To Victoria" I said.

"I am going to Finsbury Park. From there you can take Victoria Line. Let me give you a ride" he said.

For some reason, I preferred to go by taking a couple of transfers instead of going with this man.

"Thank you. I went there yesterday. I know how to get there."

The man was insisting.

"Alright, alright. I will take you there. You are considered now one of the family."

I felt that I was caught in a trap as it were. Ferdinand put on his forty-five size shoes as I guessed.

While he was starting the engine, he rolled a cigarette. He held it out to me.

"Take it"

"Nooo… I don't smoke"

"This is not a cigarette. Joint. "

That is a drug. The man was calmy and joyfully offering a drug to me. In horror,

"Thank you, I don't use it" I replied.

"How would you enjoy life without using it? Take one and try."

"Well… No, I remembered. I was going to shop here in this market before I meet with my friends."

"Okay. I will wait."

I wasn't able to keep my nerves under control.

"Don't wait. Because I don't want to go by your car" I said and got out of the car to go to the market.

I asked shop attendant Leyla to give me a daily travelling card. Leyla looked at my face.

"You are distressed" she said.

I dodged the real answer and replied: "Noo. Its sleepinees in the morning."

"Be careful with Ferdinand. He is a drug dealer." She said surprisingly. As if she saw him giving me the drug.

"A drug dealer"

"Yes"

My travelling card in my hand, and distress inside of me, I left the market. While walking to the bus stop, fear of suspicion that Ferdinand might be following me, what my mother had told me started echoing in my ears.

"Don't ever smoke a cigarette that is given to you"

What a bad beginning for today that was looking forward to it for a week. I took out immediately my mobile phone and called my mother. Hearing her voice might have consoled me.

"Mother... I am fine dear mother... My voice... Nooo. I am fine. I will meet with my friends a little later. Who are they... Mother... See there were people in İstanbul with whom I had met while we were seeking our visas... They are the ones. Özge, Mert, and Semiha."

I had already been at the stop when I hung up the phone. Yes, talking to my mother did good to me... My mother had said,

"Promise me that you will never hide anything from me" but... How could I have told her. To tell her that Ferdinand offered to me a drug. She would have urgently come her, and she would have taken me back.

I was going to meet with my friends at 11.00 a.m. It was still 9. I just left home earlier to escape from it. Since I was not in a hurry, I started waiting at the bus stop hoping that instead of using metro, I would have gone by transferred busses, and looked outside out of the window of the bus, and this way would have been able to forget about this drug offer.

As the bus proceeded, it began passing through the nicer

neighborhoods, parks and by the creek banks. Looking at the beautiful churches and the swans swimming in the creek were not a powerful sitimulus to put that drug offer out of my mind. I woul have not lived by this family. Alright, then what should I have done? Where and by whom could I stay?

When I got to the Victoria Station, there was half an hour to our meeting time. My phone rang while I was having my coffee at the cafe just near the station. The caller was Mert. I let him know the name of the café. I asked him to call Özge as well. Just the second I was taking my cup of coffee, my phone rang again. This time it was Semiha calling. They were going to a festival as a family where there would be horse races. She told us that this week she was unable to join us... She sounded sad as it were. I asked.

"I will tell you all about next week if we can meet" she replied.

While drinking my coffee, I was looking at the people running here and there, trying to have my guess for the people from where they might have come, and to get this drug offer out of my mind. For a moment, I thought how much I wanted to be sitting at a café on İstiklal Street... As I was daydreaming of the fact that I could be meeting there with dozens of my friends, greeting them, sitting with them and opening my chest to them as well as doing crazy things together, Mert arrived. I threw my arms around Mert's neck as if we have known each other for many many years. I guessed he was surprised a bit. While waiting for Özge, I started chatting with Mert. He had seen off her mother yesterday.

"Was your mother here?" I said amazedly.

"Yes. She didn't leave before she helped me settle down in the house and arranged an au pair."

"Au pair?"

"Yes… She will come three days a week, and she will do ironing, cooking dishes etc works" he said.

I heaved a sigh wishing if only I were Mert's au pair.

"How is she… I mean the au pair?"

"I have no idea… My mother told me that she was a fine girl. A French girl. She is also a student. My mother particularly preferred that the au pair was a French girl. This way she hoped I would not forget my French."

Since I didn't know French, my becoming Mert's au-per was impossible.

"Fine… I am glad" I said.

"Oh, how about you, how are you?"

"I… I don't know. I cannot say that I like my family."

"Is it… Why?"

"The girl I pick up from school is troubled. In fact, the family is a bit off."

"Where do they come from?"

"They are English but with Nigerian roots."

At that moment, Özge accompanied by a man was approaching to us. Mert seemed to be bothered by having Özge coming along with a man. The salutation part was over. The name of the young man along with Özge was Jack. An Englishman with Jewish background. He happened to be her flatmate. It's obvious that they get along well. My complaining about the family saddened Özge.

"I also get used to it with difficulty. It's not a home but a stable as it were" she said.

After hearing that Mert had very comfortable and enviable life, now the fact that Özge's making her complaints making me relaxed caused me at the same time to feel ashamed to ask this question.

"Why?"

She mentioned about her flatmates. She also grumbled about the Cypriot Turk who rented his house to four persons.

"He turned the living room into a bedroom, but he didn't get the bathroom and the kitchen repaired. Everywhere there is a need for repair. The Romanian girl is very untidy. The Pakistani boy is incredibly filthy."

She added that she only was keeping Jack's company. Jack was going to finish his university education and become a civil engineer. He looked like someone, not much talkative, serious and an earnest person. He was a socialist but at the same time he was not completely happy with Tony Blair. He was such a type only opening his mouth when it comes to politics. Mert and I were not fan of talking politics.

Taking a long deep breath at one stage, Özge turned to me and asked.

"Oh... What are you doing?"

"A moment ago, I was telling Mert. I didn't like the family. There is a problem."

"A problem? What is it?"

At the very moment I was thinking of telling them that the family father Ferdinand offered to me a drug and asking their help on that issue, Jack rolled a joint and after taking a deep breath first she offered it first to Özge and to us. I didn't accept it naturally... The only difference with him compared to Ferdinand was Jack being not insisting yet he was openly and comfortably smoking pot. I was disturbed. By speaking Turkish,

"You don't smoke it every day, do you?" I asked looking at out of the corner of him. Mert,

"No... We take it every day. Since you didn't notice it, that means there is no problem. Take it... You can try too."

"No... I don't want it."

By saying these words, I must have looked at Mert in such a way with my eyes filled with fear...I felt that he was looking at tme as if I was going to be excluded from the group of friends. And then when he was trying to belittle the ones who don't use drugs come from the lower segments of society, noticing that I was at the end of my tether, Özge asked a question as if she wanted to change the subject.

"What happened to Semiha?"

"She is not going to join us this week" I said.

Beginning to walk, Mert,

"Oh... come on, let's have fun" he said. We went inside of the Victoria Station all together.

Today's one of the most fun places was the Museum of the Moving Image. Despite being upset about my friends's drug abuse, we had great fun. I had already forgotten their great blunders. I wouldn't have dreamt of flying like Superman, sharing the stage with Nicole Kidman and act like that in the museum. Our new and earnest friend Jack was not doing crazy things but he too seemed happy. I kind of felt that he was interested in Özge.

Once we got out of the museum, we decided to go to a pub at the pier of the Fully Bridge after seeing from outside the Watch Tower, London Castle, Westminister Palace and Thames Bridge. As we were walking to the pub, Jack mentioned about the scientists, philosophers and artists who breathed the air of this city and walked on the streets we were walking now. While striding through the street stones, I was filled some sort of excitement and stir. I took heart by hitting the paving stones with my shoes as hard as possible. I collected more courage to deal with all types of troubles and to finish my education. As if the souls of the philosophers and artists who breathed the air of these places were flying over my head.

By talking we arrived at the pier of the Fully Bridge.

"Let us first eat our fill" said Mert.

Having forgotten Harringay, Ferdinand, his offering me the drug, and everything, I was in fits. I had twenty pounds in my pocket, but the HSBC credit card was tucked in my purse by my mother as a security measure, and I was cautioned not to use it unles I had to.

When I was calculating in my head whether twenty pounds would be enough to pay in order not to be embarrassed at the side of the son of the well-off family who was insulting the ones not abusing drugs and seeing them as coming from a lower segment of society, Özge turned to Mert,

By saying "Hey Mert. Let us not go to an expensive place. We ran out of money", she eased my mind.

Özge was a frank, affable, self confident and a leftist friend. It was also obvious that Jack too had to be careful with his spending. I was actually in a position to live very carefully as far as my income was concerned compared to them. But as it was the case with me since my childhood, I was trying not to let my situation known and I was creating an impression that I had plenty of money, as it were. Whereas my mother waited hand and foot for me until I reached this age. Had she known that Ferdinand offered me drugs, she would have come immediately and rented a separate house for me. She was so generous and gallant. In recent years, my inner voice was telling me that even though my mother was holding things inside, she had a bumpy ride, and I had to scrape along with my money. I didn't know my foreign land friends very well.

Even when I was in the elementary school, one of my girl friends had told me, "How you are studying in this school. You are poor." I had gone home by crying. My mother explained to me that we were not poor, that I had better toys than anyone else, that I had more beautiful school bag, yet I had not invited my school mates to our old house in Samatya until I graduated from high school. Not inviting them to the house was not covering the reality of the hidden poverty. My high school friends were going to Austria for skiing during semester break. They had insisted a lot to join them. But I didn't go with them presenting some excuses. They gathered that I was not able to go with them because we didn't have money to cover the expenses, yet they pretended to be unaware of our situation. It would have not mattered even if they knew we were not that reach, but I always hid the fact that we were poor. I was making all the efforts to become a trouble-free friend fearing that they might break up their friendship with somebody laden with social and economic problems, or maybe having a fear of losing a friend I have not been able to get over, or else for the reason of there were not many to-be friends available in this country.

Smiling delightfully Mert,

"Nooo... The price of the food is almost the same everywhere. We would be paying more or less ten pounds per head" he answered Özge's question.

"No way. Ten pounds?"

"Well... Quite cheap."

Although being a wealthy person, Mert was acting different-ly and he was not spending more than us.

Despite I was trusting Mert's palate for food, I was not skimming through the ones he suggested but the most inexpensive foods on the menu. In the meantime, Mert was informing us about the drinks.

"If you prefer to drink the traditional Enlish beer, it's not carbonated but cold. I am not recommending the draught beer" he said.

Becoming lightheaded when we come together with friends was relaxing me but I couldn't make out whot would be ensuing today's happenings such as refusing the drug offer in the morning, and getting of from the man's car as if I was fleeing. I wanted to go home this evening sober and levelheaded. Turning to Mert,

"Well... I would like to take something alcochol free. What should I drink?" I said.

"Then I am recommending to you Shandy, teetotal girl..."

There must be something in this word of "Teetotal girl", but I don't know what it was... Should I call it affection, compassion or an insult, kidding, or else envy... Oh, whatever... Mert looked at my face carefully and spoke.

"This is a mix of lager and lemonade, it has a very nice taste... Additionally, its alcohol level is very low, it's a light beer" he went on.

"Okay... No problem" I said.

"Winter Warmen" Özge ordered.

Mert and Jack too ordered the same.

We were both eating our meals and rollicking. All of us were *going to start our studies at our universities this week. Three of us were living in different neighborhoods and going to different universities. When we left the pub, the street lamps started to be turned on slowly, and the day was going from scarlet to darkness. In fact, it was just half past five. Mert bought a bottle of warm and Spring-time Muller vine from a wine-shop and invited us to his home. I wanted to spend the whole night with my friends, and I was not willing to go to the house in Harringay at all.*

Mert's house was not like the red-bricked houses in our neighborhood, and it was inside a large and very green garden with old but tall trees. It was a quite pretty house with its Victorian style architecture, and flower balconies set on the front facade of the walls adorned with ivies. The lounge in the entrance was covered with hardwood, not with the floorcloth. On the walls there were not wallpapers but they were painted with opaque satin paint like in our houses in Istanbul. The wide-screen television in the lounge was still on. The old seats, obviously not bought recently, were designed so elegantly. I thought of the fact that so many people had sat on these seats, read books, gulped their drinks or made love on them. While Mert was pouring wine into the glasses, selecting a CD, Özge and Jack came near us. Accompanied by a pleasant music, the butterflies were flying everywhere as it were. I didn't want to have this day ended. In fact, the time to go home was fast approaching. As I was reaching out to my glass and looking at the decoration of the lounge, I spoke to Mert.

"I was thinking that people of poor taste were living here."

"Why?"

"Seeing many houses still have multi-colored floorcloths, wallpapers!"

Smiling, Mert interrupted me.

"Do you think this house was like this when I rented it?"

I was surprised.

"Wasn't it?"

"Of course it wasn't... My mother had all of these parquets and wall paintings made."

"Really?"

"Yes... the English would not change furniture in every two years or the house decoration like us. The exterior of the houses is more important. They respect environment. This takes precedence. Municipalities exersize oversight. People cannot change the exterior door, their garage and the balcony at will" he said.

"You're right though...In fact, thy're doing the right thing."

"I think so... Look at İstanbul... The good old city is full of roofless, unpainted houses; devil-may-care gardens; and people eating on the newspaper spread on the roads and pavements..."

"Yes true... The seats as if belonging to a shop or store inside the roofless, unpainted houses; and television sets even in the kitchen."

"Unfortunately, we like to flash."

Mert pointed out to the seat.

"Look... They placed two seats. Who knows, maybe these seats were purchased at least one hundered years ago."

"But very elegant."

Jack immediately delved into the political side of the topic.

"The ones who take granted the historical artifacts are not the peoples, friends. As long as the governments, who whould have the peoples get used to this, would not forgo their capitalistic mentality, things would not get better. Your government is said to demolish the Haydarpaşa Train Station... To pull Ak Merkez down."

"A aaa... Is that so... I just heard about it."

I looked at Jack admiringly for the first time for his being more knowledgeable than me about what was going on in my country.

For a moment, I had the sensation that the souls of many artists like the ones on the street we were at that time, were wandering at Atatürk Culture Center.

"Why do they demolish them?"

"Because this serves somebody's purpose. This is the same like changing the seat at your home... Why do they let people get motivated to look for replacing their old seats with new ones in just five years' time?"

"Not holding onto their past and memories..."

In a manner of changing the subject, with the pretext of refreshing the wine glasses, Mert, who was not fun of talking about political issues, opened a bottle of Mulled wine and interrupted Jack.

"Come on, cheers, friends." As I was hitting the glasses, I asked Mert about that lucky French girl, I was wondering, "Where is your au pair?" Mert replied.

"Today is her day off."

When I was heaving a sigh thinking that everybody's au pairs were so comfortable, Jack was rolling again a cigarette. That was a joint. By opening the window in the lounge towards the balcony, Mert dragged heavily from the joint. I looked at their direction... As if it was bad when Fervinand offered, and it was okay when Jack did ask the same thing. Almost the same, going to bed with Brad Pitt when receiving a comment from him but being upset upon the whitewasher Durmuş making a comment...

After Özge and I talked a little bit about school, what we were planning to do after school, the professions we were going to acquire, as well as Jack's talk on world politics, we couldn't realize how time passed so quickly.

Having spent a wonderful day, we said good-bye to each other to meet again in the historical pub at the pier of the Fully Bridge every weekend.

As I was heading to Harringay, to that same house, to the same people, I had shaken off the spell of the wonderfully lived day, and I started timing of the reactions to my refusal to the offer of dragging the joint. I knew I could have not stated in this house any longer. How could I have endured until I find a soluition?

I unlocked the door with my key. Inside of the house smelled very bad. The smell of union, garlic and food was everywhere. Heading towards the stairs, without turning my head to the living room, I quickly went up to my room. The voices of Amina and Ferdinand were coming out of the living room. I set my heart at rest thinking that I was sure that Amina already knew why I didn't greet them by saying "Good night" and went up to my room since they had been frequently changing au pairs.

I entered my room. The bad smell of the house was not felt there but still there was a very light strange smell. I immediately opened the window. While I was changing my clothes, the frame of a photograph of my mother and I at the bedside was turned towards the window. I always turned the frame towards the bed and I went to sleep by looking at this photo. Never and ever I did orient this frame to that direction. Yes, they did enter my room. It was obvious they did because of the smell. I wondered which one entered. Suddenly I grew a fear inside of me that Ferdinand might have entered my room and hid drugs somewhere in the room since he was upset with me. I looked for it all around. Couldn't I sleep in this house at ease? Yes… My passport is inside the zipped section of my briefcase, but the zip I carefully kept closed was opened. I guess, they rummaged about every place and tried not to leave a trace. I needed to get rid of the distress inside of me. I held my phone and the moment I was about to call my mother, I remembered that it was here 11 but in Turkey 1 in the night. I called Özge. I told her that my room was rummaged, some nights my door was scratched, I was hearing the sounds as if someone was scratching his nails, and I was so much worried. Özge replied.

"It's normal that the family would look at every au pair's room. Of course, some polite people would not do like that… That is to say, they are free to enter your room if they want to do so. I didn't make sense of the rattling sound at your door. Do you mean someone is frightening you? Or is it something only you perceive it that way. Of course, it must me like this. Why do they want to disturb the au pair of their child?"

After hanging up the phone, I started finding fault in myself since this drug offer, my room's being rummaged were all considered normal by Özge. By thinking whether I was too much paranoid, I set the alarm at 6, and I fell asleep.

27 September

While everyone was sleeping, I placed the note on the counter: "I am going to school. I will pick Ellen up from school", and I left the house.

ON THE WAY-SCHOOL

I guess since it was the first day, I had to spend some time through asking the transfer connections between Ellen's and my schools. I was getting off from the metro and running to Ellen's school. When at the traffic lights I saw the parents and guardians having picked up their children from school, I got excited a lot. I was being late. What if they called Ellen's family! Anyway, nobody was there when I got by the school. I rand the bell. I explained the situation to the teacher in charge. The teacher handed in Ellen with a sullen face. I apologized that I made them wait. I promised that it would not be repeated. They were starting the procedures of making emergency calls after waiting for fifteen minues for the lagging parents and guardians. I felt at ease that I was there before a crises broke. Behaving capriciously all the time, Ellen this time started threatening me by saying how upset she was and she was also going to make a complaint to her father for my being late. And she would make me lose my job. Turning her sullen face towards the trees, she suddenly detoured into the road by the creek on the right. She started collecting the fallen chestnuts at the bottom of the trees and and taking out their contents.

"Come on… We are being late to get home".

She kept on collecting chestnuts just by shrugging her shoulders. She was stuffing in the chestnuts with her muddy hand.

The words the au pair company had told her came back to my memory.

"You are going to pick up the girl from school and take her home. That's it. There's no home work."

I realized at that moment that this job of picking her up from school, seemingly a very easy thing to do, turned out to be so much difficult, and now I would have preferred to do all the home works instead of picking up the child from school.

When we got home, it was almost six. I hurriedly heated

the cabbage and meat her mother cooked in the microwave and put it in front of her. Now I was not paying any attention to her whimps. While Ellen was eating, her mother arrived.

I told Amina that today I was fifteen minues late to get to school before Ellen would have said so. Amina was a little bit upset. I told her that I lost the way since it was the first day of my school. While we were talking about these things, Ferdinand burst inside. I was seeing him for the first time after he offered drugs. He seemed nervous.

"I am going up to my room" I said and headed for the stairs.

Ferdinand followed me to come up. I was just about to open my door on the narrow hole upstairs, Fedinand spoke to me unkindly,

"One minute." I turned to him by wearing a hard and decisive expression on my boot-face.

"They called me from the school. Why were you late?"

"It won't repeat."

"Good… How was your school?"

"Well… Thank you." When I was just entering my room, he put his foot to the wall and cut off my way extending a nylon bag he was holding to me.

"Look, take this… Drugs in this bag will cost only fifty pounds."

"Thank you. There is nobody using this within my circle."

"There must be. "

"No."

"Test the waters… These are very cheap. There are people ready to pay one hundred pounds for this bag."

I was at the end of my tether. While I was entering my room

angrily,

"It doesn't interest me. If you make me such offers, I will report you to the police" I said and after entering my room, I shut the door in his face.

"Ah, the police ha... You don't know me..." He shouted first... Then I heard that he said something in a huff. I couldn't make of what he had to say.

In horror, I collapsed on my bed. Noo, it's impossible now for me to stay in this house.

I immediately dialed the number of the au pair company in İstanbul, but there was no answer. Should I call my mother? What could she do? I called Semiha to find out what she was doing and also hoping that she would invite me when I told her all about what happened.

She had more troubles than I did.

"Thank God you called... Oh, my elder brother has changed a lot... He doesn't care about our brother. He doesn't have an intention to bring him here. They didn't give me even a pound... Burak is waiting for money in İstanbul. I am going to go mad. If things continue like this, I am considering to find a job and go back to İstanbul when I have enough money."

Backing out of telling Semiha about my troubles, I told her to be patient. Whom I should call? Would Mert be of any help to me? Even though I called Mert many times, there was no answer. I called Özge again at once. Anyway, she picked up the phone. I informed her about what was going on. Even tonight Ferdinand might cause a problem to me. Understanding I was too much apprehensive, Özge told me to put the nightstand to the back of the door, and to get a good sleep. She also said to me that she was going to talk to Jack and call me back. I hung up the phone by saying, "Alright."

I leapt up as soon as the phone rand. As I was assuming that it was Özge, finding a solution and now calling me, but the caller was not Özge, it was my mother when I saw the country code on the phone. Trying to place a tone of joy on my voice I replied:

"Mother."

"My daughter... Your voice sounds a little bit weird."

"No mother... I am fine."

"No you are not. What's going on my daughter. There is a distress inside of me."

Strangely enough, whenever I feel in distress here, the same goes with my mother... Now how could I have told her what was going on. What if Özge was trying to call me. And she would forgo calling again thinking that my phone was always giving the signal of being engaged.

"Mother... I am fine... I was about to go to sleep. Maybe it is out of sleepnessness."

"Alright then... Well. How is the family?"

"They are fine mother."

"Ferdinand."

Unbelievable. I had mentioned her in passing the name of that man, she kept it in the memory and now she was asking about him as if she felt that he became a headache to me...

"Ferdinand?"

"Yes. Yes... The father of the girl."

Look at that. There was no name of the girl... But the name of the father was in her memory.

"The girl, the father and the mother, all of them are fine mother. I will say hello to them for you."

"Ah, be careful my daughter. I don't feel relaxed. I wonder whether it would be good if I get there… Just to see the family, to see you being in comfort, then I would feel okay, but."

"Getting here?"

"I won't disturb you. Let's find out the hotel fees."

"Okay, come… But why now?"

"Ah, how could I know my daughter… I get anxious… I fear they migh harm you… God forbid… Anyway, if I would be disturbing you…"

"What does it mean mother, to disturb me. Come here then… There is no need to book a hotel. You can stay by me."

"Is that so… Good, now I am relaxed. Let me get my visa asap… What should I bring to you?"

"Off mother… Let me have you get your visa first."

***

Canan who left her work on the historical artifact smuggled out of the country incomplete and decided to write about Sevgi's life, met with the young girl in İstanbul Büyükada after months. Pointing out the tea garden over there by her finger, Canan talked:

"I had celebrated my birthday for the first time with my friends here. Just right here… I had organized it unbeknown by my mother, and far away from her… Just here."

"Your first birthday? Alone?"

"Yes."

"How so?"

"The year I turned 18."

"No birthday until that year…"

Wearing a bitter smile, Canan replied.

"None… Both my mother and my father wanted to live the day at home as if to pass the day I was born… It might take long… I can explain later…" After a period of short silence,

"Let us talk about you" she said and looked at the young girl with a sweet smile.

"We were left with Ferdinand… What was he doing in the girl's room at dead of night?"

The young girl was talking about what went on, right after her first diary ended…

"Ferdinand was growing the plant to make drugs.

After a while, I made complaints about my troubles, through sharing what was going on with my friends… It was such a horrible sceen for me what he was doing before the eyes of his daughter… In fact, finding out his making drugs, my friends put pressure on me to buy cheap drug from him… For their sake, I stopped giving attitude to Ferdinand."

"Alright, your mother was about to get there since she became suspicios of Ferdinand?"

"Although desiring to come by me in London so badly, for some reasons, my mother did not mention about it anymore. In fact, I found out later on that my mother had to visit the doctor when she was applying for visa since it was seen that a swell was in her breast. She eventually learnt that she had cancer. Before coming here, her radiotherapy had begun."

Sevgi's eyes filled with tears. Canan took the young girl's hand into her palm.

"If these memories make you upset… I can read them from your diary."

It was just about the sunset time… Sevgi kept on telling on the deck of the Island Boat.

"Noo… Talking to you comforts me a lot…"

She seemed to be lost for a while. She ate her meal… She drank her wine… then the young girl went on.

"Then I met with Kemal. We loved each other. Later, during the years when my mother had hidden her sickness from me, I had not told my mother that I left the family I was with. When Ferdinand was putting pressure on me to sell the drugs in school, I left them and moved to my boy friend's house… The pocket money my mother was sending to me was more than enough. Kemal and I were daydreaming of getting married. We were discussing even the location where we were going to live. After getting married, Kemal wanted to live in Turkey whereas I wanted to spend half of the year in London and the other half in İstanbul."

Sevgi heaved a deep sigh. She kept a big gulp she took from her wine inside her mouth. Canan asked the young girl affectionately.

"Do you remember your father?"

"No. Only the memories my mother told me about him."

"Memories."

Sevgi was explaining the happy and sad events she remembered with a smile on her face. As if to say, "Everything was gone!"

"Yes… Do you know, I didn't want to be born?"

If only her mother would have given birth to Sevgi through one push. Despite having gone through so many difficulties, Leman had difficulty to give birth to a child… She was pushing and pushing but the baby was being seen one moment and then it was being hidden somewhere on the other... At the same moment, she remembered her friends being under police custody... Despite all the torturing they endured, they didn't't grass on her, and they held their ground. Then her lover came to mind, she thought of Harun. If only he was by her side and holding her hand, then maybe the baby would be easily coming out. But Harun could not come. Harun was captured by a battalion of soldiers. A battalion of soldiers had restrained him. Now Harun was a detainee. Who knows whether he would be coming out from there alive or not. What did Harun do though. He didn't fill his hand with a gun. "While our poor people are not able to buy bread, I could not drive a top model car" he had said and even for once he didn't get behind the weel of the car his father had bought. He had organized meetings for better tomorrows, and he had given speeches against the government by saying "Neither America nor Russia!", "Fully independent Turkey!", He had thrown the American soldiers into the waters of the Bosphorus, and he had attended the marches. What else he would have done! The police wearing body armour had strangled him to drag him to the gallows.

It was the midnight... Leman's lover jumped from his bunk after having heard a woman's scream... He thought that they were torturing their sisters. Again, to detain hundreds of people and execute them, the bastinados, electric cables, mangles were prepared, the creatures being fed by blood took up their positions, they stripped the girls down, and while thinking now the screams would be mixed with the folk songs, he noticed a serene silence. Thinking that this was some kind of serenity but it boding no good was not giving him peace of mind. He again laid down on his bunk. He wasn't able to go to sleep. He thought about his wife he was brooding about her day and night. Those days, happy and full of hopes hand in hand. The roads they walked for the better days, the mountains and hills they climbed over. The only thing they wanted was to establish the government of people and to start a revolution. While their big hearts were being filled with the enthusiasm of love and revolution, the news of the coup, coming exactly right before their marr iage ceremony had changed not only the fate of the country but also theirs.

Sevgi's father Harun had a family as rich as Croesus. She was not sure whether they named him because they were rich. When he was born, his grandfather had sacrificed animals, and given away crops from his warehouse such as wheat, barley, hazelnut to the villagers. In fact, his grandfather was not treating his farmhands differently; he would have fed the poor during difficult times such as winter and famine, he would have provided clother for the children. His sons-in-law and his smaller sons were complaining about his character, but Harun was different. At the very early age, he had learned to share from his grandfather, an agrarian elite and wise man. His revolutionary soul had started blooming even at his childhood years. He wouldn't eat when his neighbor was sleeping hungry. Before long, his grandfather died. Around the time his uncles made the money fly, Harun was about to graduate from university. He met with Leman during that period. The family of the girl was called the vinegar makers of Samatya. They were not selling vinegar in reality, but in the past their grandmothers and grandfathers used to make vinegar. She was the daughter of a simple-hearted civil servant. She was then just a sympathizer, but she was also a gallant, courageous and loyal girl. She was steady, strong and confident.

Both Harun's father and mother liked their bride Leman a lot. Even though they didn't have tons of money now they used to have, still they had enough property to suffice the needs of their children and grandchildren. They wanted to organize a super lavish wedding event, to present to ther golden belts, golden twirling bracelets, necklaces, but Canan did accept none of them. Harun's family couldn't help thinking "Revolutionist girls are so contented, so decent." They bought a pretty house in Samatya for their son and furnished it. By trying not to eat things the people cannot afford, not to put on dresses the people cannot have, and not indulging in showing off type of behavior, Leman and Harun liked very much their house they decorated with inexpensive and simple household items. It was their cozy nest as it were. Until the day of wedding ceremony, they ran in the demonstrations, meeting without being able to hold each other's hand. Their families were afraid. The government was not in good terms with neither rightists nor leftists, and it was puting brother against brother. Every day the young people were killing one another and the government was not moving a muscle. Though it was possible to take measures, the authorities were doing nothing but watch. The struggle waged by the young people for the better tomorrows was being provoked. Many well-situated, the young people were sharing their money with the needy. They preferred to live like the common people, not in luxury. The house of Leman and Harun turned into a rendezvous point for their friends who were escaping from the police, who were being followed as it were… The quilts and pillows in the builin wardrope which were brought and organized in the house by Leman's mother came in so handy… Those mute screams not touching the silence of the night were going to change both Turkey's and Sevgi's future. Despite having brought to the labour room, Leman's delivery didn't happen, and that's why she was sent back to the maternity ward.

The following day Leman stayed in the labour room for quite a time. She had suffered a lot for days, but she was sure that she was going to give birth on that day as it were… The ones who delivered were leaving the hospital, but Leman was not able to have her baby. Doctors were claiming that the reason for this had some psychological element. The silent screams of Leman in the labour room were meeting with the screams of ther friends under police custody.

One midnight Leman gave birth to her daughter through a medical operation. The good news was sent to her father. They named their daughter altogether with their friends in the prison. See, we call her now as Sevgi.

When meting with her father for the first time while her father behind the bars at Hasdal Prison, Sevgi was only forty days old. Harun looked carefully at hisdaughter. Noticing that Harun was looking at the baby with his eyes gloed to her, Leman got emotional… Sevgi too stared at her father. She had so big eyes. Her father first looked at her eyes then herself. Her mother had put on her a jump suit with pink gloves. Her father had frozen for about ten minutes. He couldn't speak, cry or smile. What was it to made him so rigid? Long afterwards he extended his hand to his daughter. Taking off her pink glove, he touched her white skin. He seemed trembling. "For the first time, I wanted to be outside" he said. "I have no right to leave her without a father…" Leman was looking at her husband yearningly. They were not speaking but exchanging glances. Harun feasted his eyes on his wife and daughter. Then he asked after them… They sent Leman into exile. From a high school in Samatya to another school in Fikirtepe. How it was going to work? What was going to happen to the child when she was going to school? In fact, there were no friends or family to help her. The news was coming out to know that her friends were being caught one by one, some of them were being interrogated, some died of torture. Leman and people like her though themselves being outside, with their friends and relatives detained were also going through a tormenting difficulties. They were making people inside prison suffer one way, and making the others outside go through hell another way.

Sevgi's father Harun had not lived longer after his case was over and he was freed.

Sevgi's mother made tremendous efforts to have Sevgi being not conspicuous by her father's absence.

The boat took off from Büyükada collected Heybeliada passengers to head towards Burgazada.

Worried, Canan took the hands of the young girl into her palms.

"Are you still using, drugs?"

"No, I am not."

With a blissful wonderment,

"That's great… But how were you able to get rid of it?"

"My boy friend… Kemal… He worked hard for it. One night, when I used a lot of drugs, my heroin addict friends thinking that I died, panicked and after opening the door of the car they left me by a park. They called an ambulance and then went away from there. When I opened my eyes at the hospital, the police came to take my testimony. I didn't remember anything to tell the police… My drugs crises started after a while at the hospital where I was staying… The doctor prescribed for long tranquilizer, with light dosage... Those were difficult days... Without Kemal's love, I would have not been able to get it over..."

"Did you return to London for Kemal?"

"Yes... See, there was a day we met at the airport."

"Hmm... hmm."

"It was the day when we met in the plane 7 days after I had paid my final respects to my mother."

When I found out that she was sick and the cancer had pervaded everywhere, she was living on borrowed time. Oh my poor mother... I now appreciate better my only mother who sacrificed her life, her youth in order to raise me. If only she were by my side... If only she were constantly giving me her advice... If only she embraced me with her fussiness which brought me the the brink of depression... If only I would have done what my mother wanted me to do... If only I would be at the beck and call of her...

If only my mother were by my side... But she is not."

"Alright, dear... Let us go, if you will."

"No... I need to tell...

Then my mother wasn't able to speak. Her windpipe too got paralysed... She was writing down everthing she wanted to tell me. Before she was taken to the intensive care unit, she slipped this paper into my hand. She had written that when I was sleeping by her side in the night. To my surprise, she understood that I was using drugs... She held it inside. She looked at me caringly and affectionately until giving her last breath... While dying her lips were curled with a sweet smile."

The young girl had a lump in her throat... She started crying by hugging her.

***

Canan was reading the last pages of Sevgi's diary in her house's terrace.

When I was informed that my mother's illness metastasized in liver, I immediately came to İstanbul from London. I had no idea at all that she was at that advanced phase of her illness. She looked so weak and sunken, and I was not able to do anything... I wholeheartedly wanted to get her from the bed to stand up and rather be sick instead of her being in that position.

I was so desperate...In fact, my mother had endured so many difficulties when she was at my age... She had both worked and gone to university, given seminars, played a leading role in cultural associations, opened exhibitions, and did time in Hasdal after being tortured at the special branch of the police... She resisted... She succeeded... She got married... She lost her husband... She single-handedly made me go to best schools... How did she accomplish all of these? Myself on the other hand, cannot turn over my mother in this bed from right to the left... I only look at my mother who accomplished herculean tasks for me, from a distance...

My mother... When she recovered quickly after radiotherapy session, I returned to my school upon her insistence. My mother was telling me now she was fine over the phone... That she pulled through the illness... She was giving me advice that I should not be upset but I was just remembering the days when I was scolding her. Her yielding to all of my demands was haunting me all the time...

To forget completely about my mother... I didn't want to get worried, I wanted to have fun, but I was unable to act like that. Then I asked my closest friend... "What should I do?... My tem-

porary state of crying was getting more permanent, and I wasn't able to sleep for days..."

"What should I do Özge? Please help me..." She rolled a cigarette... She held out it by saying, "it's going to do good to you... There is no harm with it... Look, I have been using it for years. You were not aware of it, right?" Yes, sure... Özge was always good, and always happy... There was no such thing like a crisis... She was very clever too... Besides, one or two would not lead to anything... As soon as this depression was over, I would not put it into my mouth anymore... Here you go... Narrowing her eyes looking with the glitter of making me happy, Özge was giving me a rolled cigarette without expecting anything in return. I couldn't make of why my heart started beating so fast... Was it fear of excitement? I grabbed the cigarette with my trembling fingers in a tearing hurry... And I started using cannabis... Remember that plant, I was trying hard to escape from it...

***

Hooray... Cannabis... It was going to get a shot in the arm, and it was going to make me forget about my pains, and it was going to make me return to my normal life...

The biggest favor of my best friend was to offer the cannabis without asking money for it... I had been staying by her place for days. Even one week ago, when I still didn't start using cannabis, she didn't give me one pound for my traveling fare, then later she had offered to me the cannabis she must have paid a lot, for free... Even the rolled cigarette with cannabis she had forgotten on the coffee table when she left the house made me so happy...After finishing my cigarette, on top of it, I devoured the whole chocolate cake I happened to like a lot.

Now we were organizing the cannabis tours and meals by coming together with Özge, Jack, Mert, and others. We were cooking cakes with cannabis and eating in high spirits. I was sometimes laughing and having fun but I was keeping sight of my mother all the time... Or rather, the days I snapped at her... Perhaps cannabis was not enough... I wonder whether cocain, even poison would do good to me... Be it a pain or remorse, whatever it was, if only I would get rid this mother phobia...

***

Now my closest friends were narcotic addicts...We were having great time together. Dropping out of school completely, I started waiting tables. God forbid, my mother should not know about what I was doing.

Kemal was still after me... I couldn't tolerate his advice, or his bosom I needed from time to time...

"Let us break up."

"What!"

"I am saying, let us break up... Okay?"

"We can talk about it later."

"We don't talk about it later. Even let us not see each other anymore... Let us break up... Let us not make peace again."

"Don't do this!"

"No... I pitty you too... I am giving hope to you... You are not like us."

"What do you mean?"

"That means you are not like us."

"Does it mean that I am not a drub addict... Is this such a

bad thing ha... I should gouch out like you... being in depression all the time, dropping out of school."

"It's better for you to remain mother's darling, a wellbred child."

"Oh yeah... Being a wellbred is bad, being numb like your friends is fine, ha?"

"Off, I cannot bear with you... did you get it... go away now."

"Had I taken a puff from this cannabis you rolled, then I would be the number one person, right?"

"Indeed... try it if you will... Your pains of love would end as well."

Yes... Yes... Cannabis was not enough... Cocain... Even I should take poision and die... Our gatherings with Mert, Özge, Jack and others were getting more frequent. Even though what I was up, my lover not allowing anybody to speak ill about me approached to me one day... I befriended Kemal since the first days I got here... We were studying at the same university. I was aware of the fact that he had feelings of love for me and those feelings were for life but I was not considering both an emotional and long standing relationship anymore... Earlier, when I was a ladied and mannered girl, I had the opposite idea... Even though he was not the first man whose hand touched my hand, and that led me to thinking to start a family without getting things degenerated at that time. Now recalling what I was thinking makes me laugh. I was going to become a good and happy prosecutor with three children... My feelings and thoughts tended to be changing very often. I had talked big earlier... Now I have been living a life for one day at a time. I even didn't want to remember where and with whom I spent some of the nights. Kemal asked me, "What's going on with you?"

"What was happening to me?" I replied...

"You are getting numb in classes, and becoming aggressive during breaktime."

"You say, I am getting aggressive, ha… Get the hell out here then."

"Calm down."

"You're saying I am not calm." I replied.

He refused to take it lying down and didn't try to be calm. I already knew that he as a calm and affectionate person yet I cannot help but treat him roughly…

As he was reaching out to me by extending his hand with his looks full of love,

"Okay my dear… Come and let us walk by the river a bit" he said. I perceived these words as if he was swearing, because I wanted to get rid of him right away and get my herb immediately,

"Alright dear, let us have some icecream in our hands. Or should we eat sunflower seeds?"

Alrigh dear… You don't need icecream… You need cannabis, right?"

"What!"

"It doesn't heal you, this herb. Did you get it… You only feel that it does good to you temporarily… Now it's not enough, right? This damned herb is the precursor to other narcotics." I had become an extremely addicted person so that I would have dropped someone completely who would be opposing my herb.

"It's enough! Get out!" I shouted.

"You ought to get rid of your parasitic friends who chose this herb rather than facing the problems, my dear… Maybe you are not aware the fact that you are in an unending depression since you started taking cannabis."

"So what... Am I mad? If so, what business you have here with a mad person... Off you go..."

"I am not angry with you... You are about to lose your understanding and decision making ability. Now go get your herb... I am also going off my dear... Maybe... Maybe, I might come to you one more time... If you push my hands again... Then I will never see you again but I will remember you till the end of my life with your face before you started taking drugs... Your sparkling and as sharp as a tack looking eyes, your beaming attitudes and most important of all, your tremendous heart."

***

I did inhale the smoke of cannabis into my lungs and held it there... Now my lungs were full of smoke... even the smoke was not enogh to alleviate my damned trouble... Again my mother comes back to my mind... Her illness leapt up to her lungs... Cannabis smoke in my lungs, I was thinking of my mother... She was going to go through chemotheraphy... "Don't come... I am very well" she said over the phone... I searched in Google... Chemotheraphy, that is a treatment to wipe out the tumor through medication... Beforehand she had gone through radiotheraphy, the treatment with via irradiation... I wonder whether it was a good idea to apply chemotheraphy instead of radiotherapy... No... No... I would not feel at ease unless I went to İstanbul... my mother persistenly told me "Don't come". Oh my poor mother. She didn't know that most of the days I didn't go to school, and she was worrying that I would be neglecting my courses...

Say that I went to see her, what could I have done for her there? I have no power to help her... Why? She is such a mother! She is a woman when her 13 years old daughter's appendix was about to burst, she took her in her arms carrying to the main *street... She is a woman who waited by her daughter's side until her operation was over...*

I did inhale the smoke of cannabis into my lungs and held it there...

"Why don't I have the strength in my arms, mother?"

It has been two months since I returned from my mother whose chemotheraphy treatment had been completed at Okmeydanı Hospital... I couldn't have borne any longer her apprehensive expression and her constant bemoaning by saying, "There is something with you, it's kind of weird." After all, she didn't want me to stay... She was too much afraid of my neglecting the courses at the university. In fact, in every phone calls, I was hiding from my mother the fact that my grades were gradually getting worse, who on the other hand was telling me that she had beaten the cancer... Poor hairless woman... Had you known that I wasn't going to school in recent months, that I was zonking sometimes at Özge's, some other times at Mert's houses, that I was using cannabis, that I was sleeping with strangers, I was sure you would be dying from heart attack where you are. But what could I have done? I cannot stop what was happening... I broke up with Kemal... Did I suffer a separation pain? No... I had no idea, how a separation pain feels like. My pains were so deep... meaning that it was not strong enough to feel... The cannabis smoke was soaring over my head like a permenant halo... Now my getting relaxed and joyful state had passed so quickly.

Let me take more cannabis and stay cheerful all the time... Or else should I call Kemal? Should I lean my head to his shoulder? Yes, yes... He has not picking up my phone. Had I gone to his house, I wonder if he would embrace me or not...

Again, the smoke of cannabis was soaring over my head like a halo... Now I started rolling it in the morning, but it was not good anymore... Something was going wrongly but I could not get my head together. Some evening I went out with Kemal who extended his compassionate hand to my heart in our first reconciliation. Despite his sparing no efforts to give me his love and compassion, I regarded him as an enemy. Especially when he gave me some advice like my mother... Lately, he recognized my classes going wrong and our relationship's getting declined because of cannabis. Ah, he was not taking drugs, ha...

"From now on, perhaps I couldn't help you to quit using cannabis... you became addicted."

"Give me a break... This is as dangerous as cigarette."

"No."

"Yes."

"Your grades are lower now... You suffer learning difficulty."

"What does it to do with cannabis? I don't study. Even I don't go to school regularly.

"All of these because of cannabis."

"No."

"Why do I waste my breath? You simply have a perceptual disorder."

"Fuck you."

"See, you started again.

I argued so badly with Kemal. He would no longer call me. For all I cared!"

***

Now that old cute, smart and pretty girl was gone... Instead, an ugly girl with her dirty nails, collapsed cheeks came to the fore. I looked like as black as the ace of spades. I was feeling ashamed. I was yearning for pubs and clubs... I became thin. I hated myself.

There was nowhere I would sleep in... I was afraid. I was praying to God for having somebody rescue me but nobody was around to help me. Now I couldn't tell in which season or on which day I was. Starting my journey with a harmless drug, then years later I became a bad ass narcotic addict. I was on the street. I was going through terrible crises. I was sick... Probably I was about to die... Had I taken some heroin, I was assuming that it would have treated me...

Suddenly a hand reached out... I had to hold on to it tightly. Still I had actually a good friend. I met with Zeynep at a park, a friend from university. She helped me... She gave some advice. I promised her too. I said I will not use it again, but even at that moment, I knew that I couldn't keep my promise... She took me to a café of an acquantence at the center of London. I started working... I served as a waitress a couple of weeks. I was making money but I wasn't able to devote my attention to my work. My mind was always on cocain or heroin...I started being clumsy at work, forgetting pots on fire. One day a fire was about to break... I was fired...

"Again, I was unemployed, I had no house, no money... Again I was on the street. I was looking for a place to take a shower. I just became a true narcotic addict. I had been trying to save myself. Nobody wanted me... nobody loved me... nobody helped me... Özge didn't answer my calls... They didn't turn out to be like me. They did not use heroin ever. I had no friends. I had no house; neither did I have my work. I had no money, no lover. I had nothing. I sold even the hand-knitted sweaters at Camden... I didn't even remember to whom I gave my mobile phone... Having sold my computer, I was able for a while to fine cannabis...

Nobody was inviting me to their cocain parties... But the last narcotic addict friends told me that there was a way... They were going to sell me... By selling my body we were going to make money. With the money, we would be flying in the sky...

It was freezing cold... All of my body was trembling... I hadn't combed my hair for months, and I was itching. My bones were hurting. I din't eat at all. I was too ill... Should I knock at Mark's door?

They didn't take me inside their house for I din't have money... The doors were being closed in my face one by one... I din't have the face to go to Kemal but I had no other solution... I had to go to Kemal... No, no... I cannot go...

I knew he would not say, "I had told you so. Now you are down." But I worried mostly for his getting into trouble alongside with me, not for me seeing him being proved right... Helplessly, by protection my first love, I was going to sell my body... I would sell my body thanks to that bad friend to make money... He would too... me as well... Again we would fly in the sky.

I felt cold... I looked for my friends by my side. Where were you Özge, Mert? They were not here... Nobody was by my side... Why so? There was something I din't understand... Why Özge who introduced me to drugs had not been on the streets, why she didn't run out of money, why she didn't get sick like me, why... why? Something wasn't right about this... wasn't Ferdinand like this? A drug dealer... He lived happyly in his house with his wife and daughter... Why did I go down?

***

I don't know who threw me into the garbage dump? But I knew who saved me from dying.

I had found out after a month that it was Kemal who saved me from that garbage dump and cleaned neatly... I guess, I had met with my circle of friends, again came together with my certain narcotic addict friends, at the pub we frequented all the time, there we had drunken till morning and had fun by making love in haste... I said I guess, because I remember I was below decks of man I didn't know... I didn't recall at all what I had gone through at the pub... Did they sell me to the man... or did I want to have sex with him, I don't know. Then a garbage dump...I opened up my eyes at the hospital with the siren sound... Far away from London... A hospital in the midst of trees... A long lasting treatment... Kemal was always by my side... That Kemal, I always pushed and hustled... Where were my closest friends? Özge, Mert, Jack and others did not answer my calls anymore...

I cannot believe that I wanted to see them more than Kemal. Not Kemal, who loved me, who took care of me as if I was a delicate flower, rather I looked for the ones who threw me into the garbage dump. If they came, I knew I would get drugs from them... regardless of what it would be...cocain, heroin, doesn't matter... I still believed that these pains would end. I was constantly looking at the door...I was in agony in my bed in such a psychological state to break the person into pieces when he told me, "They don't love you, they use you." My eyes were at the door.

There wass such a deep wound on my back and it didn't get healed... It seemed that it would take long for me to get discharched from the hospital... I asked Kemal, "Where are they, whey don't they come?"

It turned out to be that I took too much drugs at that night...

Or they gave them to me... I don't know. I don't remember... The police were after drug dealers. Well, who did throw me alive into the garbage dump? Was it Özge, Mert... who was it? They didn't. I am sure they didn't, maybe someone who were by their side... After a month, I could appreciate bit by bit how terrible things I had experienced. My wounds on my back caused suffering but Kemal's touch warmed my heart... I felt safe.

***

These are the last sentences my mother wrote to me since she was not able to speak, before she entered the intensive care unit.

My beautiful daughter...

You got tired waiting by your mother's side... You were lost in thought. Your father and I got divorce one month before you were born... There was no meaning for me to live as it were... Just then you arrived in my world... When you were born, a love between us had started. I hoped it would last for life. There were so many reasons to live with you... If only you would know how sad I am for I will be gone by leaving you alone... I know, still not completing my duties of motherhood... Forgive me my daughter...

I have been thinking of things like who would set out your dowry, who is going to give you in marriage? Who will build your nest? Who will sit up with you while you are in your bed after giving birth? Who will bath your baby? I am sorry my daughter... I am sorry for I will be gone before completing my motherhood duties... Now I am not able to do anything except giving you some advise about the things that I was not able to accomplish... You will do things by yourself that were supposed to be done by your mother. Be strong for this my baby. I believe you can manage. Now in my last breath… Now while I was coming to a bad end… My dearest baby, I love you more than myself, and do you know what made me sad most? I was my getting sick and making you upset because of that… I cannot forgive myself for causing you to be introduced to drugs… I apologize to you… Forgive me my dearest baby…If you see a sweet smile curlings on my lips right after I died, and a relaxation on my face, then be assured, that would be because of my strong belief that you are going to ged rid of this malice of drugs, my baby…

***

Following her return to İstanbul from her London travelling, Canan sent the email of her recently finished novel to the publishing house. With a feeling of sweet tranquility inside, she stopped by her mother's house. She had bought for her the umbrella chocolates because her mother liked them so much. With her habitual way of cheerful attitude in the arbor under a vine tree, Fevziye had stretched out one of her legs on the chair and the other on the garden wall. She was talking with her plumb and fat cats which descended on the boiled chicken pieces she had thrown them haphazardly on the large pot on the ground.

Approaching to her quietly, Canan closed her mother's eyes with her hands… She had brought things from London, her mother liked most…

As Fevziye was managing to open the chocholate wrappers in the shape of an umbrealla and and eating them heartily, the young friends entered through the garden gate with their hand full, actually there were the ones they all met when

Fevziye was seeing off her daughter at the airport. Canan was surprised. Fevziye turned to her daughter.

"Do you remember them? After having seen you off to London, we had coffee together at the airport."

Canan smiled as if she remembered at both her mother and the newly arrived people. Her mother had already forgotten about her being there and delved into a conversation cheerfully with her new friends. Until the moment she heard the music that took her by storm.

At that very moment, when Canan put the CD of Frank Sinatra's "From The Bottom of My Heart" into the CD player. Canan had found out that this piece of music was the special song of her mother and her mother's fiancé she never forgot… Fevziye's looks searched for her daughter. The ice of those invisible mountans was melted, the questions werer answered, and when the charming melody of the music being the harbinger of the eternal peace filled the room, the mother's and daughter's glances with full of love had eventually met.

THE END